PRAISE FOR THE #1 BESTSELLING NYPD RED SERIES COAUTHORED BY MARSHALL KARP AND JAMES PATTERSON

"*NYPD Red 2*, like its forebear, stands out due to
Karp's unmistakable style. Karp, already one of my favorite
authors because of his wonderful Lomax and Biggs mysteries,
gets a chance in the mega-selling spotlight with this terrific series,
and he soars with the opportunity."
—SCOTT COFFMAN *LOUISVILLE COURIER-JOURNAL*

"In the case of *NYPD Red*, there is simply
too much fun—in the form of inventive murder,
sex, chemistry, investigation, more murder, more sex,
and the like. Though the book is complete in itself,
there are plenty of interesting characters who could
carry this as a series for as long as Patterson
and Karp will want it to go."
—BOOKREPORTER.COM

"Patterson and Karp spare no plot twist in this page-
turning thriller…Love triangles, mafia ties, and political
entanglements abound, layering this character-driven
mystery in such a way that no dull moment ever arises."
—*HAMPTON SHEET MAGAZINE* ON *NYPD RED 2*

"Patterson and Karp once again prove that this is
one crime series that's not to be missed—the literary
equivalent of your favorite summer blockbuster movie."
—NIGHTSANDWEEKENDS.COM ON *NYPD RED 2*

"Better than mostly anything on the market...
The Rabbit Factory is, quite simply, stunning...
Worth every single second it takes to fly through...
632 pages of unadulterated magic."
—CHRIS HIGH, *TANGLED WEB* AND *SHOTS MAGAZINE* (U.K.)

"This is a nigh-on flawless first novel—I thoroughly enjoyed
both the story and the writing style of the author
and I implore you to simply read it!"
**—DEBUT BOOK OF THE MONTH,
CRIMESQUAD.COM (U.K) ON *THE RABBIT FACTORY***

"...just the right blend of belly laughs and suspense...
Karp's second offering is every bit as funny
and fast-paced as *The Rabbit Factory.*"
—*BOOKLIST* STARRED REVIEW FOR *BLOODTHIRSTY*

"...wickedly funny...this quirky, off-kilter novel also has
a really big heart...[and] an emotional core that will make
readers care about these tough but vulnerable crime
fighters and keep them hoping for a sequel."
—BOOKREPORTER.COM ON *THE RABBIT FACTORY*

"Blending the gritty realism of a Joseph Wambaugh
police procedural with the sardonic humor of
Janet Evanovich, Karp delivers a treat that's not only laugh-
out-loud funny but also remarkably suspenseful."
—*PUBLISHERS WEEKLY* ON *FLIPPING OUT*

"*The Rabbit Factory* was a joy to read...
[It] has been compared to the work of Carl Hiaasen,
but I'm happy to say it's much better."
—THEBOOKBAG.CO.UK

"A plot that reaches 7.5 on the Richter scale...a host
of brilliantly cast characters...[and] switchblade sharp dialogue.
Lomax and Biggs are two of LAPD's finest, as fine
a pair as have ever come out of the city's fiction"
—BOOK OF THE WEEK, *DAILY SPORT* (U.K.) ON *THE RABBIT FACTORY*

"The frenetic plotting and outrageous
characterisation are in [Carl Hiassen]'s line...
but the anti-establishment humour is reminiscent
of another darkly humorous novelist, Joseph Heller."
— *PUBLISHING NEWS* (U.K.) ON *THE RABBIT FACTORY*

"I strongly suspect that Marshall Karp is the secret
love child of Raymond Chandler and the Marx Brothers,
with some Dorothy Parker around the edges. Karp
should be considered a national treasure."
—CORNELIA READ, EDGAR NOMINEE FOR
BEST FIRST NOVEL ON *BLOODTHIRSTY*

"Unplug the phone, pull up your favorite chair, and settle
in for the best mystery novel this year. This strong debut
is an often hilarious head-scratcher, and features a smartly
drawn cast of characters...a page-turner."
—SCOTT COFFMAN *LOUISVILLE COURIER-JOURNAL* ON *THE RABBIT FACTORY*

"Karp craftily engineers a statement on ethical values,
both institutional and personal."
— *KIRKUS* ON *THE RABBIT FACTORY*

"*The Rabbit Factory* is beautifully written, with lifelike characters, humor, and a sense of intimacy that only good research and experience can provide...fun to read, full of humor along with accumulating suspense. And even with that many pages, you'll be sorry there aren't more!"
—WHO-DUNNIT.COM

"Marshall Karp needs a blurb from me like Uma needs a facelift. This guy is the real deal, and *Bloodthirsty* is a first class, fast, funny, and fabulous read by a terrific writer. Great entertainment, highly recommended to one and all."
—JOHN LESCROART, *NEW YORK TIMES* BESTSELLING AUTHOR

"*Bloodthirsty* is worthwhile as much for the repartee between its main characters as it is for its mystery plot....will further Karp's reputation as a humorous mystery writer in the vein of Elmore Leonard, Kinky Friedman and Carl Hiaasen."
—BOOKREPORTER.COM

"...features the funniest detective duo around...a seamlessly plotted caper that hooks you on page one and never lets go... Karp is a true talent who understands how words entertain, and *The Rabbit Factory* does just that."
—*CANNON BEACH GAZETTE*

"Laugh-out-loud funny, realistically portrayed, break-neck-paced, and powered by literally hundreds of hilarious one-liners...Karp has hit the jackpot with Lomax and Biggs. The most endearing and wildly entertaining protagonists to grace the pages of a mystery novel in years."
—PAUL GOAT ALLEN ON *BLOODTHIRSTY*

"With this fifth long-awaited book in the Lomax
and Biggs series, we see Marshall Karp return in full force
with his poignant trademark humour that never seems to leave
the room, even under the direst of circumstances.
Karp really has the coveted talent of being able to turn
virtually any situation into something worth
laughing at, helping to create a balance with
the numerous dark places the story goes to."
— DAVID BEN EFRAIM, *QUICK BOOK REVIEWS* ON *TERMINAL*

"Murder mysteries should all be this much fun.
Full of quirky dialogue, action and well-developed characters,
Karp has created a book that's impossible to put down."
—POPSYNDICATE.COM ON *BLOODTHIRSTY*

"Blending edge of your seat mystery and laugh-out-
loud humor in such a way that neither steps on the
other's toes is not easy, yet once again Karp proves
himself a master of that delicate operation in *Cut, Paste,
Kill*. So what are you waiting for? Buy, Read, Enjoy!"
— ELIZABETH A. WHITE, *EDITING BY ELIZABETH*

"Marshall Karp is the Woody Allen of the murder mystery.
He's up there with Carl Hiaasen and Donald Westlake
and Janet Evanovich—smart, fast-paced, clever,
and really, really funny."
—JOSEPH FINDER, *NEW YORK TIMES*
BESTSELLING AUTHOR ON *BLOODTHIRSTY*

"Nobody writes smart criminals
and smarter cops better than Marshall Karp."
—NYPD DETECTIVE JOHN CORCORAN (RETIRED)

SNOWSTORM IN AUGUST

ALSO BY MARSHALL KARP

THE LOMAX AND BIGGS MYSTERIES

Terminal

Cut, Paste, Kill

Flipping Out

Bloodthirsty

The Rabbit Factory

COAUTHORED WITH JAMES PATTERSON

NYPD Red 6

Red Alert (aka NYPD Red 5)

NYPD Red 4

NYPD Red 3

NYPD Red 2

NYPD Red

Kill Me If You Can

For details and sample chapters, please visit
www.KarpKills.com

MARSHALL KARP

SNOWSTORM IN AUGUST

BLACK STONE PUBLISHING

Copyright © 2022 by Mesa Films, Inc.
Published in 2022 by Blackstone Publishing
Cover and book design by Kathryn Galloway English

Printed in the United States of America

First edition: 2022
ISBN 979-8-200-71401-8
Fiction / Thrillers / Terrorism

Version 1

CIP data for this book is available
from the Library of Congress

Blackstone Publishing
31 Mistletoe Rd.
Ashland, OR 97520

www.BlackstonePublishing.com

For Emily with love.
And for Adam, Lauren, Zach, Sarah, and Jim,
with love from Emily and me.

CHAPTER 1

New York City
August 21, 12:14 p.m.

Aurelia gladstone twisted her silver hair up in a loose bun and pinned it in place. She smiled. The granny look, which she had been sporting for decades, was suddenly in. Women sixty, even seventy, years younger than she were dying their hair gray.

"I'm ninety-two years old," she had said to Maddee at dinner last night, "and all of a sudden, I'm trending!"

"Just your hair, Miz G. Just your hair," her housekeeper had snapped back. "But that dusty rose lipstick you insist on wearing screams World War II."

"Jerry loved it," the old lady responded. "The lipstick, not the war."

That ended the discussion. Whenever Aurelia played the dead-husband card, Maddee immediately backed off.

But maybe she was right, Aurelia thought. She leaned forward and stared at her pale-pink lips in the vanity mirror. Okay, so it was a tad ghostly, but . . .

That's when she caught the first glimpse.

Impossible, she thought, turning around in her chair. She stood up and walked slowly toward her bedroom window ten stories above 5th Avenue.

And there it was, swirling in powdery funnels, leaving a white blanket on the cars below and the green trees that stretched across her beloved Central Park.

Snow.

In August.

"Maddee," she called nervously. No answer.

"Maddee!" she said again, raising her voice a notch and putting some urgency into it.

No use, Aurelia thought. Maddee was in the laundry room with the dryer spinning and those damned earbuds attached to her head. *There's no way she'll hear me.*

Or believe me.

It didn't snow in August. Hadn't in the ninety-two years since Aurelia arrived on the planet, and while she hadn't paid a hell of a lot of attention to all that global-warming business, she didn't think that glaciers melting in Antarctica translated to snow falling over New York City in the middle of summer.

But there it was. Snow. Not dust or soot or any of the usual crap you might see eddying around the yellow-gray skies of New York. This was the white, flaky stuff that everybody was hoping would arrive on December 25, and here it was four months ahead of schedule.

For a second she thought about calling her nephew, but she dismissed it immediately. Giles, with his pandering phone calls and his obsequious "How's my favorite auntie?" compliments, was the last person she should be calling. He and his odious little wife Kimberly were waiting for her to die.

Barring that, he'd be happy to tuck her away in a nursing home—correction: *assisted living facility*. Fuck him. She was old, but she didn't need any damn assistance living, thank you very much. She had Maddee and Mr. Philips, the building super, and four very lovely door-men, and a kitchen drawer piled high with menus, which let her order whatever kind of food she was in the mood for, whenever she wanted.

Call Giles and tell him I think it's snowing in August, and the son of a bitch would have me committed.

"Maddee!" she demanded as loudly as her rheumy voice could go.

"For God's sake, Miz. G., I can hear ya. No need to carry on."

Aurelia turned around. Her short, squat, sharp-tongued house-keeper of thirty-seven years was standing in the doorway.

"Sorry, Maddee," she said. "I thought you were in the laundry room."

"I was. And now I'm on my way to the kitchen to fix us some lunch. I can make a nice tuna salad, or I could call down to the diner, and . . ."

"Lunch can wait. First, come over here and look out the window."

"What's going on?"

"It's snowing."

"Ha!" the housekeeper bellowed. "What's *really* going on?"

"You tell me," Aurelia said, stepping aside so Maddee could get close to the window.

"Holy Mary, Mother of God. It's like a winter wonderland out there," she said.

The two women looked down at the cars, their wipers on high. A bike messenger peddling furiously and weaving in and out of traffic skidded on the slippery streets and plowed into a woman with a baby carriage who had been trying to cross against the light. People were pouring out of the park. Those who had managed to get to the east side of 5th Avenue were ducking under awnings.

"It's supposed to hit ninety degrees today," Maddee said. "What the heck is going on?"

"I don't know," Aurelia said. "Turn on the Weather Channel. They'll know."

They didn't. Not yet. But half a mile to the west, Officer Brian Saunders of Central Park's Twenty-Second Precinct was about to find out.

He had pulled his three-wheeled scooter up to the Loeb Boat-house and jumped out of the cab when he spotted a jogger caught by the sudden storm drop to the ground. As he approached the man, a second jogger went down and, seconds after that, a cyclist. Someone at the café outside the boathouse yelled for help. A child lay face-down on the cobblestone path. Two more people were sprawled on the no-longer-green lawn.

Saunders realized what was happening. He didn't understand, but his job wasn't to figure it out. It was to call it in.

He ran back to the scooter, his uniform dusted with flecks of white, climbed inside the cab, and grabbed his radio.

"Central, this is Two-Two Precinct scooter. I need ESU forthwith. I have a hazmat condition outside the Loeb Boathouse. At least eight people down, maybe more."

"Unit, we are receiving numerous calls about a freak snowstorm falling in the park," the dispatcher replied. "Can you confirm if—"

Saunders cut her off. "Central, be advised that it's definitely coming down hard, but it's not snow that is falling in the park. It's . . ."

He took a breath, only barely believing what he was about to report.

"It's cocaine."

CHAPTER 2

Ten days earlier

LIKE MOST COPS, I HAVE TWO PHONES. The ringtone on the one I use for the job gets changed once a month. Metallica, Black Sabbath, Slayer—I bounce around. The only criterion is that it has to be shrill, aggressive, and loud enough to bring me out of a coma.

The ringtone on my personal cell is the polar opposite. It's the telephonic version of an Ambien and a glass of warm milk, but I haven't changed it since Deirdre uploaded it to my phone fourteen years ago.

I met her on a hot August night a lot like this one. *Met* is an exaggeration. She was one of 300,000 people who poured onto the Great Lawn in Central Park for a Neil Diamond concert. I was one of about two hundred cops pulled in from the other boroughs. As a sergeant, I could easily have dodged the assignment, but I volunteered. After seven years working the crime-riddled streets of the South Bronx, I was happy to get away from the crack whores, gang wars, and housing project stabbings so I could scan the crowd of latte-drinking music lovers and look for pickpockets, drug dealers, and other Upper East Side miscreants. And being twenty-nine and single, I was also hoping to spot something more interesting than an easy collar and eight hours of OT.

And then I saw her. A blue-eyed redhead with a mischievous

smile and an infectious laugh that lit up the sea of drab blankets and vinyl-strapped beach chairs around her.

She first noticed me looking her way when Diamond was singing "Girl, You'll Be a Woman Soon." Deirdre was twenty-seven at the time and very much a woman, but she reacted to the lyrics as if she were just coming of age. And when the words "soon, you'll need a man" filled the air, she looked at me and shyly turned away.

Flirty as all hell. Girls do that with cops. At least, they did back then. She didn't look at me again until three songs later—"Sweet Caroline," the one the fans can't listen to without singing along. She was on her feet at that point. We locked eyes for "touching me, touching you," and if there had been a pickpocket working that night, he could have taken my wallet, my badge, and my gun, because I was mesmerized as she moved her lithe body, pumped her arms, and cried out, "so good, so good, so good."

I sized up the people she was with. Three other women and a guy with a 35mm camera around his neck, who was more into taking pictures than listening to the music. I was pretty sure that he was gay, which meant he was a work friend or a friend-friend, but definitely not a *boy*friend.

I was thinking about how to strike up a conversation when a loud, angry "Fuck you!" cut through the music and pierced the air. I scanned the people nearby and saw that at least a dozen of them had turned away from the stage and were looking at a hot-dog cart about seventy feet to my left.

The vendor was maybe five-six, no more than 140 pounds, and dark-skinned. The customer, a white male in his early twenties, was nearly twice his size.

I headed toward them at a brisk pace. Walking. Nothing panics a crowd faster than seeing a cop on the run.

The hot-dog guy held up both hands and appeared to be trying to solve their issue diplomatically, but the big man wasn't interested in diplomacy.

"Why don't you learn to speak fucking English, you little shit-brown camel jockey," he yelled, bumping his disorderly conduct up to a bias charge. He then gripped the underside of the cart, jerked it up, and toppled it over. The vendor stumbled backward and fell to the ground, barely avoiding being crushed.

The bully wasn't satisfied. He bent down, reached into the overturned mess, and came up with a foot-long stainless-steel, two-pronged barbecue fork.

I ran, pulling my expandable baton from my belt as the crowd scattered.

"Goat fucker!" the white guy snarled.

I came up behind him just as he raised his arm high, and smashed the baton across his wrist.

Steel connected with bone, the man shrieked in pain, dropped the weapon, turned toward me, and, in one fluid motion that I had perfected in boot camp on Parris Island when I was eighteen years old, I put my forearm to his chest, slipped my foot behind his leg, flipped him to the ground, and cuffed him.

Five minutes later we were in a squad car on our way to the nearest precinct, Manhattan's Nineteenth. That's the thing about being a cop. You come into contact with hundreds of people every day, and invariably you get to spend your evening with a shit-faced racist instead of the sexy redhead who was so good, so good, so good.

The next day, I was back at the Four-Four in the Bronx. I got to the precinct a half hour before my shift, and the desk sergeant stopped me on the way in.

"Hey, Doc, someone here to see you." He nodded in the direction of the waiting area.

I turned. It was her.

"Hi," she said. "Remember me?"

I smiled. I couldn't have held it back if I wanted to. "It's my job to remember people," I said. "Some I remember better than others. How can I help you?"

"My friend Nick took about a thousand pictures last night. I thought you might like a few."

She handed me a black-and-white photo—a close-up of me taken with a long lens. "Wow," I said. "I don't look this good in real life."

She gave me a sly wink that said she disagreed. "There's more," she said, handing me half a dozen color shots.

It was me again. In action this time. Running, coming up behind the enraged man wielding the barbecue fork, taking him down to the ground, cuffing him, and hauling him off to jail as the concert-goers who had seen it all gave me a round of applause. "These are incredible," I said. "Your friend Nick should do this kind of thing professionally."

"He does. He's got eight pages in this month's *GQ*. I'm Deirdre Solomon," she said, extending a hand.

"Danny Corcoran," I said, taking it. "How'd you track me down?"

"Easy-peasy," she said, pointing at the black-and-white close-up of me and tapping it on the brass 44 insignia on my collar and the name tag on my chest.

"Hmm," I said, giving her my best steely-eyed TV-cop look. "You know that stalking is a crime."

"I'm an ADA with the Queens District Attorney's Office," she said. "My father is a judge. Don't try to enlighten me on the criminal justice system."

"Well, you caught me by surprise," I said. "Why don't we have dinner Saturday night, and I'll try to come up with something more enlightening?"

"For starters," she said, "you can tell me why the guy at the front desk called you 'Doc.'"

We met at a little Parisian bistro in the middle of a quiet side street on the Upper East Side. As soon as the waiter poured us some wine, Deirdre got down to business.

"So, what kind of doctor are you, or do you just play one in your free time?" she said, giving me the same mischievous smile that had knocked me dead at the concert.

"I'm afraid your version is more interesting than mine," I said. "I'm a cop in a specialized unit. We're on the radio a lot, and it's smarter to use code names instead of our real ones. So Chris Redwood is Sequoia, Dennis Wiley is Coyote, and then there's me, Daniel Orion Corcoran— D. O. C. Doc."

"Your middle name is Orion, like the constellation?"

"He was a Greek god before he was a constellation," I said.

"You're named after a Greek god? Now *your* version is more interesting."

I'm pretty sure I fell in love with her when she showed up at the precinct with those pictures, but by the time we finished our main course, I was 1,000 percent positive.

Dinner on Saturday ran into brunch on Sunday, at which point Deirdre felt she knew me well enough to program Neil Diamond singing "Sweet Caroline" as the ringtone on my phone.

A year later, we were married. Ten years after that, we were on vacation in Wyoming, and Deirdre, who grew up on horses and had been riding since she was a young girl, was on a mountain trail when her horse threw her. She died instantly.

The loss of a loved one is devastating in any form. But the suddenness and senselessness of Deirdre's death overwhelmed me with a flood of negative emotions—anger, despair, disbelief, and finally, the most crippling of all: guilt.

Some people fall into drugs, alcohol, or depression after losing a spouse. Some turn to God. I did my best to fill the emptiness with work. I've never shied away from living on the edge. I always welcomed the high-risk assignments. After Deirdre's death, I craved them. But finding that challenge, in a department bound up in bureaucracy, steeped in tedium, and hamstrung by politics, seemed impossible.

I wonder if Police Commissioner Trace Baker knew that about me when he invited me down to his office at 1 Police Plaza that morning three years ago. I walked in disenchanted, disheartened, one of four hundred captains in the department, stuck in the middle of the pack with a countdown clock on my phone that reminded me I had 753 days before I could retire. Two hours later, I walked out energized, filled with purpose, a member of the PC's inner circle, and commanding officer of a new unit that would be the top priority, and the most closely guarded secret, in his department.

With only sixteen of us in the squad, we split the workload into two shifts, eight to four and four to midnight. We're off nights and weekends, but since no other team has the training to take our place in an emergency, we're on call 24/7. That's why the ringtone on my work phone has to be as loud and annoying as possible.

It was two hours before dawn when the raw, distorted sounds of Exhale the Demon, an underground heavy-metal band I had recently discovered, jolted me awake.

"Corcoran," I said, hitting the speaker button and jumping out of bed.

"Captain, you're mobilized. US Park Police observed six unknown subjects landing on Liberty Island. They're armed with 9mm submachine guns, have scaled the base, and entered the statue. Pick up at Field Forty-Three."

CHAPTER 3

WHEN YOU DO WHAT I DO for a living, there are some basic rules to live by.

Rule #1: Keep your tactical gear within arm's reach. I have multiple sets—at work, in the trunk of my car, and in my bedroom closet. Less than three minutes after the call came in, I had suited up—cargo pants, shirt, boots, ceramic-plate vest, Kevlar helmet—strapped on my 9mm Glock, and was out the door.

Rule #2: Never depend on an elevator. The building I live in is twenty-seven stories high. My apartment is on the third floor. I took the stairs two at a time, forty pounds heavier than I was going up the night before.

I got to the lobby, where Tibor, the white-haired night man, had seen my ride pull up and was holding the front door wide open.

"*Legyen biztonságban,*" he said as I raced past him. It's Hungarian for "be safe"—his usual send-off when he sees me dashing through the lobby dressed in black and outfitted with body armor.

Rule #3: Never assume your driver knows what he's supposed to do: I jumped into the front seat of the marked SUV and recognized the man behind the wheel: Larry Perkins, an ESU veteran, a total pro. It didn't matter. "Do you know where we're going?" I asked as he pulled out onto York Avenue.

"Yes, sir. Randall's Island. Field forty-three. FDR, RFK Bridge, Central Road, Sunken Meadow Loop."

"Lights and sirens," I said, punching the lights. At this hour, I doubted I'd have to hit the siren more than a few times.

Rule #4: Focus on the mission. It was impossible not to. I'd been obsessively focused on this mission since the day the PC briefed our team two months earlier.

"How hard do you think it would be for a bunch of fanatics to blow up the Statue of Liberty?" he had asked. It was a rhetorical question. We knew better than to respond. But Baker didn't say a word for a solid thirty seconds. He didn't want an answer. He wanted us to think about the unthinkable.

"Her security system is full of holes," he finally said. "During the day, the Park Police are there in force, but at night their number dwindles down to a skeleton crew."

"Doesn't make sense," Chris Redwood said. "Why would they—?"

"Money," Baker cut in. "The feds already spend twenty-five million to maintain and protect Liberty and Ellis Islands. It would cost another eight, maybe ten, to do it right, and no politician is going to ask for that kind of dough. They'd be accused of overkill and laughed out of the room."

"So you're saying the price of Liberty is twenty-five mil," Redwood said. "And not a nickel more."

The team responded, some with laughter, some shaking their heads, and one who simply grumbled, "Assholes."

"Your job," Baker barked, silencing the room with a steely-eyed glare, "is to plug the gaps in their security, not get tangled up in the politics that put them there." He turned to me. "I want a live run-through in sixty days."

"Yes, sir," I said.

"One more thing. It goes without saying, but I'll say it anyway." Baker squared up and addressed the squad. "Priests, lovers, and dying mothers."

He turned and left, his final words reverberating through our collective brain.

Trace Baker was the most hands-on New York City police commissioner since Teddy Roosevelt. And this team of thirteen men and three women was living proof of his commitment, his dedication, and the size of his balls.

When he was appointed PC three years earlier, he had made it his mission to fix what he saw as one of the department's most glaring deficiencies.

"Our Counterterrorism Bureau falls short of what this city needs," he said when he first recruited me. "Their website does a convincing job of making them sound badass, but it's mostly smoke and mirrors aimed at intimidating potential enemies. The public feels safer when they see these guys with their M-4s and their Kevlar helmets patrolling high-profile targets, but in reality, the backbone of the division is an army of people sitting at keyboards, gathering intelligence."

I nodded, clueless where the conversation was going.

"And they're damn good at it," he said. "But if there's a militarized attack on this city, no amount of intelligence is going to win the day. New York is a top-tier target, and we need a corps of cops that has the resources and the training to respond to whatever crazy shit the enemy throws at us. We need a unit that rivals the Navy SEALs, the Green Berets, or the Marine Raiders."

"Sir," I said, "if you ever put that unit together, sign me up. I want to be part of it."

"I don't want you to be *part* of it," Baker said. "I want you to head it up."

Head it up? I would have let out an ear-splitting *oorah*, but he wasn't finished with his appraisal, and I was enjoying it too much to interrupt.

"I've done my research, Corcoran. You're a highly decorated marine; you've got three combat crosses with the NYPD, *plus* the Medal of Honor. And if that's not enough, you haven't taken a sick day since you joined the department."

I smiled. "I haven't been sick."

"That doesn't stop most cops from taking off time they think they're entitled to. You're a team player. And when you're sitting behind this desk, that means a hell of a lot. Let me be straight with you. Not only are you my first choice, you're my *only* choice."

"I'm honored," I said.

"Do you want the job?"

"Absolutely, but—"

"'Absolutely' is a complete sentence," he said. "Add the word 'but,' and you've undone the absoluteness of it all."

"Sorry, sir. The 'but' is a question. Putting together a unit on a par with the SEALs or the Berets won't come cheap. My first thought was, who's paying for all this?"

He laughed. "Well, I could ask the mayor, but he wouldn't cough up a dime. Knowing him, he'd say, 'You want a Special Forces unit? Call the Pentagon.'"

"So, then, to repeat the question," I said, "who is going to pay—"

"That's my problem," Baker said. "Yours is to comb the department looking for candidates, run them through a battery of medical, physical, and psychological tests, and handpick the best of the best. You in?"

"Yes, sir. Absolutely."

CHAPTER 4

THREE MONTHS LATER, WE HAD THE FINANCES, the facilities, and the firepower we needed. Baker dubbed us "Direct Report One," or, in cop shorthand, DR-1—an innocuous name that could easily get lost in the alphabet soup of NYPD bureaus, divisions, and agencies.

Everything about us was secret—who we were, what we did, and how we got it done. The oath of office was simple: Tell no one, and that included, as Baker was prone to reminding us, priests, lovers, and dying mothers.

On the org chart, we were folded under Emergency Services Unit, so we got our fair share of rescue work and emergency calls. But our real mission was to be trained and battle-ready to secure our little five-borough homeland in the event of another surprise attack.

It took us four days to come up with a master plan to storm Liberty Island. Working with a detailed schematic, we went over every inch of the statue's infrastructure and calculated that it would take a terrorist team forty-five minutes from the time they came ashore till the moment they could detonate the Semtex that would obliterate the iconic beacon of democracy that had stood in New York Harbor for almost a century and a half.

The second part of the mission was a lot dicier. Devise a

counterattack, train for it, and do a series of trial-and-error practice runs at a three-hundred-foot tower on Randall's Island until we got it as close to perfect as possible.

Now, on a warm overcast night in the early hours of August eleventh, we were doing it for real.

Eight of us converged on Randall's Island. Seventeen minutes after my phone rang, we were in an unmarked Viper Attack helicopter flying low over the Hudson, practically skimming the water. Only when we were issued red-barrel rifles, and sidearms loaded with Simunitions that would fire paint pellets instead of bullets, did we know for sure that this was a drill.

The helicopter zeroed in on the island, rose 150 feet in the air, and lowered four of our team to the top of the pedestal. As soon as they touched down, the chopper shot up another 200 feet and lowered the rest of us to the crown of the statue.

A quarter mile offshore, Baker sat at a console aboard a thirty-two-foot customized Metal Shark and watched the operation unfold as our night-vision cameras transmitted the action in real time.

For the next nineteen minutes, he watched as our rescue team made a dynamic entry into the statue, and a daring tactical assault on the saboteurs. Thirty-nine minutes and forty-two seconds after the invasion began, five of the terrorists were dead and one had been captured.

I radioed the news. "Lady Liberty is secure."

Ten minutes later, his boat docked, and Baker, wearing the only NYPD field jacket with five stars across each shoulder, jumped off and strode briskly across the plaza. My team and I were there to meet him, along with the six faux terrorists and three Park Police recruited for the mission.

"Great job," he said. "Eighteen seconds under forty minutes."

"We could have been faster," I said. "The chopper should have gotten thirty feet closer to the crown."

"We can go over the video later this morning," he said. "TARU's been filming the entire exercise."

I looked up. A second, smaller helicopter was hovering over the torch in Lady Liberty's outstretched right arm.

"Someone should tell them the exercise is over," I said as a series of flashes went off inside the chopper.

"What the hell is going on up there?" Baker asked.

I took my binoculars and peered at the aircraft as another barrage of flashes went off. "I'm not sure," I said, "but it looks like DCPI Walton is having a photo shoot."

"I told Tony to travel with the film crew. If anyone from the media got wind of what we were doing here, his job was to kill the story," Baker said, training his binoculars on the open chopper door. "Jesus F. Christ. Who is that idiot, and what the hell is he doing out there?"

A young man dressed in black had stepped out onto the skid of the chopper and was posing for pictures with the statue below him.

"Is he out of his tiny fucking mind?" Baker bellowed.

And then, as if to answer the question beyond any shadow of a doubt, the man in black did the unthinkable. He detached his safety harness and spread his arms heroically.

Baker keyed his mic and exploded. "PC to Aviation One. Get all personnel inside the chopper and return to base forthwith!"

Through my glasses I could see the pilot turn around and shout an order. DCPI Walton immediately reached out in an effort to grab the man and pull him aboard. But the young daredevil wasn't ready. He turned and waved at the onlookers below.

I knew him. In fact, everybody knew him. Brady Lebeck, an Uber driver/wannabe actor from Brooklyn, had lit up the screen four years earlier in his first movie, a summer blockbuster. He had followed it up with three hit action films and was now a bona fide megastar.

Lebeck gave his audience a mock salute. The PC returned the gesture with an angry arm pump that said *get the hell inside that bird.*

Lebeck stood up, waved again, and took one more step. His last. Misjudging the height of the doorway, he stepped into the open space between the skid and the helicopter.

Arms flailing, his screams lost in the drone of the rotors, he plummeted through the predawn sky and landed with a bone-crushing thud on the statue's crown.

NYPD's top-secret nighttime maneuver would be public by sunrise.

CHAPTER 5

WE FROZE. THE LOT OF US, warriors all, armed to the hilt, trained to handle every possible emergency, and we just stood there. Speechless. Motionless. Powerless.

Two high-intensity searchlights—one from the helicopter above, the other from the patrol boat below—swept the sky and zeroed in on Brady Lebeck, the twenty-nine-year-old Hollywood golden boy who, only heartbeats ago, was convinced he was king of the world. Now he lay draped between the third and fourth rays of the halo of light on Miss Liberty's head, his body broken, his neck twisted at an angle that left no doubt.

"He's dead," Baker said, his voice barely a whisper. "And so are we."

He radioed the chopper, and the pilot set the aircraft down on the plaza.

Trace Baker had two choices. He could have gone ballistic and stormed the helicopter, screaming questions to which there could never be answers that would change the outcome. Instead, he took the high road.

The pilot killed the engine, and Baker stood there, his body ramrod straight, waiting for the silence.

DCPI Tony Walton stepped from the helicopter and walked toward us. He was in his midforties, good-looking, outgoing, charming, funny, and if that weren't enough, he had the key to the innermost circle of the premier police force in the country.

Everyone wanted a piece of Tony. He was the deputy commissioner of public information, the top cop's guardian at the gate. If a reporter, an editor, or a politician wanted to know what was going on behind closed doors at 1PP, Tony was their man. He knew it, and so did Baker. But they also knew that the conduit of information flowed both ways, and Walton was skilled at getting more information than he parted with, at placing more stories than he gave up.

A job like that can go to a guy's head, and those of us who knew him had watched it happen. Tony was a star-fucker. He enjoyed rubbing elbows, clinking glasses, and occasionally bumping uglies with the rich, the famous, and the powerful. They in turn loved rubbing, clinking, and bumping back. I had no idea what the quid pro quo was between Brady Lebeck and DCPI Walton, but I knew I was about to find out.

Walton, head down, shoulders slumped, approached us and didn't look up until he was in front of the PC. His eyes were red-rimmed from crying.

"I'm sorry, Trace," he said. "Sorry beyond words. You'll have my letter of resignation within the hour."

"This is a crime scene," Baker said. "Investigations before resignations. The District Attorney's Office will be up your ass for the foreseeable future. Their primary goal will be to blame that man's death on you, so being out of a job will be the least of your problems. They might not charge me, but the press, the mayor, the City Council, and Lebeck's family will be coming at me with a vengeance. They're going to have a lot of questions, and there's one I can't answer: What the fuck was a civilian doing on board that chopper in the middle of a highly classified counterterrorism operation?"

Walton closed his eyes, took a deep breath, and let it out slowly. I recognized the tactic. I'd seen it from hundreds of perps who have their alibi rehearsed and need a few quiet moments to pull it out of their head. Truth cascades from people's mouths. Lies ooze like beads of flop sweat.

"A couple of months ago, I got a call from the Mayor's Office of Media and Entertainment," Walton said, opening his eyes and gazing intently at Baker. "Brady Lebeck was going to be starring in a remake of *Dirty Harry*. The original was shot in San Francisco, but Lebeck was thinking it would be much grittier if they shot it in New York. Lebeck is a cop junkie, and NYPD versus San Francisco? No contest. So I sent him on a couple of ride-alongs with some uniforms from the Nineteenth. I told you about that."

"And you spent July Fourth weekend at his place in Easthampton," Baker said, tripping him up immediately. "You forgot to tell me about that. Cut to the chase, Tony. A ride-along on the Upper East Side is ho-fucking-hum to someone like Lebeck. He wanted more action. So you thought, I've got just what he's looking for: a simulated terrorist attack on the Statue of Liberty. He probably shat his pants when you dangled that. And what was the payback? A weekend in Malibu? A stroll down the red carpet at some Hollywood premiere?"

There was no dodging the question. "He said he had two empty seats at his table for the Golden Globes next January," Walton said, opting for the truth. And then he tried to spin it. "I thought, what's the harm? I took his cell phone away so he couldn't record it, and all I did was agree to take a few pictures of him on the skid with the statue in the background. Nobody could connect it to our operation. Plus, he was harnessed. Who knew he'd be crazy enough to unhook himself?"

"And you did all that so you could sit next to some asshole actor at a fucking awards show?"

"You're making it sound like it was only about me. There are five Dirty Harry movies in the franchise. If they shot them here, it would be worth millions to the city."

"Well, I can guarantee they won't be shooting any of them here," Baker said, "and by the time the lawyers are done, it'll *cost* the city millions."

"I'm sorry, Trace."

"You're sorry? Oh good," he said taking out his cell phone and punching the speed dial. "I'll be sure to pass that along."

"You calling the district attorney?" Walton asked.

"Not yet. First I've got to call the man who's going to pay for all the damage you've done. Also, now seems like as good a time as any to give him the opportunity to fire me." He turned to his cell phone. "Hello, Mr. Mayor. This is Commissioner Baker. Yes, sir, I know what time it is. We've got a situation."

Baker didn't try to sugarcoat it. He spelled it out, detail by grisly detail. About thirty seconds in, a voice called out. "Commissioner!"

It was Detective Jeff Fowler, the helicopter pilot, double-timing it across the plaza. "Commissioner," he repeated as he reached us.

I put a finger to my lips. "Keep it down. He's on the phone with the mayor."

Baker had stopped talking and was listening now. He held the phone just far enough away from his ear that I couldn't quite make out the words, but I could make out the tone. The mayor, bombastic at the best of times, had kicked it up a few notches to all-out batshit crazy.

Baker rolled his eyes, hit the mute button, and looked at me. "We've got a movie star with twenty million Twitter followers, hanging like a side of beef off the Statue of Liberty, and all the mayor cares about is how much time he has for damage control."

"Sir," the pilot blurted out.

"Just a second, Mr. Mayor," Baker said into the phone. He muted it again and turned to the pilot. "What have you got, Jeff?"

"Sir, I've been monitoring the radio traffic. A helicopter is on the way here. He's four minutes out."

"One of ours?"

"No, sir. It belongs to Channel 7 Eyewitness News."

"Mayor Richardson," Baker said into the phone. "I don't know what you have in mind for damage control, but you've got four minutes to get it done."

CHAPTER 6

NINETEEN HOURS AFTER I BOLTED OUT OF my apartment that morning, I finally staggered back in. I grabbed a beer from the fridge, collapsed on my unmade bed, and turned on the TV just in time to catch the eleven o'clock news.

In the news business, they like to say, *if it bleeds, it leads*. And when it's the blood of a hot young international action movie star and it's spilled on the copper crown of the quintessential symbol of American liberty, the media will milk it for all it's worth.

I flipped to the channel that had the most to milk. The one whose traffic reporter broke the story and whose camera was rolling a solid seven minutes before any other news source showed up.

The anchorman had on his most somber face. "Good evening," he said. "Back in 1994, when O. J. Simpson's white Bronco led police on a seventy-five-mile chase along a Los Angeles freeway, ninety-five million people watched it unfold on national television. That number was shattered today as an estimated half billion people around the world stayed glued to their TV sets, their computers, their tablets, and their smartphones to watch three brave officers from the NYPD's Emergency Service Unit retrieve the body of actor Brady Lebeck from the crown of the Statue of Liberty. And our cameras were the first on the scene."

"Mother *fucker!*" I yelled, drowning out the rest of his opening. "Way to spin it, Eyewitness News." By drawing the comparison to the iconic O. J. chase, they had managed to turn their predawn scoop into a historic event worthy of the TV news archives.

They then cut to the video that had already been shown again and again and again since it was shot at dawn. It was network TV, so the camera kept a respectable distance from Lebeck's body. If you wanted a bloodier close-up, it was available on LiveLeak or any one of dozens of other websites that cater to those who want the gory details. I, of course, had seen it all firsthand. I had been one of those three brave police officers.

Bravery didn't have much to do with it. Responding to high-risk situations is what we do every day. But in my case, I was handpicked to retrieve the body because ever since I was a kid, I've been a wiz at tying knots.

Back then it was a simple skill set that earned me a Boy Scout merit badge. But at ESU, knowing the right knot is a matter of life and death. If you're setting up a Z-drag hauling system to lower a two-hundred-pound man from the top of the Statue of Liberty, you'd better get every step of that complex procedure right, or the body will drop to the ground in seconds, dragging the rescuers down with it.

It took two of my strongest guys and me more than an hour to harness ourselves, climb out onto the crown, bag the body, strap it to a stretcher, and then, using a one-ton winch, carefully guide it inside the statue, where the medical examiner and the forensics team were standing by.

After milking the recovery operation for a solid five minutes, the broadcast then segued from body-bag journalism to the blame game.

"How did it happen," the anchorman said, "that a civilian, an actor who played a heroic cop in the movies, was aboard an NYPD helicopter on a secret maneuver that many say was illegal? We have someone here in the studio who can shed some light on the subject. Former NYPD Detective Jason Harding."

"Fuck," I said, and downed the rest of my beer in three swallows.

Harding had left the department two years earlier under a cloud of suspicion after ten kilos of uncut heroin disappeared during a routine chain-of-custody transfer. Nothing was proved, but a month after the drugs went missing, he retired and joined a big firm as a private security consultant. Since then, he had been a frequent critic of the NYPD, its policies, its practices, and its leadership. He was known throughout 1PP as Jason Blowharding.

The camera cut to his lantern-jawed head with its shock of red hair and matching mustache and goatee. "The tragedy that occurred today is irrefutable proof of the continued mismanagement of our city's police force, and its growing lack of concern for the lives and safety of the very people it is paid to protect," he said, scowling like a Texas DA arguing for the death penalty. "Last night, when almost everyone in the city that never sleeps slept soundly in their homes, the NYPD brazenly, wantonly, and unlawfully flew weaponized aircraft over hundreds of thousands of innocent civilians to execute a military operation that is far outside the scope of a city police force."

I was debating whether to switch channels when Neil Diamond interrupted. My personal cell. I looked at my caller ID. It was Kirsten, Deirdre's sister.

I muted the TV and took the call. "Hey, Kirsten. How are you?"

"How are *you*?" she said. "I just saw you on the news. Are you watching? That cop who is always shitting all over the department is on Channel Seven."

"I know. Thanks for calling. I needed a reason to turn him off. What's going on?"

"Look, I know you've got your hands full, but I need a favor."

Kirsten was a strong, smart, capable woman. When she reached out for help, it was almost always because her creep of a husband had done something stupid, illegal, or both. Phil was a hotshot Wall Street trader and a coke-snorting skirt chaser. I had bailed him out of more than one jam. Two years earlier, Phil was cruising the fuck zone in Hunt's Point after dark when he spotted a young pavement princess and negotiated a forty-dollar beejay. He paid her, but instead of reaching into his pants, she reached into her purse and pulled out her detective shield.

Phil played the "my brother-in-law is a cop" card. The detective recognized my name and gave me a call.

"Danny, it's Elyse Rhodes. I'm working Whittier Street, and I just collared a john by the name of Phillip Grissom," she said.

"That's my asshole brother-in-law," I said.

"We've confirmed the asshole part, but I needed you to verify the rest."

"Have you booked him yet?"

"No. Right now I've got him on ice, but my lieutenant is going to swing by here in about ten minutes, so if you want me to cut him loose . . ."

"Elyse, what I want is for you to bring him to my house so I can nail his balls to the wall, but after what his wife has gone through the past couple of years, I'd like to spare her the agony."

"Is that Deirdre's sister?" Rhodes asked.

"Kirsten," I said. "She's had it rough. Two years before Deirdre died, their brother Toby OD'd on heroin."

"Oh, Danny, I didn't know."

"Well, Dad's a judge, so they kept it under wraps. Listen, Elyse, thanks for the call. Nothing would make me happier than to have you drag Phil through the ugliest part of the system, but that would mean dragging Kirsten, her kids, and Judge Solomon along with him."

"Say no more. Let me uncuff him and send him packing before the boss shows up."

"I owe you one, Elyse. Thanks."

"Don't thank me," she said. "*He's* the one who should be thanking *you*."

"He should," I said. "But he won't."

And, of course, he never did. Now Kirsten was calling for a favor, and I wondered what hell Phil was putting her through this time.

"What's up, Kirsten?" I said. "What can I do for you?"

"It's Dad," she said. "The cancer's back."

"Oh, shit," I said. "Look, he beat it before. He can beat it again."

"I hope so, but it kicked in again months ago. He didn't tell me about it until tonight. I was furious at him, but you know how he is. He said Dr. Yang had him back on radiation, and he didn't want me to worry."

"Sounds like the judge."

"He took me out to dinner. We had such a sweet time together talking about the old days, about Mom, and Deirdre, and Toby. He said he's ready to put down the gavel. He's going to rule on this god-awful Alboroto case tomorrow, and as much as he hates to go out on this colossal FBI clusterfuck—his words, not mine—he doesn't have the strength to take on any more work."

"What can I do?" I said.

"You know how much he loves you. He could use some moral support. Do you think you could find the time to make it down to the courthouse tomorrow for his last hurrah?"

"I'll make time," I said.

"Thanks. Call me afterward and tell me how it goes. Then maybe you and Dad could come over for a barbecue on Sunday with me and the kids."

Me and the kids. Not *me and Phil and the kids.* Their marriage had been going south for years, and a family gathering without him was just another sign of the inevitable.

"It's a date," I said.

I hung up and turned the sound back up on the TV. The blowhard ex-cop was just wrapping it up.

"Thank you very much, Detective Harding," the anchorman said.

"One more thing, if you don't mind. I'd like to say something to Mayor Richardson on behalf of the people of New York."

He didn't wait for an answer. "Mr. Mayor, election day is less than three months away, and from where I sit, you're in a close race. I think you can win the hearts and minds of the voters and a second term if you act now to fire your out-of-control commissioner and reassign his band of quasi-military storm troopers to a unit where innocent civilians won't get killed." He smiled, his face oozing with hollow compassion and goodwill. "I hear there are some openings in motor vehicle repair."

I wanted to put my fist right through the flat screen, not just because I despised him, but because I knew he was going to get exactly what he asked for. Trace Baker had called me twenty minutes before I got home.

"Danny, it's over," he said. "I'm out. DR-1 is history, and if you decide to stay on, your new PC will be Martin Ennis. Mayor Richardson will announce it at a press conference tomorrow at nine a.m."

He hadn't invited me to be there, so I figured I'd watch it on TV. Now I wouldn't do either. Kirsten's phone call had upset me. There was something foreboding about that sweet father-daughter dinner where the judge talked about the old days with his only surviving child.

I suspected that the cancer was worse than he was letting on, and right now spending some quality time with a man who meant as much to me as my own father was more important than flicking on the TV set and watching my twenty-two-year career with the NYPD go down the drain.

CHAPTER 7

I CAN'T BEGIN TO COUNT the number of times I've been to the US District Courthouse at 500 Pearl Street in Lower Manhattan. It has never been one of my favorite places. But this time was different.

I wasn't there to sit on the witness stand for hours or even days on end and be badgered by slick defense attorneys doing their damnedest to discredit my testimony, impugn my character, or convince a jury that I was just another angry, racist cop.

No. This time I was there because it was the only place in the world I wanted to be.

I arrived at 8:30 and checked my gun with security. Most of the guards are retired NYPD, so I can never get through the gauntlet of blue blazers without fielding a few questions about the latest department gossip. That morning, with the front page of the *Post* screaming, SHOCK AND AWFUL!!! ACTOR DIES AS NYPD'S SECRET MILITARY OP GOES HAYWIRE, the questions came fast and furious.

I told them I didn't know much more than what they already saw on TV, which was a lie, and that the mayor's press conference at nine o'clock would answer most of their questions, which may or may not have been the truth.

"Was Lebeck drunk when he took the dive?" one of them asked, following me down the corridor as I headed toward the elevator.

"His BAC was 0.17," I said, giving him some inside information that would go public soon enough. "More than twice the legal limit."

"I knew it," he said.

The elevator arrived, and I stepped in.

"Catch you later," he said, which meant I'd be bombarded with more questions when I came back for my gun.

I rode up to the twelfth floor and immediately ran into Wesley Claiborne, who was waiting for an elevator heading down. Thirty years ago Wesley played goalie for a professional football team in Haiti. One morning, he was jogging on the beach at Port-Salut when he saw another jogger coming toward him. She was tall and athletic, and the closer she got, the more beautiful she was. As soon as she passed him, Wesley did a 180, caught up to her, and turned on the charm.

Anna-Maria turned out to be a fifth-grade teacher who was passionate about her job and, as far as Wesley could tell, about everything that came her way. She had only one drawback. She was in Haiti on holiday and lived an inconvenient fifteen hundred miles away in the Bronx. Wesley didn't hesitate. He cut his career short, immigrated to America, married Anna-Maria, and became a court officer. Judge Solomon saw his potential on day one. Thirty years later, Wesley is still the judge's right-hand man and still very much a footballer—physically fit, fast, with a knack for assessing a situation in a heartbeat.

"Danny, I saw all that Statue of Liberty craziness on television. How are you holding up?" he said, his Creole heritage ever present in his voice.

"Lousy, but thanks for asking. Where are you off to?"

"Brooklyn. The judge asked me to run these papers over to the Eastern District. I'll be back in a few hours."

"I thought he had court this morning."

"He does. Nine o'clock."

"None of my business," I said, "but I have to ask. If he has court, why is he sending his senior court officer off to deliver paperwork? There are at least a half-dozen paralegals who could do it, and none of them would be missed."

A bell dinged, announcing the arrival of an elevator heading to the lobby. Wesley was about to get on, hesitated, and then stopped. The door closed, and he let the elevator go without him. "Let's talk in private," he said.

I followed him down a corridor, and we stepped into the stairwell, shutting the door behind us.

"It's this Alboroto hearing," he said. "It's eating him up inside."

Sebastián Alboroto was the only son of the man they called *el Carnicero*—the Butcher—Joaquín Alboroto, the head of the largest drug cartel in Mexico. A few months ago, the FBI got a tip that Sebastián was meeting his girlfriend on a yacht off the shore of Longboat Key on Florida's West Coast. As soon as he showed up, they stormed the boat, arrested him, and flew him to New York. Judge Solomon was currently presiding over the hearing to determine whether he should go to trial.

"I only know the bare bones of the case," I said. "Is the judge upset because it's narcotics? I mean, his son died of an overdose. He could have recused himself if he thought he couldn't be fair, but he didn't."

"That's the problem. He's *too* fair. Which is why this morning he's going to step into that courtroom and set Alboroto free."

"Holy shit. What . . . how . . . ? It looked like a slam dunk."

"The feds fucked up, Danny," Wesley said. "One in particular: Special Agent Frank Delaqua. He got a tip six months ago that Sebastián was having an affair with Camilla Uskar, the Spanish supermodel. Both of them are married, and Camilla is constantly hounded by paparazzi, so their *affaire de coeur* had to be kept under wraps. Delaqua asked the US Attorney for a warrant to tap Camilla's phone so they could track Alboroto. They turned him down."

"No surprise," I said. "She's a law-abiding citizen of a foreign nation, and the FBI can't violate her privacy just because they heard she's shtupping some drug dealer."

"Delaqua bugged her phone anyway," Wesley said.

I instinctively threw my hands up in the air in my go-to how-stupid-can-one-person-be reaction.

Wesley went on. "As soon as Delaqua caught the first call from

Alboroto, he ran back to the US Attorney, said he scored Alboroto's number from a CI, and got his warrant. After that, every time Alboroto changed burner phones, the warrant was reissued. Then it was just a matter of staying on him until he planned the rendezvous on the yacht, and they nabbed him."

"Illegally," I said.

"Illegal as all hell."

"And the judge knows this?"

"He found out yesterday. The defense team is good, Danny. They traced the DNA of the arrest back to the illegal tap on Camilla's phone. Delaqua didn't just bend the law. He pissed all over the Constitution."

"So the judge has no choice but to cut Alboroto loose," I said. "That still doesn't explain why he's sending you off to Brooklyn."

"NYPD traced the heroin that killed Toby to the Alboroto network. Now the judge has one of the men responsible for Toby's death in his courtroom, and he has to bang the gavel and say, *Vaya con Dios*. I think he's sending me off on this bullshit errand so I don't have to witness the darkest day of his career."

He opened the stairwell door, and we headed back to the elevator bank.

"He may be able to get you out of the courtroom," I said, "but it won't be so easy to get rid of me. Thanks for filling me in. I'm going to be there for him whether he likes it or not. Where is he now?"

"In chambers. He's expecting you."

"How is he expecting me? I didn't even know I was coming till late last night."

The elevator stopped, and Wesley gave me a wide, toothy grin as he stepped inside. "Oh, please, Danny. The man is amazing. Even when he's down, he still manages to stay three jumps ahead of the rest of the world."

CHAPTER 8

HARVEY SOLOMON, my father-in-law, friend, and closest confidant, was sitting behind his desk. "Danny!" he said, getting up and giving me a hug. "What brings you here on this auspicious day in my waning career?"

"I ran into Wesley. He said you were expecting me."

"The man talks too much. Kirsten called me last night. She told me you'd be swinging by. I've been following this actor's death on the news. How could something like that happen?"

"A confluence of bad decisions."

"Any of them yours?"

"No, but I still ended up inside the blast radius."

"Is there anything I can do to help?"

"Thanks, but it's riddled with politics. Keep your distance. Anyway, I didn't come here to talk about me. Kirsten said the cancer kicked up again. What's going on?"

"That's what I love about you, Danny: no foreplay. I remember the time we were all up at the lake, and the whole family was tiptoeing around me because—"

"And that's what I love about you, Harvey. You're a master at dodging the question. Let's get to the elephant in the room. What did Dr. Yang say about the cancer?"

"He reminded me that the surgery and the radiation I had the first time around bought me twelve good years, and then he said something to the effect of 'you can't expect it to last forever.'"

"That sounds harsh."

"I may have paraphrased. He's actually a good guy. I guess I'm just a little pissed off at the cards I've been dealt."

"You told Kirsten that he has you back on radiation."

"It's the tried-and-true method," he said. "I don't know if it'll work, but I'm willing to give it the old college try." He capped off the run of bullshit clichés with a jaunty smile.

"Let me see the tats," I said.

"What?"

"Harvey, the therapy team pinpoints the precise spots on your body where you'll get the radiation, and then they mark it with tattoos or permanent ink. Let me see yours. And don't try to show me the ones that are twelve years old. I want to see the new ones."

He grinned. "Y'know, sometimes you fucking cops are too smart for your own good."

"You're not getting radiation, are you?"

"No, Danny. That ship has sailed."

"Which brings me back to the first question. What did the doctor say?"

"First, he said that this time around, the story is not going to have a happy ending. Then he told me to get my affairs in order. Funny, I thought only doctors in tearjerker movies used that old saw, but Dr. Yang actually said it."

"So last night when you and Kirsten went out to dinner and reminisced about the old days, was that you getting your affairs in order?"

"My legal affairs have been buttoned up for years," the judge said. "Last night was about connecting with my only surviving child."

"And this Sunday you can connect with your grandchildren and the only son-in-law you're not embarrassed to introduce to your friends."

"I doubt if I'm going to have any friends after I rule on this Alboroto case."

"Bullshit. Nobody is going to lay this on you, Harvey. Wesley told me about the illegal wiretap. If you cut Alboroto loose, it's because you have no legal grounds to hold him."

"No legal grounds," he repeated, shaking his head. "Every day, I would sit up there, looking down at him with his arrogant smirk and his fuck-you-judge attitude, and I kept thinking, how can he be so smug? And sitting right behind him in the first row was his mother, who was also taunting me in her own little special way—clutching her rosary, wringing her hands, letting out the occasional wail. Wesley calls her Mother Teresa, but it's pure theater. The woman's been sleeping in the same bed as el Carnicero for forty years.

"The prosecution had a solid case. Then yesterday, the defense dropped the bomb that the FBI never had a warrant to tap the girl-friend's phone. I think Alboroto knew they had that ace in the hole all along. That's why he was so cocky. He was just fucking with the system.

"So now, after thirty-eight years on the bench, I get to throw out the case, and in less than an hour Sebastián Alboroto and his mother will be on a private jet back to Mexico."

"If it's any consolation, I'll be in the courtroom for moral support."

"Fuck moral support. I'd be happier if you beat the shit out of Special Agent Delaqua."

If he was angling for a laugh, it worked.

He looked at his watch and stood up. "It's time. Do me a favor, Danny. Go to work. Go home. Go anywhere. I hate the thought of having you watch my career end in a blaze of ignominious defeat."

"With all due respect, Your Honor, if you don't want me in your courtroom, you are going to have to officially bar me from entering. Kirsten wants you to see one friendly face when you look out onto the gallery, and for better or worse, it's going to be mine."

He reached his hand out, and I took it.

"Thanks," he said. "And tell Kirsten I said thanks for not sending my other son-in-law."

CHAPTER 9

THE HEARING WAS A MEDIA MAGNET. At least fifty diehard trial junkies were lined up outside who didn't stand a chance of getting inside the jam-packed courtroom. I simply strolled in, and one of the court officers ushered me to a front-row seat behind the prosecutor. It pays to know the guy who runs the show.

I looked around the vast space, at the hundreds of expectant faces all waiting to be the first to hear one man's decision—a judgment that would echo around the world only minutes after he delivered it.

I felt as if I had walked into a theater filled with people waiting to see a movie I'd already seen. I knew the ending. I looked over at the prosecution team. They had their game faces on, but I'd be willing to bet they were smart enough to know they were about to go down in flames.

I turned around to check the gallery behind me. Three rows back, I spotted the man who had blown their case: Special Agent Frank Delaqua. I recognized him immediately. The press had thoroughly documented the scene when he delivered Sebastián Alboroto to the federal lockup. Only now Delaqua wasn't looking nearly as smug. His career was down the toilet, but his once-a-cop-always-a-cop sixth sense was still intact, and within seconds he picked up on my stare and returned it, no doubt wondering who the VIP was who had been escorted to a ringside seat.

I looked away and zeroed in on the heir to the throne of the evil empire, sitting at the table to my left. Sebastián Alboroto seemed to have stepped off the cover of *GQ*. His pitch-black hair was oiled and slicked back, his white teeth flashed against a bronze canvas that glowed with health, and his cream-colored bespoke linen suit would have set me back two months' salary.

Arrogance oozed from every pore, and I hated knowing that in only minutes, his self-satisfaction and blatant narcissism would reach a new high. He turned in his chair and reached out to the woman in black who sat on the other side of the rail behind him. She clasped his hand with both of hers, and he responded with a tender reassuring smile. The moment screamed *Photo op!* and cameras clicked like a swarm of beetles.

The touching mother-son moment was interrupted with the cry of "All rise. The Honorable Judge Harvey J. Solomon presiding."

My father-in-law took the bench. "Be seated," he said.

He waited a solid twenty seconds for everyone to settle in. For better or for worse, this was Harvey's last hurrah, and he made sure all eyes, ears, and minds were on him.

"Yesterday's revelation of an improperly obtained wiretap on the part of the FBI is irrefutable," he began. "All the evidence against the defendant is fruit of the poisonous tree, which makes it completely and unequivocally inadmissible. Therefore . . ."

He cleared his throat with all the finesse of an awards-show presenter about to announce the winner. "Therefore," he repeated, as if his audience could have forgotten where he left off, "I am ruling that the arrest of Sebastián Alboroto was unconstitutional."

The room exploded, and the judge pounded his gavel, demanding order.

The lead defense attorney stood. "Your Honor, the defense moves to have *all* charges against my client dismissed and requests that he be released immediately. Based on your ruling, it would be unfair for the government to hold him in custody for another moment."

The judge nodded. "I see, Mr. Navarro. You'd like your client to be released immediately so he can once again return to his life of kidnapping, killing, and destroying millions of lives with cocaine and heroin."

"Your Honor!" Navarro snapped back. "I object! The court has no right to assail my cli—"

The judge banged his gavel. "Sit the fuck down and shut up, Counselor!"

I heard it. I saw it. But I couldn't make sense of it. Harvey Solomon had gone off the rails.

"Your Honor, I will *not* sit down!" the attorney yelled back. "Your attack on my client is grounds for us to file charges of judicial misconduct to the—"

Sebastián Alboroto stood up and put a hand on his lawyer's shoulder. "It's okay, Tino. Sit. I got this."

Navarro took his seat.

"Go ahead, Judge. Get it off your chest," Alboroto taunted. "I can handle it. We all can handle it." He turned to his mother.

Luciana Alboroto rose to her feet. She was taller than I expected. Earlier, I had only seen her leaning forward toward her son, but standing erect and proud, she was about five-ten. She lifted her head defiantly at the bench.

"Knock yourself out, Your Honor," Alboroto said. "Lay it on me."

"I've had vermin in my court, Mr. Alboroto," he said, "but none as vile or despicable as you. But I took an oath that I would administer justice under the Constitution no matter how rich or poor, how saintly or satanic, the defendant may be. And today, I honored that oath. I fulfilled my obligation as a judge."

"Sounds to me like Your Honor is saying . . ." Alboroto turned and played to the room. "Justice has been served."

"Far from it," the judge said. "Everyone in this courtroom knows you are guilty of the charges brought against you, and many more. I only afforded you the protection of the Constitution of a country whose citizens are the tragic victims of your criminal enterprise. My ruling upheld the law. But justice was most definitely not served."

There was a large envelope on the bench. The judge opened it, slid out an eight-by-ten photo, and held it up. It was Toby.

"This is my son. *Was* my son—young, alive, and full of promise—until you murdered him. You weren't in the room when he died. You weren't even in the country. But as far as I'm concerned, it was you who plunged that needle into his arm."

"I'm sorry for your loss, Your Honor," Alboroto said, and then turned to the gallery, the self-satisfied grin still on his face. He was savoring this. It was theater, and he was the star. "But I take no responsibility for people who abuse drugs irresponsibly. You know what they say when a kid dies of an overdose? 'Where were the parents?'"

There was an audible gasp from the room, and Harvey set the picture of Toby on the desktop.

"Now, if you're through trashing me," Alboroto said, turning back to the judge, "let's get back to business. You just tossed my arrest. So I'm guessing that means I get to walk now."

Harvey leaned forward in his chair. "As a federal court judge, I am bound by law to let you go. But as a grieving father, I'm going to make sure that the only place you go is straight to hell."

He stood up, reached into his robe, pulled out a gun, and pointed it at Alboroto.

The drug dealer's instincts were fast, and he dived to the left just as the judge pulled the trigger. The bullet struck Mother Teresa in the neck, and a geyser of blood sprayed across the defense table as she fell.

I did what I've been trained to do when there's an active shooter: bring him down, even if he's your dead wife's father. I instinctively reached for my gun. But by the grace of God, it was twelve floors away with security.

There were nine court officers in the room, all bound by the same protocol: neutralize the threat. Three of them were in the rear, and with the crowd stampeding toward the exit doors, their guns were useless.

But the six at the front had drawn their weapons, and at least half of them had a clear shot. They could have—should have—opened fire immediately. But they didn't. Or couldn't. They screamed at him. A chorus of "Your Honor, drop the gun! Put the gun down! Drop it, drop it, drop it!" rang out.

Maybe they hesitated because none of them could bring themselves to mow down a beloved man who had served his country with such distinction and dignity for nearly forty years.

Or maybe they gave him the few extra seconds it would take to finish what he had started. He aimed his gun again. I could see now that it was a Glock 45—a 9mm semiautomatic with a seventeen-round magazine. He had sixteen bullets left.

He needed only one.

Alboroto had flattened himself against the rail to get as low as he could. But the bench was two feet above the floor. The judge aimed down, pulled the trigger, and opened a gaping hole in the swaggering young drug lord's head, streaming an arc of blood, brains, and bone from his cream-colored suit to the gold brocade draperies fifteen feet away.

A second later, a hail of gunfire rang out as almost every court officer in the room emptied their gun, shredding the judge's robe, splintering his desk, and shattering the carved US District Court shield behind him. Most of the spectators were gone or scrambling to get out. Only the court officers, a few intrepid photographers, and I made our way in the other direction.

The bloodied body of the Honorable Harvey J. Solomon had pitched back against the mahogany wall, and his chin dropped to his chest. Over the course of my years in the marines and the NYPD, I've seen my share of carnage—IED explosions, mob violence, school shootings—but I have a built-in defense mechanism that keeps my emotions in check.

Not this time. I wouldn't cry openly, but I could feel the pain of immeasurable loss coursing through my body. I wanted to scream at him. I wanted to tell him how much I loved him. Most of all, I wanted to apologize to him for not stopping him, but I had failed to see the signs.

Now, in hindsight, they were crystal clear. "Get your affairs in order," his doctor had said.

And so he did. Last night, he connected with Kirsten, and this morning, he connected with Deirdre, through the only conduit that mattered to him. Me.

"My legal affairs have been buttoned up for years," he had reminded me. But there was still one piece of unfinished business: avenging Toby's death. And once that was done, Harvey Solomon was ready to meet his Maker.

He knew it would be at the hands of the court officers who, only minutes earlier, had vowed to protect him. I'm sure he regretted putting that burden on them, but the one thing he couldn't do was put it on the man who had been his protégé, his loyal deputy, and one of his closest friends for thirty years.

And that's why, right about now, Wesley Claiborne would be walking into a courthouse in Brooklyn with an envelope full of meaningless papers under his arm.

CHAPTER 10

Mexico City, 1962

"Soy un hombre simple que vive una vida simple," Alejandro Alboroto said when he was interviewed for the job.

The interviewer almost smiled. His question had been, "Tell me about yourself," and the best Alboroto could come up with was, *I am a simple man living a simple life.*

"*¿Qué más?*" the interviewer said. What else?

Alboroto shrugged. He had a wife, Catalina, a five-year-old boy, Joaquín, and . . . He stopped. That was all he could think of.

That was all the interviewer needed. "You start Monday morning at six," he said.

Alboroto beamed. He was now a transporter for the Quintana cartel. He would drive the trucks filled with cocaine to the Mexican border towns where they would be offloaded for the next leg of their journey to the United States. It was the perfect job for a man with very little education, even less ambition, and humble needs for his small family.

And for the next seven years, he did it perfectly. Until the ninth of November, 1969, when he and five other drivers were rounded up and shepherded into a warehouse on the outskirts of the city. Their hands were zip-tied behind their backs, and they were lined up against a cinder-block wall.

A man entered, and they all froze. Vicente de la Plata was known as *el Hombre de Negro*. Black shirt, black pants, black boots, black heart.

"*¿Quién lo llevó?*" he demanded. *Who took it?*

Alboroto was confused. Took what?

"Yesterday's delivery arrived a hundred kilos light," De la Plata said, answering the question as if he'd read Alboroto's mind. "Only six drivers had access to that shipment. One of you was stupid enough to think I wouldn't notice the shortage. I want that fool to step forward now."

Nobody moved.

De la Plata clasped his hands in front of his chest and looked at the trio of guards who were covering the drivers with their PM md. 63 assault rifles. "*Todos inocentes,*" he said, his face as close to angelic as it could ever get.

The minions gave the boss man a hearty laugh.

"One of them is lying," he said. "But which one? *¿Quién sabe?*"

He stepped in front of the first driver. "*Buenos días,* señor Flores, did you take my cocaine?" he asked graciously.

"No, señor."

"I don't believe you," De la Plata said, and put a bullet through Flores's brain.

He stepped in front of the second man. "Ah, señor Velázquez, do you happen to know where my missing cocaine is?"

Velázquez was sobbing. "No, señor, I swear on the life of my—"

A bullet silenced him.

One by one, the drivers denied stealing the drugs, and one by one, they were shot through the head.

Alboroto was the last in line. "Today is my son's birthday," he said. "He's twelve."

That got a response. "*¿Cuál es su nombre?*"

"Joaquín."

Alboroto braced himself for the next question. Did you take the cocaine? But De la Plata smiled and said nothing.

And then Alejandro Alboroto, as uneducated as he was, understood that the question no longer had to be asked. If he answered yes, he would be shot. If he answered no, he would still be executed like the others.

"*Soy un hombre simple que vive una vida simple,*" Alboroto said.

The man in black pulled the trigger.

He turned and left the bodies for the others to dispose of. He would call his superiors and tell them that he had found the man who stole the cocaine, and had made sure that he would never steal again.

It would matter to no one that five innocent men had to die to be certain that justice was done.

CHAPTER 11

On the day after his twelfth birthday, Joaquín Alboroto accompanied his mother to the local police station.

"When did you last see your husband?" the detective asked as he filled out a missing-persons report.

"Yesterday morning when he went to work."

"What does he do?"

"He drives a food delivery truck for Comestibles Mexicanas."

The detective put down his pen, and Joaquín knew that the investigation was closed before it began. Comestibles Mexicanas was owned by the Quintana cartel. The cop, whether he was on their payroll or not, wasn't going to waste his time looking for a low-level drug runner who went missing.

The detective shrugged. "Men leave, señora," he said.

"Not Alejandro."

The cop turned to Joaquín. "Take care of your mother."

That afternoon, they went to church with five other families to ask Father Hernández what they could do to find their loved ones.

"Pray," he said.

And in that instant, Joaquín had his epiphany. Nobody looked after the working people—the farmers picking coca in the fields, the packers, the truck drivers. Not the police. Not even God. People like his father were disposable.

He knelt to pray. Not for Alejandro Alboroto, a good man, a simple man, whom he knew he would never see again. He prayed for his destiny—to be everything his father was not. Rich. Powerful. Invincible.

It took only a week for the Lord to answer his prayer.

For two years, Joaquín had worked after school for Héctor Díaz, the local butcher. First sweeping and taking out the trash, but the boy was too smart to keep behind a broom. So Díaz, whose seventy-year-old hands were racked with arthritic pain, began to teach him the art of butchering. Young Joaquín was a quick learner, and soon Díaz began to supplement his minimum wage with a weekly ration of meat scraps.

The night Joaquín Alboroto's life changed forever, he left the butcher shop at six and walked home. "Where's our dinner?" his mother said as soon as he entered the kitchen.

"It's Tuesday," Joaquín said. "I don't get paid till Saturday."

"I know, but I called Héctor this morning and told him to send you home with a pound of ground beef. I told him I would pay him for it."

"He said nothing, mamá."

His mother threw up her hands. "Crazy old man. I told him to write it down."

"Should I go back?"

"I'm sorry," she said, putting a soft hand on his cheek. "But you must either go back or go hungry."

Joaquín went back. Héctor would be there. He always stayed at least an hour after closing, to tally the receipts and check the inventory for the next day.

When Joaquín arrived, the lights were on, the shades were drawn, and he could hear the buzz of the band saw coming from inside. As soon as he opened the rear door, a man grabbed him by the collar, yanked him in, and pressed a gun to his head. A second man slammed the door and bolted it.

"Who the fuck is this, Díaz?" the first man demanded.

"It's okay. *Está bien*," Héctor said. "He's my apprentice. I sent for him. I could use some help. Joaquín, *por favor*, give me a hand with this."

The boy looked at the carcass stretched out on the massive butcher-block table. It was human. Or at least what remained of one.

He turned to Díaz in horror.

"Come on, muchacho, you've done this before," Díaz said, hoping the boy would catch on. "Put on your apron and show these men how good you are at carving up the meat."

Joaquín knew better than to protest. He nodded. He understood. Slowly he advanced toward the dead body.

"Are you sure this *niño* knows what he's doing?" the man with the gun asked.

"No worries," Díaz said. "He's smart. He's good. Pretty soon, he will be better than me. You want this done in a hurry? With two of us, we will be done twice as fast."

And so, with Díaz guiding him, Joaquín butchered his first body. The two men bagged the remains and left.

Joaquín stood there stunned, his heart pounding, his apron drenched with blood.

"They work for the Quintana cartel," Díaz said.

"And they brought you a dead body?"

"Not one. Many. These people are ruthless. They will kill another man as casually as you would squash a bug. And the *Federales* don't want to deal with their victims littering the streets. But a man gone missing? Nobody cares. He ran off. He crossed the border. A man found dead on the sidewalk? Now, that's a problem. They pay me good money to help them get rid of the problem." He laughed. "You think I can survive selling chickens to peasants? What are you doing here at this hour anyway? Why did you come back?"

"*Carne molida*," Joaquín said meekly. "Mamá wants me to bring home some ground beef."

"No!" the butcher boomed.

Joaquín trudged home, exhausted, blood spattered, and reeking of gore.

"Where were you?" his mother asked as soon as he walked through the door. "I was worried."

"Sorry, *mamá*. El señor Díaz needed some extra help."

"It's late. Where's our dinner?"

He handed her a package and watched as she unwrapped the butcher paper.

"*¡Dios mío!*" she said, staring in wonder at the thick red, beautifully marbled T-bone steak.

She turned to her son. She said nothing, asked no questions. Tears streamed down her cheek, and a look of intense pride swept over her as she gazed at her boy.

And she knew he was no longer a boy. He was a man. But unlike his father, Joaquín Alboroto was not a simple man.

CHAPTER 12

THE FOLLOWING WEEK, the same two men brought another body to the butcher shop. Ten days later, they showed up with another. A week after that, they carted in two more.

"Five dead in less than a month," Joaquín whispered to the butcher. "Are the Quintanas at war?"

Díaz shook his head. "No, it's just business as usual. Those two," he said, nodding at the pair who delivered the cadavers. "This is their full-time job."

Armando Galdós was essentially a beast of burden who was paid to lift dead weights and keep his mouth shut. He did both well. César Villablanca, who was in charge, was much more sociable.

"I've told them about you," he said to Joaquín. "Even Fernando Quintana knows of the boy who dismembers cadavers with the skill of a surgeon."

"El señor Quintana knows my name?" Joaquín said, his eyes wide.

"Not your name. Just your reputation. To him you are el Carnicero Pequeño."

Joaquín filled with pride. The head of the syndicate knew him. The Little Butcher.

Six months into his new role, Joaquín arrived at the store after school.

It was quiet. No customers. No Héctor. He put on his apron, swept the floor, and opened the thick refrigerator door to look for his boss.

Héctor Díaz was stretched out on the concrete floor. No wounds. No bruises. No signs of violence. *A sad end to a sad life,* Joaquín thought. Fifty years a struggling butcher, and he drops dead in the meat locker, his legacy to be consumed at dinner and flushed down the crapper before he is in the ground.

He called Héctor's wife, and an hour later, the body was in the funeral home. Joaquín was about to close up when Villablanca burst through the door.

"*¡Carajo!*" he growled. "I heard Díaz is dead."

"Yes, sir," Joaquín said. "God rest his soul."

"To hell with his soul. I need a butcher."

The boy hesitated. "I'm . . . I'm a butcher."

"And is this your shop? You open every afternoon when school is done?" Villablanca said, mocking him.

"I don't need a shop. Do you think I want to spend my life selling chickens to peasants?" Joaquín said, quoting his late mentor. "All I need are the tools of my trade and a private place to do my work. Someplace safe, where you don't have to worry about people sticking their noses in the door."

Someplace like the Quintana compound, he wanted to say, but he held back, hoping Villablanca was smart enough to figure that out on his own.

He was. But he wasn't so sure it was a good idea. Quintana might think he was a fool for suggesting it. So Villablanca played it safe. "Mi Jefe," he said to Quintana later that evening, "the butcher dropped dead, and the kid, el Carnicero Pequeño, had this *idea completamente loco.*"

"*¿Loco?*" Quintana said after Villablanca spelled it out. "*¡Es brillante!*"

Quintana lived in a 45,000-square-foot mansion with his wife, his daughter, and an army of chefs, maids, butlers, gardeners, dog handlers, and other household help.

Three other massive buildings stood on the property. The largest was a second mansion that housed more than a hundred traffickers, enforcers, soldiers, and bodyguards. They worked around the clock, half of them on duty while the other half slept, ate, showered, drank, or fucked. On the outside, it was almost identical to the main house, but on the inside, it was strictly functional, and the men who lived there called it *el palacio del pobre*—the poor man's palace.

Behind the crew quarters stood a windowless steel structure that was only a single story high. Seven stories belowground were an impenetrable vault, office space for the money launderers, and easy access to a tunnel that extended a mile beyond the compound's outer gates. And finally, there was the hangar where Quintana kept his fleet of cars, trucks, motorcycles, two Boeing 737s, and a Sikorsky CH-53 Sea Stallion helicopter.

A week after the death of Héctor Díaz, a section of the hangar had been walled off and converted into a workstation for Joaquín. There were two stainless steel autopsy tables with perforated surfaces for fluid drainage, a wall-mounted dissecting sink, and an extensive assortment of knives, scalpels, bolt cutters, and bone saws.

Despite the fact that it was a state-of-the-art morgue, it was still called *la carnicería*—the butcher shop. Four days after it was ready, Joaquín welcomed its first two visitors. One was Norberto Abril, a journalist who had published a column that morning condemning the cartel for bribing politicians and police officials throughout the state. Mr. Abril was wearing jeans, sneakers, and a guayabera shirt that had fourteen fresh bullet holes in it and had gone from pure white to a dark reddish-brown. The second visitor, who walked in under his own steam, was none other than Fernando Quintana, who wanted to get a firsthand look at his newest facility.

When he walked out ten minutes later, he spoke to Lucatero, his second in command. "The boy is too smart to be cutting up dead bodies. Bring him along. Slowly."

And so, every day after school, Joaquín would head straight for the compound, where his job was to help out the crew. He'd polish their boots, wash their cars, make their coffee, empty their ashtrays—whatever they needed.

Many of the men genuinely liked him. But every one of them knew that he was el Jefe's favorite, so they'd give him a smile, a pat on the back, and a few pesos to show their appreciation. Add that to the money Quintana paid him, and he was bringing home more than men twice his age.

Catalina Alboroto always accepted it gratefully, never asking her son for any of the details about the job. Nor did she ask why, three or four times a month, a car would pull up to their house after dark, and Joaquín would disappear for hours.

At sixteen, he left school to work for the cartel full-time. This was the life he had chosen, and he decided to follow the example of his new friend, Galdós. Speak only when spoken to. The best way to learn was to listen.

One night, he heard something that shook him to the core. Villablanca and three other men had been playing dominoes, drinking tequila, and telling war stories for hours. Joaquín was behind the bar washing glasses when he caught a snippet of Villablanca's chatter.

"So he killed *all* of them. Six fucking good drivers."

Joaquín stood there frozen, waiting for more.

"One of them stole from us," one of the men said. "His friends paid the price."

"Bullshit," Villablanca said. "Nobody stole the hundred kilos. He just fucked up the count. Maybe intentionally. It's not enough for him to kill for business. He kills for pleasure. Who does that?"

The second man picked up an empty bottle and yelled, "*¡Muchacho, más tequila!*"

Joaquín didn't move. He wanted to scream, "Who killed the six drivers?"

"*¡Ándale!*" the man waiting for more tequila yelled.

The story was over. Joaquín rushed over with another bottle, and the men returned to their domino game.

Joaquín's heart was racing. Not ten feet away, laughing and getting drunk, were a group of men who knew what happened to his father. And they knew who did it.

But he didn't dare ask.

And then he looked across the room. Galdós sat in a cushy armchair, quietly waiting to be summoned if there was a body to be picked up. His coworkers called him *el gigante silencioso* because he hardly said a word. Not to them. But in private, he spoke to his young butcher friend.

Joaquín brewed two fresh cups of espresso and carried one over to the big man, who thanked him with a nod.

"It's a beautiful night," Joaquín said. "I'm going to drink my coffee under the stars."

Galdós considered the idea, shrugged, then stood and followed Joaquín out to the porch.

The moon was high, and the sweet scent of nightshade was in the air. Joaquín sat gazing at the sky for a full five minutes. Finally, he said, "You don't like him, do you?"

"Who?" Galdós asked.

"The one that got Villablanca all pissed off."

There was a flicker of recognition in Galdós's eyes as he figured out who they were talking about.

"The cartel kills to protect its interests," Joaquín said. "Not for pleasure."

"*Es verdad*," Galdós said.

"I respect you, Armando," Joaquín said. "You have a job to do, and you do it. You're a professional. But that asshole . . ." He stopped. "I'm sorry. I shouldn't talk like that about one of our own."

"Don't worry," Galdós said, draining his coffee cup. "Nobody likes De la Plata."

Joaquín could barely breathe. He knew Vicente de la Plata. Always steered clear of him. And now, more than four years since the night his father didn't come home for his twelfth birthday, Joaquín had a new purpose.

Six months later, just before daybreak on the ninth of November,

Joaquín was on a cot in the communal sleeping quarters when he heard the commotion outside. He got out of bed, showered, put on clean clothes, and sat down to wait.

Ten minutes later, two men came for him. They didn't say a word. They searched him for weapons, then walked him out the door and through the courtyard, where a dozen or more men milled around a six-foot-high wooden stake. Joaquín didn't stop to look at it. He already knew what was there.

The bloodied head of Vicente de la Plata was impaled at the top.

CHAPTER 13

JOAQUÍN HAD NEVER BEEN INSIDE EL JEFE's home before. It was beyond anything he could have imagined. The vast rooms, the marble floors, the rich tapestries on the walls—it was a king's palace. The men escorted him down a corridor to an ornately carved wooden door with a brass devil's-head knocker as the focal point. The door opened before they could knock.

He entered. El Jefe was sitting behind a big desk. He didn't look like a man who was worth billions. He was wearing shorts, a Harley-Davidson T-shirt, and a pair of weather-beaten huaraches.

He took a cigar from a humidor, positioned the blades of a stainless-steel guillotine cutter just inside the cap, and made a quick, decisive cut. Joaquín's hips involuntarily pulled in as the tip snapped off and flew to the floor.

Holding the cigar at an angle, Quintana flicked his lighter and applied heat to the foot of the cigar, rotating it slowly. Then, without touching the flame to the tobacco, he puffed a few times, making sure it was evenly lit.

"You killed one of my men," he said, setting the cigar down on a glass ashtray.

"And he killed six of your men," Joaquín said. "Good men. Men who worked hard on your behalf."

"I don't remember asking you to settle the score for me."

"One of those men was my father. I didn't do anything for you. I did it for me. For my mother."

"But you killed one of my workers. You knew there would be repercussions."

"I would rather die avenging my father's death than live knowing I failed."

"I'm surprised you didn't die," Quintana said. "You went up against an experienced killer—with a kitchen knife."

Joaquín inhaled sharply, caught off guard. It had been a fourteen-inch *cuchillo cimitarra*, a hand-forged butcher's knife whose curved blade and upturned tip allowed him to cut through the greatest amount of flesh in a single slicing motion. It was far from a kitchen knife, but he didn't correct Quintana. He was too stunned by the fact that el Jefe knew the details of his middle-of-the-night showdown with De la Plata.

"How did you know what I . . ."

"I have eyes everywhere—human and electronic," Quintana said. "I saw you kill him. What I don't understand is why you gave him a fighting chance. You could have slit his throat in his sleep."

"No, sir. He had to know it was me. So I waited until I was strong enough to go against him mano a mano. Also, today is my birthday. Five years ago, my father was murdered on this day. Now we are both at peace."

Quintana took another puff on his cigar. "Are you done wreaking vengeance, or should I be concerned that more of my men will end up with their head on a stake?"

"No, sir. Justice has been done. Whatever you do to me, please tell my mother that my father's death has been avenged."

"Tell her yourself. And come back tonight."

Joaquín looked puzzled. "Señor?"

"Suffering is bitter, but its fruits can be sweet. The stupidity of one of my men has caused you great pain. But that pain has helped you find a new life. You should not spend your birthday in *el palacio del pobre*. You should celebrate with your new family."

That night, Joaquín met el Jefe's daughter Luciana. He'd seen her briefly only once, three years earlier, when she left to study at the Barcelona Academy of Art. Now she was back. A tall, stunning, vibrant woman of twenty-one. But the difference in their ages, backgrounds, and social standing couldn't stop them from falling in love. Three years later they were married.

Twenty-seven years after that, Fernando Quintana was flying to Mexico City when a blood clot dislodged from his leg, traveled to his lungs, and formed a massive pulmonary embolism. He was dead in an instant.

There was no question that his son-in-law, whom he loved like a son, should assume the reins. Over the next fifteen years, the organization tripled in size to become the most powerful drug-trafficking syndicate in the Western Hemisphere, and Joaquín Alboroto became one of the most loved, most hated, most feared men on the planet.

Fifteen minutes after he learned that Luciana and their only child, Sebastián, had been murdered in a courtroom in New York, Joaquín walked to the sprawling green *ahuehuete* tree that made a canopy over his mother's grave.

He dropped to his knees, bowed his head, and, as he had done decades ago when he learned who had executed his father, uttered a single word.

"Venganza."

But this time, the object of his wrath was not one man. This time, the sworn enemy of el Carnicero was the entire city of New York.

CHAPTER 14

AT ALMOST THE SAME MOMENT as I watched Harvey Solomon go from judge to jury to executioner, Mayor Lloyd Richardson got up in front of a packed pressroom at City Hall and announced that Trace Baker would be stepping down as police commissioner. None of the reporters looked surprised.

With just a few scant words of praise for Baker's decades of service, the mayor quickly moved on to announce his new top cop, Martin K. Ennis, "a distinguished veteran of thirty years, an innovative thinker, a proven leader," and a handful of other hollow phrases that also were utter bullshit.

The real Martin K. Ennis was an administrative hack. Early in his career, he had been a borough inspection sergeant for Manhattan North. His only job, which he seemed to relish, was to pop in unannounced at a precinct and bust balls for deficiencies in a cop's appearance—things like a bad haircut, sloppy shave, missing tie clip, or unshined shoes. Rarely did he leave a station house without barking, "What did you polish those with, Officer—a chocolate bar?"

One afternoon, he had just reamed the day tour at the Three-Three on Amsterdam and was in the parking lot filling up his gas tank, when he saw two cops walk out of the precinct with their hats clipped to their duty belts. Always on the prowl for new victims, he jammed the gas cap of his Chevy Caprice under the pump handle to keep the gas flowing, yelled at the two cops to stop, and stormed over to dress them down.

A word about the fueling stations at NYPD precincts is in order: The gas is such cheap crap that no sane person would put it in their personal car, and the equipment is so antiquated that there's always a bucket of kitty litter handy to sop up the inevitable spills that happen with no automatic shutoff valve.

That afternoon, there wasn't a spill. There was a flood. And while Sergeant Ennis was giving hell to the two men who had the audacity to leave the precinct without their hats on their heads, at least fifteen gallons of bargain-basement gasoline gushed onto the parking lot and ran downhill to the spot behind the building where cops go for a quick cigarette—sometimes so quick that they don't get more than a few drags before someone yells at them to get back inside and they flick the half-smoked butt to the ground.

The rest is department history—and not just NYPD, but FDNY as well. Before the men of Engine Company 67 could get it under control, the fire destroyed six police cars and thirteen personal vehicles belonging to the cops on duty—including the precinct commander's three-week-old Lexus.

From that day forward, Martin K. Ennis was known as Ennis the Menace, and his reputation for being a petty, pencil-pushing bureaucrat was legend.

Twenty-three years later, that supreme fuck-up was chosen to guide the 38,000 members of the NYPD and protect our city's eight-and-a-half million citizens and its millions of visitors from around the world.

I knew it was not based on his qualifications. The last thing our mayor wanted was another police commissioner with a brain and a backbone. He needed someone who would be thrilled to have the title and happy to do whatever he was told. And Martin K. Ennis was a natural-born puppet.

After the mayor introduced him, Ennis peacock-walked his way up to the mic and announced his first order of business.

"Effective immediately, I have dissolved the unit responsible for the tragic operation on Liberty Island. The men and women assigned to that squad will immediately be reassigned based on the needs of the department."

The needs of the department. That's a catchall phrase the brass uses when they give someone highway therapy—a transfer to some remote precinct in Brooklyn or Staten Island.

I, of course, didn't watch the press conference until much later that day. At nine a.m., while Ennis was dismantling Trace Baker's most significant contribution to the safety of New York, I was in the middle of sheer bedlam.

As soon as the last shots were fired and it was determined that the only active shooter had been eliminated, the court officers shut down the entire twelfth floor, sealing stairwells and cutting off elevator access. At least 150 spectators had been in that courtroom, and whether they bolted as soon as the bullets started flying, or ducked for cover and stayed behind, every one of them was a witness who had to be questioned by detectives. They were quickly rounded up and sequestered in another courtroom on the same floor.

Cameras were confiscated, and with dozens of journalists in the room, there were plenty of them. But of course, hundreds, probably thousands, of images and videos were transmitted to media outlets within seconds of the shooting, and they quickly made their way across the global network of electronic communications.

Law enforcement officers poured into the building—a federal tactical unit, NYPD's Emergency Services Unit, a forensic team, at least a dozen detectives, countless uniforms, and finally, because there's never a quota on how many assholes can show up at a clusterfuck, Martin K. Ennis burst onto the scene. I had not yet seen his coronation, but Baker had given me the bad news the night before, so I wasn't surprised to see him and his phalanx of security officers show up.

I had dealt with him in the past, and while I wouldn't say there was bad blood between us, he knew I was Baker's right-hand man, so there definitely was no *good* blood. As soon as he saw me, he headed straight at me.

"This judge was your father-in-law," he yelled out as he approached. "Did he tell you he was going to do this?"

I didn't think. I lunged at him. "You insensitive cocksucker!" I screamed, determined to bring him down no matter the consequences. I was an arm's length away when two of his security people jumped between us.

"Captain, I gotcha, Captain," one of them said, wrapping his arms around my chest and doing his best to save me from self-destruction. "We all just need a minute to cool down."

"I don't have time to cool down," I said, my voice bouncing off the walls. "I have to go tell my two nephews that their grandfather is dead."

"My office, eight a.m. tomorrow, Captain Corcoran," Ennis said, standing safely behind his defensive line, three of whom had worked for Baker until this morning.

"I can't make it," I said. "That's when the pension section opens. I'll be there putting in my papers. I'm done."

I took the elevator down to the lobby, retrieved my gun, left the building, and skirted the media madness that had sprung up outside the courthouse.

My feet took me down Pearl Street, to the cobblestone pathways of the South Street Seaport, where tourists and locals went about their day, unaware of the chaos that had rocked my life.

Over the course of a single day, I had been the point man on a high-level police operation gone horribly wrong, the father figure I loved dearly had committed a heinous crime and essentially taken his own life, and my twenty-two-year career in the NYPD had come to a crashing, ignominious finale.

I made my way to the East River and found a secluded spot under the iconic Brooklyn Bridge. Shell-shocked, I stopped trying to make sense of what happened, and asked myself where my life was going from here.

All I knew was that my first responsibility was to help Kirsten bury her father, and be there for her and her two sons. But then what?

My work phone rang. I had no intention of answering it, but out of habit I looked at the caller ID. It was Trace Baker.

"Trace," I said. "How are you?"

"I'll be fine, but you . . . Doc, I know how much you loved the judge. How are you holding up?"

"I don't know. Somewhere between heartsick and homicidal."

"I heard you tried to unleash some of that anger at our new PC."

"Yeah, it didn't go quite as well as my first meeting with you."

"And now you're putting in your papers?"

"I had a good run. And the best part of it was working for you. But my days with NYPD are over."

"In that case, you're going to be looking for work," Baker said.

"You and me both," I said.

"Well, I've just been offered something. Hell, it's more than *something*. It's huge. I can't give you the details over the phone, but it's big, Danny. It's important, and I want you with me. Are you interested?"

Interested? Trace Baker was the best leader I ever worked for. The kind of man I would follow to the gates of hell in a gasoline suit.

"Absolutely," I said.

"Fantastic," he said. "Mary Beth and I are getting out of Dodge and going off the grid. The PC job took a lot out of me, and I need to recharge my battery before I jump back into the fray. You should do the same. Get some rest, and we'll regroup after Labor Day."

"Looking forward to it, boss."

"One more thing, Danny. It goes without saying, but I'll say it anyway."

I knew what was coming next, and I knew what it meant.

"Priests, lovers, and dying mothers," Baker said.

And just like that, I went from one top-secret job to another. "Got it," I said.

"Good. I'll see you in three weeks."

He hung up, and I stood there staring out at the East River, the hum of traffic on the roadway above echoing off the stone arches of the bridge, and I exhaled slowly, letting the rush of hope surge through my body.

CHAPTER 15

August 21, 11:47 A.M.

THE FIRST PERSON TO SPOT THE HELICOPTER was an eleven-year-old boy. Kevin Burlingame and five of his best friends had piled into his father's Grand Cherokee in Valley Stream that Saturday morning and headed for New York City to celebrate Kevin's birthday at the Intrepid Sea, Air & Space Museum.

After boarding the decommissioned aircraft carrier, the kids went straight to the hangar deck to ride the G-force simulator. They spent another forty minutes bouncing from one exhibit to the next until Dave Burlingame announced that it was time to head up to the flight deck for their tour of the Concorde.

Kevin was the first to get topside. "Dad, Dad, look at this!"

His father, who was bringing up the rear of the pack, stepped out onto the deck and took in the sleek turbo-powered supersonic passenger airliner. "It's a beauty, isn't it?" he said. "It could fly twice the speed of sound."

"No, Dad, not that. Look out *there*," Kevin said, pointing.

Dave Burlingame turned his attention from the Concorde and gazed out at the Hudson River. A helicopter was flying no more than fifty feet above the water. Having spent the past eighteen years as an air traffic controller at LaGuardia, Burlingame knew that it was a twin-engine Bell 412—the civilian version of the military's UH-1Y Venom, the Super Huey. But this one was like none he had ever seen flying through New York City's air space. It was outfitted with four sets of arms extending twenty feet on either side of the aircraft. Each arm contained dozens of nozzles.

"Dad, what are those pipes on that chopper?" Kevin asked.

"Boys, stay right here. Don't move," Burlingame said, pulling his cell phone out of his pocket. He dialed a direct line at the LaGuardia tower.

Mike Grassi picked up.

"Mike, this is Dave Burlingame."

"Hey, Dave, I thought this was your day off. What are you—?"

"Mike, I'm on the Intrepid with my son, and we just saw an agricultural helo flying northbound."

"*Agricultural?*" Mike repeated.

"Yeah. A cropduster."

"Hold on . . . I've got nothing on my screen, Dave."

"He's well under your radar, practically scraping the waves."

He could picture Grassi grabbing his binoculars and scanning the horizon from his glass cab two hundred feet above the airport tarmac.

"Got him," Grassi said. "Stay on the line, Dave."

"Dad," Kevin said. "It starts in five minutes."

Burlingame dug into his pocket, pulled out the tickets for the Concorde tour, and handed them to his son. "You guys go in there. I'll either catch up with you, or I'll be right here when you come out."

As the boys disappeared under the eighty-four-foot wing of the giant airliner, he heard Mike Grassi's authoritative voice.

"Unidentified helicopter six miles west of LaGuardia northbound at low altitude, this is LaGuardia tower. Acknowledge and identify."

There was no response.

"Mike, I lost him," Burlingame said. "Where is he?"

"He's over the Sanitation Marine Transfer Station at Pier 99 and he's climbing. Hold on, I just picked him up on my radar. His transponder is off. No identification. He's at eight hundred feet, and he's heading east over 59th Street."

"He needs the altitude to clear the buildings," Burlingame said.

"Roger that. He just crossed 12th Avenue." Grassi radioed the pilot again. "Unidentified helicopter, this is LaGuardia tower. Contact us immediately on 118.7. Repeat, contact LaGuardia tower immediately on 118.7."

Five seconds passed.

"He's not responding," Grassi said.

"Mike, I can see him from the *Intrepid*. Jesus—he's headed inland. Call NYPD Command Center forthwith!"

"I've already alerted them to get a chaser helo up there. Calling it in to the Coast Guard and Homeland now. I don't know what's going on, Dave, but get your boy and get out of Manhattan."

Grassi hung up, and Dave Burlingame watched as the rogue helicopter flew past the Time Warner Center, turned north, and began to descend.

Just before it dropped out of sight, he saw the trail of white powder as the pilot opened the nozzles wide and began to empty the two nylon bags, each of which held five hundred kilos of cocaine, harvested and processed for the occasion by the Alboroto cartel.

CHAPTER 16

Joaquín alboroto sat in his office and stared intently at the bank of monitors as four cameras livestreamed the flight of the Bell 412 helicopter from three thousand miles away.

This was his operation and his alone. No deputies. No lieutenants. Every aspect of the seismic event that was about to befall the city of New York had emanated from his brain, his soul, his grief, his rage.

Choosing the target was easy. New York was a city of over one million buildings—too many places for people to hide, too many rooftops to contain the cocaine until it could be safely disposed of by a legion of rescue workers in hazmat suits.

But one look at a satellite map confirmed what he already knew. There in the center of Manhattan was a patch of green and blue two and a half miles long by half a mile wide—Central Park, the crown jewel of the city that attracted more than thirty-five million visitors every year. It was vast, open, unprotected, and, most important, it was symbolic.

Every meadow, every body of water, every grove of trees, every exotic animal in the six-acre zoo in the southeast corner of the park, had been meticulously planned. It was, the Central Park website informed him, "a defining monument to the idea of American democracy. A place where one may truly pursue life, liberty, and happiness freely. A place where all men are equal."

Destroying it would be like ripping the very heart out of New York. Just as New York had done to him.

His choice of that Saturday, nine days after the death of his wife and son, had also been strategic. It was the day of the New York City corporate challenge, a 5K race to raise money for charity, which would attract more than fifteen thousand bankers, Wall Streeters, and corporate commandos.

"You'll be killing some of your best customers," Huberto Miraval told him as Alboroto laid out the plans for the attack. Miraval was his pilot and the best man for the job—a man who, Joaquín knew, would give his own life to guarantee the success of the mission.

"And yet," Alboroto said with the first hint of a smile on his lips since the loss of his family, "I could walk into the office of the chairman of Goldman Sachs on Monday morning, tell him I want to take the cartel public, and he'd have his top people working on the IPO before I left the building. I have no *best* customers. I only deal with degenerates and drug addicts. I could kill a million of them, and a million more would take their place."

Now he watched as Miraval leveled the helicopter at thirty feet above the park. "*¡Para Luciana y Sebastián!*" the pilot proclaimed over the air as he made his first pass directly over the entire length of the racecourse crowded with power brokers of the city's financial structure.

Runners by the hundreds dropped to the roadway as they were strafed with the pure, uncut, deadly white powder. Then Miraval banked the aircraft, and flying just above the treetops, he crisscrossed the park, raking the 842 acres of wooded urban paradise with precise swaths that Alboroto had determined would render the most damage.

El Carnicero sat emotionless as he watched the carnage. People writhed on the ground, some going into convulsions while others, whose respiratory systems were already compromised, went into cardiac arrest. Birds fell from the sky. Horses that had been plodding along pulling hansom cabs broke into a full gallop, throwing passengers from their carriages and trampling anything in their path.

On the ground in New York, two of Alboroto's men monitored all radio transmissions, keeping the pilot apprised of how much time he had left before an NYPD response team was on its way to intercept the helicopter. On the sixth pass, with the first responders still three miles away, Miraval drained the last of the cocaine and headed north at his top speed of 150 knots.

Ninety seconds later, he was over Riverbank State Park. This was tiny by comparison—a mere twenty-eight acres built over a sewage treatment facility in Harlem. It, too, was filled with humanity, mostly people of color playing ball, picnicking, swimming, jogging, or just basking in the summer sun.

Miraval set the Bell 412 down on a softball field, almost at the fence in right center. Then he jumped from the aircraft and ran.

Alboroto watched the livestream from the camera strapped to Miraval's chest. People in the park had no idea who Miraval was, but a dark-skinned man running away could mean only one thing: The cops were after him. The crowd cheered him on as he sprinted to the parking lot and jumped into a waiting black Suburban. The rotors of the helicopter were still spinning as the SUV turned out of the lot and disappeared into the southbound traffic of the Henry Hudson Parkway.

Dalvin Serrano and Mariano Cordoba, both members of the Monte Plata Boys, a Dominican street gang, had pulled into the lot a few minutes earlier and watched it all unfold.

"Dalv," Cordoba said, eyeing the helicopter. "That dude took off in a fucking hurry."

"Let's find out what he left behind," Serrano said, getting out of the car.

But they weren't the only ones to hear the knock of opportunity. One of the softball players had already climbed into the cockpit, looking for anything worth liberating. A few seconds later, he stepped back out, waving a white-powdered hand and yelling to his teammates. "Coca! Coca! Coca!"

With news of the attack flashing on everyone's smartphone screen, he confirmed what many had begun to suspect. The helicopter sitting on softball field number 9 was *that* helicopter.

People raced madly toward it. The melee resembled the Black Friday insanity that happens every year when the stores open their doors to frenzied bargain hunters.

But in this case, the bargains were worth killing for. The two Monte Plata Boys had already made their way onto the aircraft. Serrano grabbed the softball player and flung him to the ground, while Cordoba drew a semiautomatic pistol, pointed it at the advancing mob, and fired three shots over their heads.

"Get the fuck back," he yelled. "This shit belong to the Monte Plata—"

A hail of bullets ended his life in an instant. Serrano reached for his gun, but he, too, was cut down.

The crowd dived for cover as four members of a rival gang, Loco DR 140, their guns still smoking, ran to the helicopter. Clavo, the smallest of the four, scrambled into the cockpit. "Holy fuck!" he said, dumbstruck by what he saw.

The nylon bags feeding the spray arms had been depleted, but they were far from empty. With each bag large enough to hold over a thousand pounds of coke, the residue alone, which appeared to be as much as ten kilos per bag, had a street value upward of half a million dollars.

He cut the bags free, dragged them to the door, and dropped the first one to the ground. A white cloud billowed up, and like kids darting into a sprinkler, the gang members let it waft over them, sucking it in deeply and letting the fine mist settle on their mustaches, eyebrows, and tongues.

Clavo, too, was feeling the buzz as he dropped the second bag to the ground. And then he saw it. A squad car from the Thirtieth Precinct careened into the parking lot, which was separated from the ballfield by a chain-link fence.

"Five-O," he yelled as two cops rolled out of the vehicle and crouched low, maneuvering their way toward the helicopter using the parked cars as cover.

"Police! Don't move!" one yelled.

Clavo jumped down and joined his crew as a second squad car arrived, followed by two more. Galloping toward them from the opposite direction were two mounted New York State Park Police.

A voice boomed from above. "Police. Drop your weapons." It was the NYPD Response Team helicopter that had taken off from Floyd Bennett Field when the first alert went out from the LaGuardia tower.

The thugs were boxed in, outnumbered. Even in their kill-or-be-killed world, logic would have dictated that they give up or at the very least run, knowing that the cops were there for the drugs, not for them.

But there was no logic. Not with a treasure trove of cocaine at their feet, and a generous amount up their noses.

"Loco DR One-Forty, mother fuckers!" Clavo screamed, and all four gang members began shooting.

The cops responded with a barrage of gunfire that killed two of them instantly. The other two went down as they ran toward the barrier that separated the park from the highway.

"Live stupid, die young," Alboroto said, looking away from the monitors.

He turned to a man sitting silently off to the side, his fingers poised over the keyboard of a laptop.

"*Para mi esposa. Para mi hijo,*" Alboroto dictated as the man typed into an untraceable Twitter account. "*Así no es como termina. Así es como empieza.*"

He nodded, and the man hit Send. Within minutes, Alboroto's words would go viral as people around the world translated the chilling message.

For my wife. For my son. This is not how it ends. This is how it begins.

CHAPTER 17

LIKE ANY HURRICANE, WAR, or can of soup, a disaster needs a label. The Great Chicago Fire, the Johnstown Flood, and Chernobyl are all brand names that conjure up horrific events of the past. The media wasted no time coming up with a handle for this latest catastrophe.

Cokestorm.

The videos of people emerging from thick clouds, coughing, choking, and covered with toxic residue, would lead you to believe that nobody in their right mind would want to be within miles of the kill zone. And yet, even before the dust settled, thousands flocked to the scene, hoping to scoop up as much of the deadly blizzard as they could.

The NYPD, even at full force, was ill equipped to contain the frenzy. The governor declared martial law, and within hours, three thousand National Guard troops had created a secure ring around the vast plot of contaminated earth that had already been dubbed Powder Park.

I was watching the drama unfold on TV, aching to be part of the action, when the opening chords of "Master of Puppets" by Metallica blared from my work phone. It was Trace Baker, calling me two weeks sooner than I expected.

"Trace," I said into the phone. "Where are you?"

"Mary Beth and I were on a sailboat in the middle of the Caribbean when the cartel attacked the city. We finally made it back to Barbados, and we're on our way to the airport. I should be back in New York by about two a.m."

Translation: He was not flying commercial.

"I know I said this new venture wouldn't start till after Labor Day, but things have changed. Are you ready to jump in?"

"With both feet," I said.

"I'll pick you up tomorrow morning at seven. Pack a bag. You're going out of town for a few days."

I didn't ask where.

The next morning at 6:55, I was standing in front of my apartment building on East 88th Street. Vehicular traffic into Manhattan was prohibited. People could get out, but no one could get in. The West Side Highway, the FDR, the Harlem River Drive, and the avenues from Lexington to Amsterdam were closed to all but emergency vehicles. Major crosstown streets from 14th to 125th had been converted from two-way to one-way. Subways and buses had been canceled or rerouted, and TV newscasters warned the public that unless you were a first responder, getting around New York would be next to impossible.

Baker pulled up at exactly 7:00. I wasn't surprised. Officially, he was a private citizen, but as a former commissioner who had earned the respect of the rank and file, I'd bet every cop he encountered had waved him through and snapped him a salute as he passed.

He was driving a black Audi Q7 SUV that had to cost upward of eighty grand, and since it would be tricked out with all the communications and security modifications that Baker was used to, it would easily have run to six figures.

"Nice ride," I said, getting in and inhaling the new-car smell.

"Company car," he said, poker-faced.

"Sounds like a great company to work for. I'm surprised they didn't spring for a driver."

"That would have been a deal breaker. For me, having a full-time guy behind the wheel was one of the worst parts about being PC. Driving clears my head. The next time I ride in the back of a car, it's going to be a hearse. So, how are you doing? You miss being part of this craziness, don't you?"

"The worst part of it is being out of the loop—not knowing what's really going down. The TV newscasters have been speculating and contradicting one another nonstop. You're better wired than any of them. Fill me in."

His expression turned serious. "The Park Precinct lost three scooter cops," he said. "They were on patrol, got caught in the deluge, and instead of getting out of harm's way, they pulled at least sixty people under bridges, into the boathouse—any place they could find shelter until they passed out themselves. By the time other units got to them, they were dead.

"EMS and the National Guard are out there right now, retrieving bodies. It's slow going because they're wearing hazmat gear. There are three tents serving as interim morgues outside the Office of the Chief Medical Examiner on 1st Avenue. So far, they've processed more than seven hundred dead, but there are at least another twelve hundred missing or unaccounted for, and it'll take more than a week to comb every inch of the park.

"The decontamination tent that was set up outside the Museum of Natural History has treated more than four thousand men, women, and children who were exposed. They had to strip naked and were hosed down, dried, and issued hospital scrubs. Most have been released, but about three hundred were transferred to hospitals across the tri-state area.

"Most of the animals in the Central Park Zoo either died in the attack or had to be euthanized. And I just spoke to Lucy Evans, the president of the Central Park Conservancy. She was in tears. Told me that the park will be a barren desert in less than a year. The good news is that arrests were twenty-five percent of normal. But that's partly because there aren't enough cops to enforce the law."

I looked at him, shaking my head, unable to say anything meaningful.

"Danny, this attack is just the beginning," he said. "I know how much you loved your father-in-law, and I know this is not what he intended. He was avenging his son's death. But Alboroto also lost a son and his wife, and I know for a fact that he will take vengeance to a whole new level."

"What have you got?"

"Jávier Ceteño called me last night from Mexico City."

I knew, respected, and trusted Ceteño. Two years earlier, Baker had sent him down to Mexico to be the NYPD liaison to the Mexican Federales. His job was to gather intel about cartel activities that could impact New York.

"He called *you*?" I said. "He's had a new boss for more than a week."

"I know, but his new boss almost got him killed. Did you see Ennis's press conference yesterday? I didn't, but I heard it was a disaster."

"That's an understatement," I said. "Ennis isn't a cop, boss. He's a bureaucrat, and he's definitely not the wartime consigliere we need now. Instead of updating the public on the threat level, he tried to intimidate Alboroto by saying, 'NYPD is on top of this. We have a man in Mexico, and our informants are keeping us abreast of the situation.' I started screaming at the TV. 'Our informants? Why don't you just paint a target on their backs!'"

"He did. That's why Ceteño called me. There was a driver working for the cartel, Julio Núñez. He'd been giving up shipment schedules to the Federales and providing Ceteño with a list of stash houses on the receiving end in New York. He was too low-level to get wind of the attack on Central Park, but he was onto something big, and Ceteño was supposed to meet with him again today. As soon as Ennis talked about our informants down there, Alboroto didn't bother ferreting out the mole. He just eliminated all the possibilities, and this morning twenty-six of them—including Núñez and his family—were found hanging from an overpass, each wrapped in a US flag, every one of their tongues cut out. And that's not all. Alboroto put a price on Ceteño's head."

"Fucking Ennis," I said. "No wonder Ceteño called you."

"He's okay for now. The Federales moved him to a safe house, and he's still trying to figure out Alboroto's next move. He's a good investigator, but we're at war. We need a military strategist down there, and that's you. Your flight to Mexico City leaves at noon."

By now we were in Lower Manhattan, heading toward the Battery Tunnel to Brooklyn. "But we're not heading to the airport," I said.

"No. First, I want to show you around our new office space. It's on Staten Island, about ten minutes past the Verrazzano Bridge."

"Pretty far off the beaten track," I said.

"It's the most cop-friendly part of the city."

"I thought we were ex-cops," I said.

"Only on paper, Doc," he said, his tone as serious as it ever gets. "Only on paper."

CHAPTER 18

BAKER TURNED INTO A QUIET STREET in the Dongan Hills section of Staten Island, pulled the car into a wide driveway, and stopped in front of an imposing three-story edifice.

"Here she is," he said. "Your new home."

The building looked more like a citadel than like office space. With its limestone-and-brick balconies, ornate cornices, and arched windows, it was a throwback to the New York City that opened its doors to immigrants over a hundred years ago. Yet as grand as it may have been in its day, it now had a quiet, stately manner about it—the kind of structure that doesn't get noticed in a world of glass, steel, and architectural flash.

"Great find," I said.

"She's a decommissioned firehouse," Baker said. "Built in 1903, back when the city took a lot of pride in its public buildings. The inside is a little more twenty-first century."

He tapped a button on his cell phone, one of the three bay doors went up, and he pulled the Audi inside. The space was deep enough to accommodate a hook and ladder truck. At the far end was a large room, separated from the parking area by a glass wall.

"That's the parlor," Baker said. "It's nice and comfy-cozy, totally innocuous, and if anybody stumbles in here by mistake, that's all they'll ever see."

As soon we got out of the car, a woman inside the parlor tapped on the glass and waved at us. Baker waved back, and we walked toward her.

"That's Kaori Piper," he said. "Her mother's a Japanese physicist; her father is an American CIA officer, happily retired. Kaori is the total package. She's smart, knows how to think outside the box, tenacious as a pit bull, has a great sense of humor, and she's totally dedicated to our mission. You'll love her."

"What does she do?" I asked.

Baker gave me a sly smile. "She pays the rent."

He pushed open a glass door, and we entered. "Comfy-cozy" was a good description. It reminded me of one those concierge lounges in the better hotels, with tastefully furnished seating arrangements, and private dining tables for two or four people peppered throughout.

Kaori came bounding toward me. She was in her late thirties, petite, wearing a black skirt and blazer, a beige blouse, and a pair of oversize glasses set in a dark burgundy frame. It was a look that told the world she was all business, but the smile on her face said *totally approachable*. "Captain Corcoran," she said, her arm outstretched.

"Danny," I said, shaking her hand. "Nice to meet you."

"I've heard so much about you," she said. "But from the look on your face, Trace has told you very little about BAG."

"Bag?" I said looking at Baker. In cop-speak, the bag is your uniform, and once a cop gets used to working in plain clothes, the last thing he wants to do is go back in the bag.

"Not '*BAG*,'" he said. "B, A, G. It stands for 'the Baltic Avenue Group.' I'll explain later. First, let's take the tour."

The three of us walked up a flight of cast-iron stairs that had the same ornate Beaux Arts features as the outside of the building.

At the top of the stairs, Kaori leaned into an electronic iris scanner. I heard a loud thunk, and a door opened to a vast room.

"Déjà vu," I said, taking it in. "It looks a lot like the Joint Operations

Center at 1PP. Same configuration, identical layout—even the workstations look familiar."

"We used their model as a blueprint," Kaori said. "But we've got a few things under the hood that they don't."

"Like what?"

"Basically, if it exists on a computer network, we can access it. Criminal databases, arrest histories, DMV files, commercial flight manifests, INTERPOL records, immigration and customs documentation—"

"Sorry to interrupt," I said, "but what do you mean by 'we can access'? Because the last time I looked, most of the databases you just rattled off are not accessible without a court order or a series of excruciatingly painful interdepartmental negotiations."

"I know," she said, not answering the question. "We also have eating and sleeping quarters on the third floor, a complete arsenal vault, as well as a print shop that can produce driver's licenses, passports, Global Entry cards, or any other ID you might need."

"And you put this all together in the week since Ennis disbanded our unit?"

"No," Baker said. "About a year ago, I knew the clock was running out for me. I was too strong for Mayor Richardson, and I knew he'd find a reason to dump me and replace me with some flunky who would undo everything I've done and leave the city more vulnerable than ever. So I went to the only people I knew who could keep that from happening."

"That would be this Baltic Avenue Group," I said. "What can you tell me about them?"

"Not much. What do you want to know?"

"Well, I kind of figured out that they're rich as hell. Probably billionaires, because I don't think mere millionaires could afford the upkeep on this operation."

Baker nodded in silent agreement.

"And while I appreciate their generosity, the cynical cop in me has to ask, what's in it for them?"

"Fair question," Baker said. "Do you have any idea what kind of economic impact the September 11 terrorist attacks had on this city?"

"I'd guess it was in the billions," I said.

"Closer to three trillion. And since the individual wealth of each of our donors is directly tied to the financial and political stability of New York, they want to make sure they don't go through that again."

"So they're using their millions to safeguard their billions," I said.

"Yes, but it's not all business. Danny, these are the strangest bedfellows you'd ever want to meet. Politically, they're polar opposites—two on the right and two on the left—but they do have one thing in common. None of them started out rich. They're all self-made, and every one of them is quick to say that this city gave them the opportunities they needed. They've been quietly paying back for years, creating jobs, supporting education, funding the arts. A lot of what they do is under the radar, and in this case they want complete anonymity."

"The world has changed," Kaori said. "Politicians on both sides are no longer willing to support a strong police presence, but this group trusts Trace Baker, and they believe in our mission to keep New Yorkers safe from the kind of catastrophic event that happened yesterday in Central Park. Were you curious about why they called themselves the Baltic Avenue Group?"

"Baltic is the cheapest piece of property on the Monopoly board," I said. "I just figured they're not without their sense of irony."

"No," she said. "It's because none of them were born on Boardwalk or Park Place. They never forgot where they came from, and they want to be reminded of what can be achieved if people are willing to put in the work."

"For now, the only thing you need to know about them is that they've given us a healthy budget," Baker said, "but if you need something above and beyond, ask Kaori. She's our go-between."

I looked around the state-of-the-art command center. "Well, they didn't stint on anything so far. Who else is on the team besides the three of us?"

Baker perked up. "I've been waiting for you to ask. Ever since this pipe dream became a reality, I've been thinking about the people I've worked with, respected, and trusted over the years."

It was a classic Trace Baker statement. In one short sentence, he had created the perfect inverted pyramid so I could track his thinking process. At the top of the pyramid were the thousands of people he'd worked with. Below that was the smaller group of those he respected. And at the bottom of the funnel were the special few who had also earned his trust.

"Remember Kevin Cavanaugh?" Baker said.

I nodded. Cavanaugh had been a detective at Midtown South, the precinct that covers Times Square. Crime happens all over the city, but when it happens in the Crossroads of the World, it gets a lot more airtime. For Cavanaugh, it was a dream job, and he got in front of the cameras every chance he got.

As soon as he retired, he became an investigative reporter for Fox News and found a niche covering the most wanted criminals in New York. The segments were so popular, the network gave him a weekly show.

"It's hard to forget a legend," I said. "But the last I heard, Cavanaugh was a TV star living in Hollywood."

"A TV star still using his contacts and his resources to catch bad guys," Baker said. "In his gut, he's still a cop. How about Marina Whitney? You worked with her, didn't you?"

I nodded again. Marina was another legend. She had been a captain with NYPD Computer Crimes.

"Did you know that the day Marina retired, she had half a dozen job offers?" Baker said. "Think about it. Black, female, over forty, with serious computer-crime chops—she could have written her own ticket, but she turned them all down and opened her own consulting firm.

"Right now she's in DC, testing the cybersecurity of the Pentagon's global armament network. So far, she and her team have breached it twice. As soon as they crack the code, they show the DOD how to correct it. She's still fighting crime, Danny.

"I spoke to Marina, Cavanaugh, and nine more of the best cops ever to wear an NYPD uniform. A few live in New York, but the bulk of them have moved on—Boston, London, Tel Aviv—and Billy Templeton is eight thousand miles away in Johannesburg. All eleven of them want to be part of this new task force."

"So we're all retired NYPD," I said.

"'Retired' is what you say when something is old, worn out, and useless. These people have cracked the biggest cases, outsmarted the most cunning adversaries, and they're still at the top of their game. None of them are sitting around waiting for the phone to ring. They've all reinvented themselves. They're vital, talented, productive—"

"So, then, how much of their time do we get?" I said.

"As much as you need. They're on call twenty-four-seven, like world-class surgeons."

"And they're just a click away," Kaori said, pointing at the bank of monitors.

"Of course, you'll also need boots on the ground right here," Baker said. "I'm sure there are people from your DR-1 team you'd like to bring. So . . . any questions before you leave for Mexico?"

"Just one," I said. "When I chased bad guys for the city, I knew my jurisdiction. Now I'm doing it for a bunch of billionaires, and as much as it makes my heart sing to find out I can hack into—I'm sorry, *access*—any database on the planet, I find myself wondering, is *any* of this shit legal?"

Baker was about to answer, but Kaori held up her hand.

"Captain Corcoran . . . Danny," she said. "Working for NYPD, what has been the biggest roadblock to getting your job done?"

"That's easy," I said. "Bullshit restrictions, petty departmental regulations, and undue due process."

"Those will no longer be an issue for you," she said. "Working here, you will be totally autonomous. It's a revolutionary mandate for peacekeepers, but these are revolutionary times."

Translation: The only rule is that there are no rules.

"Of course, with that autonomy comes a calculated risk. You won't have the bureaucracy to drag you down, nor will you have them to intervene if something goes wrong." She paused. "Do you understand what I'm saying?"

"Yes ma'am," I said. "I've heard it before. Should any member of our team be caught or killed, the secretary will disavow any knowledge of our actions."

She clapped her hands, laughed out loud, and turned to Baker, who had a shit-eating grin on his face.

"You see?" he said. "I told you you'd like him."

CHAPTER 19

THREE HOURS LATER I was on a flight to Mexico City. My new identity was Timothy Randall, a rare-book dealer from Princeton, New Jersey. One of the best parts about being Tim was that he flew first class. I didn't know whether it was because that's the way rare-book dealers travel, or because I was now employed by a bunch of money-is-no-object billionaires instead of the penny-pinching City of New York.

Or maybe it was because first class allowed me to stretch out in solitude in one of those solo-seat mini suites, with no seatmates to look over my shoulder while I scanned my laptop.

Kaori had put together a six-page document, which she titled "Antiquarian Bookselling for Dummies." It had more information about rare books than anyone in Mexico was ever going to ask me. This was not one of those undercover assignments where I had to become an expert in a world I knew nothing about. Essentially, I'd become Tim Randall, so there would be no trace of Danny Corcoran leaving the country.

I ate well, read the bios of the retired cops already committed to the unit, mulled over half a dozen of my own candidates, watched a movie, and still found time for a forty-five-minute nap. We touched down at General Abelardo L. Rodríguez International Airport, and I breezed through Immigration and Customs.

"Señor Randall," a woman's voice called out as soon as I stepped into the terminal. "So good to see you again."

She was in her early thirties, about five-five, with piercing brown eyes, perfect makeup, and long dark hair that fell gracefully to her shoulders. She didn't look like a cop, but she carried herself like one.

"Sergeant Inés Bolano, Policía Federal," she said shaking my hand. "Thank you so much for coming. My partner is waiting outside."

An unmarked black Chevy Caprice was parked directly in front, and as soon as we exited, the trunk popped open, and the driver came around and took my suitcase.

"Detective Luis Vadillo," he said, putting my bag in the trunk and shaking my hand. He was lean and wiry, not much bigger than his female partner, but I've met bantamweights who can kill you with their bare hands, and Vadillo exuded an inner grit that said, *don't let my size fool you.*

"I've got a hotel room booked," I said, "but my first order of business is to get face-to-face with Jávier Ceteño."

"You and about a dozen of Alboroto's enforcers," Vadillo said. "Jávier is a marked man. He's waiting for you at the safe house about forty minutes away."

"He told us a lot about you," Bolano said. "It's an honor to work with you."

The two of them spent the first ten minutes of the ride telling me what a solid guy Ceteño was. They admired his smarts and his willingness to dedicate himself to fighting crime in a foreign country where he had no authority.

"Most cops, they do something good, they want the glory," Vadillo said. "Not Jávier. Since he's here, he's helped us lock up twenty-two *pendejos* we wouldn't have caught without him. Other cops get the credit. He's happy to just work on the next case."

We spent the rest of the trip talking about Alboroto, about how vast his empire had grown, and trying to come up with scenarios about how he'd make good on his threat to get even with the city that murdered his wife and son.

We were only a few miles from the safe house when Vadillo braked the car. "We're under attack," he said.

Bolano and I both looked up. It was dusk, and through the fading sunlight, we could see smoke billowing a mile away. I rolled down the window, and even over the hum of the Chevy's AC, I could hear the *brap-brap-brap* echo of automatic gunfire.

Bolano pulled a pair of binoculars from the glove compartment. "Alboroto's men. They're inside the compound. The guardhouse is destroyed, and I can count at least a dozen firing at the house."

"What's burning?" Vadillo said.

"The garage and every vehicle in it. The house is still intact, but fuck, they're launching grenades at the windows. One just hit, but it didn't penetrate." She turned to me. "Every window is fortified, but they won't hold up long."

She reached for the radio.

"Don't," Vadillo said. "They'll be monitoring our frequency. We don't want them to know we're here."

"They can't monitor this," I said, handing her my phone.

Vadillo hit the gas. "Grab the Serpents from the trunk."

I flipped the center armrest down and pulled the handle on the hatch behind it. A light went on, illuminating the pass-through to the trunk. I reached in and grabbed three guns along with three ballistic vests.

"FX-05 Fire Serpents," Vadillo said as I passed two to the front. "You know them?"

"Yeah. Just never got up close and personal with one." I looked the gun over. Same whore, different town. "I'm good," I said.

"Air support, ETA twelve minutes," Bolano said, returning my phone.

Vadillo turned off the road and plowed through a thick wall of mesquite and catclaw. A hundred yards in, he stopped at a padlocked gate.

"It's the back of the compound," Vadillo said. "Looks like it wasn't on their radar."

The house was two stories, an incongruous mismatch of old-school masonry and high-tech polycarbonate windows. Bolano opened the lock and swung the gate open just as a barrage of grenades hit the compromised windows and opened up two gaping holes. A cheer went up from the attackers.

Vadillo hand-signaled his strategy: Bolano to the left, me to the right, and he'd go straight up the middle.

"Welcome to Mexico," he said, and the three of us raced toward the attackers.

We had the advantage of surprise and killed three of Alboroto's men before they even knew where the bullets were coming from. They were tough, but they were guerrillas, thugs with no training, their brains wired with PCP courage, like a hundred gangbangers I'd watched go down in flames at NYPD.

They fired fearlessly, many of them standing in the open, blowing out one window after another, completely disregarding the basic concept of taking cover. Within minutes, they had demolished most of the ballistic glass and began launching grenades into the house.

Ten minutes into the battle, the distinctive rumble of helicopter rotors cut through the air. The gunfire stopped, replaced by cries of "*¡Vámonos! ¡Vámonos!*" Discharging their weapons haphazardly, five of them retreated to a pair of Range Rovers, piled in, and barreled past the charred remains of the front gate. They didn't get far. Two black choppers swooped in from the darkened sky. Each released a missile, and within seconds what remained of Alboroto's army was obliterated in a pair of white-hot explosions.

Bolano yelled into her radio. I knew enough Spanish to get the gist. She gave the men inside the all clear, letting them know it was safe to come out. And I knew enough about tactics to know that they wouldn't just take her word for it.

A voice called out, "Who is Montezuma?"

Bolano smiled. "He's the one-eyed cat that lives off the generosity of the entire squad."

The front door opened, and one of the Federales stepped out, his face lacerated with cuts from flying debris, his rifle lowered but at the ready. A second Federale followed. Then another. And another.

All four of the guards inside the house had made it out alive.

I stared at the open door. Waiting.

The first Federale, the oldest of the four, spoke. "Domingo Ordóñez." He lowered his eyes. "I'm sorry," he said. "We failed."

I shook my head. We all had failed.

"He could have stayed safe in the cellar," Ordóñez said, "but he refused. He fought with us side by side. He was one of yours, but he was also one of us. Your loss is our loss."

"We lost two more," Vadillo said. "They took out Bibiano and Nogueras when they stormed the gate. Alboroto sent twenty of his *pendejos*. Sixteen are dead, four wounded."

Ordóñez nodded to his men, then turned to me. "I'll take you to Jávier."

He led me into the smoldering building. Ceteño's body was upstairs on the floor of the bedroom where he fell. A bullet had torn through his jugular vein.

I dropped to my knees in the pool of blood, the two most gut-wrenching words in every cop's vocabulary racing through my brain. *Officer down.*

"Our Father, who art in heaven," I began.

Ordóñez knelt beside me. "Hallowed be thy name," he said, joining me.

A burst of automatic gunfire rang out.

"Thy kingdom come," Ordóñez said, not missing a beat.

A second burst of gunfire.

We continued praying together while police officers, sworn to protect the citizenry and maintain law and order, executed the four wounded guerrillas.

I felt a million miles from New York.

CHAPTER 20

IF THERE'S ONE THING I KNOW after twenty-two years with the NYPD, it's that when you're on a case being bombarded left and right with information, some of it real and some of it bullshit, you need to keep track of everything you saw, heard, or thought. And there's no way you can entrust it all to memory.

Ceteño had to have kept a written record of his meetings with his informant, and my gut told me they were somewhere in this room.

Ordóñez and I finished praying, and we both stood. "Would you mind giving us a few minutes alone?" I said, gesturing at my dead comrade.

"Take as much time as you need," he said, nodding respectfully. "I'll make sure you're not disturbed."

He was a smart cop. He knew what I was up to, and he was letting me know I had his silent approval.

He left, closing the door behind him.

I scanned the room. It was stark—a bed, a desk, a small dresser, and a closet. The attack on the safe house had come suddenly. Ceteño wouldn't have had much time to hide his notes, but since Alboroto's men wouldn't know enough to search for them, all he had to do was stash them somewhere in a hurry. I started with the least obvious: the bed. It didn't take long. I found his notepad, ID, and shield tucked inside one of the pillows.

I dropped to my knees one more time, put my hand over Ceteño's heart, and thanked him for his service. Then I sat down at the desk and pored over the details of his sessions with Núñez.

Twenty minutes later, I called Trace Baker in New York.

He took Ceteño's death hard. "I don't call the shots any more," he said, "but I'm still wired to the people who do. I'll make sure he gets a hero's funeral. He was an exceptional cop."

"Right to the end," I said. "He left a detailed account of his meetings with his CI, Julio Núñez."

"What have you got?" Baker said.

"Ceteño knew how Alboroto moved the coke around. If he had five thousand kilos, he wouldn't put it all in one shipment. He'd send out fifty trucks with a hundred kilos apiece, knowing that the Federales don't have the manpower to intercept more than a handful. They, in turn, have a ploy. They stop a truck, and no matter how small the load, they threaten the driver with life in prison. Once he's sufficiently terrified, they offer him a deal. They'll return the coke and set him free if he agrees to be their eyes and ears inside the organization.

"It almost never works. Most of the drivers would rather rot in jail than risk being caught by Alboroto. But Ceteño had an idea. Instead of stopping a random truck, target a specific driver. He picked Julio Núñez, twenty-two years old, his wife about to have their first child. Three days after she gave birth, they stopped Núñez's truck, confiscated the drugs, and offered him the get-out-of-jail-free deal. He knew the risk of turning against Alboroto, but he couldn't bear the thought of never seeing his newborn son again. He folded, and he became Ceteño's go-to informant.

"A few days after Alboroto's family was killed, Núñez told Ceteño that instead of transporting drugs, he was now the cartel Uber."

"What does that mean?" Baker asked.

"Drug dealers from the States were flying into Mexico: Jamaicans, Russians, Italians, Dominicans—about forty altogether—and Núñez was relegated to picking them up and driving them to a compound in the middle of the desert. Núñez had no idea what the gathering was about, but it wasn't all business. There was food, booze, women—whatever the men needed to keep them happy—and Alboroto spared no expense."

"Holy shit," Baker said. "Drug dealers don't work together. And they certainly don't *get* together under one roof to party. What the fuck were they doing there?"

"That's the same question Ceteño asked. But before Núñez could come back with any answers, Ennis signed his death warrant."

"So we're at a dead end?" Baker said.

"Maybe not. As soon as I read Ceteño's notes, I called Marina Whitney in Washington, told her about the secret meeting in the desert, and asked her to get the manifest for every flight out of Alboroto's territory: New York, Philly, Boston—his entire Northeast distribution system. She's amazing. She pulled it all together in minutes. Núñez got it right. A shit ton of drug kingpins all arrived within a few hours of one another on that Tuesday. And they all left Thursday morning. Except the Russians."

"Why do you think the Russians stayed behind?" Baker said.

"They didn't. Oleg Malenkov and two of his lieutenants flew back on Tuesday a few hours after they arrived."

"Guys like Malenkov know it's a red flag to make a round trip to a foreign country in one day. They hang around for a few days so it looks like a vacation," Baker said. "Something must have gone tits-up and they bolted. Do you think all these drug dealers were in on Cokestorm?"

"No. There's no way that many people could keep that big a secret for four days. I don't know why Alboroto wanted all these kingpins down here, but whatever it was, the Russians didn't want any part of it. We have to find out what they know. Who's our best source on the Malenkov cartel at NYPD?"

Baker didn't hesitate. "George Delamater. He's a lieutenant out of intel down on Vesey Street. He's smart, but you can't trust him. You tell him about a group of renegade ex-cops looking into the Russian mob, and it'll work its way up to the fourteenth floor of 1PP in twenty minutes."

"In that case, who's our second-best source? Someone we can trust."

"You're not going to want to hear this, Danny, but your best resource for intel on the New York Russians is Special Agent Frank Delaqua from the FBI."

"Trace, Delaqua is the idiot who started this whole fucking mess."

"I know, and I can guarantee you he's eating himself up over what that one fuck-up led to. But he's not an idiot. He's just a cop hell-bent on breaking up drug syndicates. I know you don't like him, but if you have any hope of finding out what Alboroto is planning next, track down Delaqua and tell him you need help."

CHAPTER 21

I STAYED AT THE SAFE HOUSE until the American embassy sent a hearse to pick up Ceteño's body. Then I drove with Bolano and Vadillo back to Mexico City, where we rehashed the day's events over tequila shots. I checked into my hotel at two a.m., checked out three hours later, caught a cab back to the airport, and dragged my body onto the first flight out. I didn't wake up till we landed at JFK, exactly twenty-four hours after I'd left.

It's what's known in the law enforcement business as *a long fucking day*, but I had no choice. There was nothing more I could do in Mexico, and Frank Delaqua was with the New York office of the FBI.

Or at least, I thought he was.

"I'm sorry, but Mr. Delaqua is no longer with the Bureau," a cheerful female voice informed me when I called.

"Do you know how I can get in touch with him?" I asked.

She didn't know. And if she did, she wasn't going to share it with the likes of me. So I called someone at the Bureau who would.

I met Prescott Ames at Parris Island, and we served together for the next four years, including more than a few memorable nights getting shit-faced in a tavern ten kilometers outside of Ramstein Air Force Base in Germany.

"This is Special Agent Ames," he said, picking up on the first ring.

"Oorah," I barked. "*Kann ich dich für ein bier interessieren?*"

"Danny Fucking Corcoran," he said. "Last time I saw you, you were on the eleven o'clock news, hanging off the side of the Statue of Liberty. Some cops'll do anything for attention. What's happening?"

"For one thing, I'm no longer a cop. But I'm glad to hear you're still with the feds, because I need a favor."

"Your German still sounds like it's right out of a Monty Python sketch, but I did pick up on '*bier.*' How about we meet at Maxwell's?"

"Not this time, bro. Too many patrons with dark suits, lapel pins, and inquisitive minds."

"Ahh, so now we're talking hole-and-corner shit. I'm intrigued. There's a bar uptown in Harlem—one and a half stars on Yelp. But the guy who owns it, Moses Morrison, gets five stars for discretion. How soon do you want to meet?"

"How soon can you get there?"

"Give me an hour. I don't have the exact address, but it's on Frederick Douglass Boulevard between 132nd and 133rd. The sign outside says *Morons.*"

"Sounds like our kind of place," I said.

I didn't even have to step inside to know that Moses Morrison had a wicked sense of humor. At one point, the large neon block letters out front had read *Morrison's.* But over time, half the letters had gone dark, and Moses had capitalized on the new identity.

"Welcome to Morons," the aging Black man with a close-cropped white beard said as soon as I walked through the door. "I'm Moses. Prez is waiting for you in the back."

I didn't have to ask him how he knew I was there for Prez. I was the only white guy in the place.

"We got Rheingold on tap," Moses said, drawing one and passing it over the bar to me without waiting for an answer.

"Sounds good."

"The back" was not just the rear of the bar. It was a quiet little room behind that. There were four tables, three of them empty. Prez, who was waiting at the fourth, stood up.

He's linebacker big and puppy-dog friendly. I set my beer down as he came in for a big bro hug.

"Dan the man," he said. "When did you leave the department?"

"About ten seconds after I tried to take a swing at the new PC."

"I hope you connected. He's worthless. The mayor's working him like a sock puppet," Prez said. "So what's next? You got a plan B?"

"I didn't, but I got lucky. Something big fell in my lap, and I signed on right away."

He raised his beer mug and tapped it against mine. "Congratulations. Tell me all about it."

I shook my head. "Private enterprise. I can't give you any of the details except to say I'm still one of the good guys, and I can use your help."

"What do you need?"

"A sit-down meeting with Frank Delaqua."

"You, the *New York Times,* the *Washington Post, 60 Minutes* . . . Delaqua is the most famous former agent since J. Edgar Hoover."

"When did he leave the Bureau?"

"He resigned the same day as the shooting in the courtroom."

"Do you know where he is now?"

"I might. Why are you looking for him?"

"I already told you, Prez. I can't talk about the nature—"

He cut me off. "Spare me the top secret, national security crap. I hear it all day long. Try to see it from where I'm sitting. If it weren't for Frank Delaqua, your father-in-law would still be alive. So I'm wondering if you're thinking about evening the score, because if you whack the fucker, that would make me an accessory before the fact, and the Bureau tends to frown on that kind of shit."

"Good point," I said. "I'm not planning on whacking anybody, and for the record, I don't blame Delaqua for the judge's death. Harvey did what he did on his own, and he knew the consequences."

He drained the last of his beer. "I can help you. But at least tell me what you can tell me."

"Like I said, I'm not a cop, but I'm still dedicated to serving this city. The reason I can't give you the details is the same reason I couldn't do anything about it when I was with the department. But I can tell you this. I just got back from Mexico. The attack on Central Park was only the beginning, and the only people who might have been able to help me figure out what Joaquín Alboroto is going to do next were all murdered."

"By Alboroto," Prez said.

I nodded. "I have some leads, but I'm not deep enough in that world to make the most of them. Delaqua is. He can help. I don't know him, but right now I trust him more than I trust anybody who takes orders from Martin K. Ennis."

"Delaqua's got a cabin tucked deep in the woods somewhere up in Buttfuck, Pennsylvania," Prez said.

"Would you happen to have a street address, or at least a zip code for Buttfuck?" I said.

He laughed. "From what I hear, his driveway is a half mile long, and you wouldn't get twenty feet past the Trespassers Will Be Shot sign before he unleashed the dogs, the heavy artillery, or both."

"He sounds a little paranoid," I said.

"And with good reason. He took a lot of scumbags off the street, many of them for life. I can think of half a dozen drug kingpins who would like to see him dead. And now he can add Alboroto to the list."

"Prez, I've gotta find this guy and talk to him."

"Then you've got to catch him when he leaves the house."

"Does he?"

"Oh, yeah, and I can tell you for a fact that there's one place he likes to hang out at, every day of the week."

"A gin mill?"

"Hell, no. This place is definitely alcohol-free. I can get you an exact address," he said, pulling out his phone. He was about to tap on the screen but changed his mind. He put it down on the table and looked square at me.

"What's the matter?" I said.

"I just need to repeat this loud and clear, Marine. Ever since I know him, Frank Delaqua has been one of those agents who's always looking over his shoulder. If you spook him, you may not get the chance to explain that you're one of the good guys. Just promise me you'll be careful."

"Hey, of course I'll be careful," I said. "Just because I hang out at Morons doesn't mean I am one."

CHAPTER 22

BUTTFUCK, PENNSYLVANIA, TURNED OUT to be a little town called Matamoras, population 2,400, most of whom were white, blue collar, and living on a lower-middle-class income. It's a two-hour drive from Manhattan and only minutes away from one of the highlights of the region: a two-and-a-half-foot-long hunk of granite that marks the point where New York, New Jersey, and Pennsylvania meet.

If Delaqua wanted to get away from it all, he picked a good spot. The tiny town was surrounded by more than five hundred square miles of dense woods. I called Marina Whitney, who sent me a satellite photo of Delaqua's fortress in the wilderness.

As far off the beaten path as it was, the area was not without its amenities: affordable bars and restaurants, a Walmart Supercenter, and, most important to Delaqua, a gun range.

"Guns are like religion to him," Prez had said. "He shows up at the range every morning. If you're trying to talk to him, that's the place."

"Just walk up to him while he's holding a loaded 9mm in his hand and say something like 'Remember me? I was in the courtroom when your career went down the crapper,'" I said. "What could possibly go wrong?"

Prez laughed. "I know you, Corcoran. You've got much more

elegant ways of getting someone's attention. You'll come up with something."

The following morning at 7:30, I was sitting in the diner across the street from the Tri-State Gun Range, working on a stack of buttermilk pancakes, a carafe of coffee, and a plan on how to approach Delaqua. Nothing about the diner or the plan felt particularly elegant.

The range's website said that they opened at nine. At 8:45 I saw a maroon pickup truck heading in my direction. It was a 2018 Ford F-150 with an aftermarket camper top, which matched the description Marina had given me. As it got closer, I could make out Delaqua behind the wheel. He drove straight past the range without even slowing down. Three blocks later, he turned right and disappeared. Five minutes after that, he drove by again, and this time he turned left after a few blocks.

On the third go-round, satisfied that he wasn't being followed, Delaqua pulled into the parking lot, got out of the truck, slung a backpack over his shoulder, and walked through the front door of the range just as someone unlocked it from the inside.

Prez wasn't kidding when he said religion. Delaqua was there just in time for nine o'clock mass.

Ten minutes later, I followed, showed my permit to the man at the front desk, paid my way in, and was assigned to slot number 7. Delaqua, the only other shooter on the range, was in slot 4.

He had already put a tight grouping of holes in the middle of his first target. It would have been impressive at any distance, but at a hundred yards, it was jaw-dropping. I watched as he sent a fresh silhouette downrange and reloaded.

He got into his stance and drew aim. But before he could squeeze the trigger, a shot exploded with a deafening boom and reverberated through the building. I had fired my Desert Eagle, which is more of a statement than a practical handgun. It's oversize and overweight, with a fierce recoil, and sounds more like a cannon than a pistol. Real cops don't carry them. Movie cops, video-game supervillains, and real-life assholes do.

Delaqua lowered his gun, pulled out his spotting scope, and zeroed in on the .50-caliber hole I'd left. "Dead center, dude," he said. "Good shot—if that had been your target instead of mine."

I fired again. A second hit ripped directly into the bullseye. "It *was* my target," I said.

"Why would you want to do that?" he said.

"I was trying to get your attention." I put my gun down and stepped back out of the stall so he could see that my hands were empty.

"I know you," he said.

"Danny Corcoran. Judge Solomon was my father-in-law and my friend."

"I know. I'm sorry. Very sorry. I was trying to bring down a drug dealer who was killing thousands of people. I broke the rules, and it cost me my career. My biggest regret is that my actions led to the judge's death."

I knew he meant it. I nodded a silent thank you.

"You're NYPD," Delaqua said.

"Recently retired."

"So you're coming after me as a private citizen?" he said, his gun still about hip high.

"I'm not coming *after* you. I'm coming *to* you. For help. I just got back from Mexico. Alboroto is organizing something big down there, and I'm trying to put the pieces together."

"Alboroto's not my problem any more."

"Oh, sorry," I said. "I heard he wants to kill you, but if that doesn't seem to be a problem . . ."

"Pack up your gear," he said. "Let's take this conversation off the grid."

A half hour later, we arrived at his place. Up close, it looked like any typical sportsman's cabin: post-and-beam construction, stone fireplace, leather sofa, fishing poles in the corner—rustic as hell. But the land around it—two hundred yards in all directions—had been cleared so nobody could sneak up undetected. And there were eight cameras and three dogs just in case anybody tried.

Delaqua made a pot of coffee, and I spent the next twenty minutes filling him in on my trip to Mexico, and about twenty seconds explaining that the group who was funding this operation wanted to remain anonymous.

"At least for now," I added.

He listened intently and didn't say a word until I was finished.

"It sounds like fake news," he said.

"I was there," I said. "There was nothing fake about the three cops who were gunned down."

"Sorry. No disrespect. I'm talking about this story from your CI about all those drug lords from the US flying down to Mexico. How do you know he didn't make up a bullshit list just to give your man Ceteño something to chew on?"

"Because the night he was killed, my tech person verified that every name on that list landed in Mexico City and cleared customs. And the next day, she got access to the videos—both arriving and departing."

He sat there shaking his head, and finally, he dropped a single f-bomb. But it came out low and slow and it took about six syllables before he got from the initial "F" to the final "K."

"How can I help?" he said.

"Whatever Alboroto is planning, the Russians didn't want any part of it."

"Oleg Malenkov hates Alboroto," Delaqua said.

"I was hoping you'd say that."

"Right. So now you're probably wondering if he hates him enough to tell us what's going down."

"Exactly."

"Never happen, Danny. Malenkov doesn't go to the feds to solve his problems. He settles things in his own sweet time, in his own savage style."

"Shit," I said.

"However," he said, holding up his index finger, "there is one Russian who is always happy to talk to me: Dmitri Volkov. He runs a successful travel agency catering exclusively to his countrymen in Brighton Beach. Malenkov is one of his best customers. Two years ago,

I started to wonder if maybe Dmitri was doing more for the cartel than making travel arrangements."

"Laundering money," I said.

"That was the dream. No such luck. It turns out Dmitri is totally legit. But he does have one little failing that caught my attention."

"What's that?"

"He was fucking Malenkov's wife. Every time the boss went out of town, Dmitri and Yelena were getting it on. I mean, it's easy to see why. She's a beautiful woman married to a short, fat, ugly swine, and Dmitri is tall, good-looking, and quite adept at making her scream. And if you don't believe me, I have the videos to prove it."

"So you own Dmitri Volkov," I said.

"Let's just say that Dmitri and I have developed a very healthy quid pro quo relationship. He keeps me informed, and I keep him from getting his johnson hacked off and shoved down his throat."

CHAPTER 23

"Do you like swedish meatballs?" Delaqua asked, with a hint of a smile for the first time since I'd met him.

"Um . . . sure," I said, trying to make sense of the question. "Are you serving hors d'oeuvres?"

The smile broadened. "Dmitri and I have a dozen different places where we meet up, all of them as far from the Russian ghetto in Brighton Beach as possible. I just texted him and told him to meet me at noon at the IKEA in Paramus, New Jersey. I'm not a big fan of their furniture, but the meatballs and mashed potatoes at their restaurant are fantastic."

"Prevent a terrorist attack on New York *and* get a fantastic meatball lunch in the bargain?" I said. "Win-win."

I'd meant it as a joke, but the humor escaped him. "I know," he said.

The rendezvous spot was a little over an hour away. We took separate vehicles and drove to the top floor of the IKEA parking garage. Our informant was waiting for us in a black Lexus SUV with tinted windows. Delaqua got in the front seat, and I got in the back.

Dmitri Volkov was every bit as good-looking as Delaqua had said he'd be, but not nearly as accommodating.

"Hello, Frank," he said. "I'm surprised to hear from you. I thought you were not with the FBI any more."

"Correctamundo, my friend. I'm not with the Bureau. I'm with him," he said, pointing at me.

"And yet you still need information?"

"*He* needs information. Same rules apply."

"You mean, if I don't cooperate, you'll inform Malenkov of my indiscretions with his wife."

"Like I said, nothing changes."

"You're out of touch, Frank. Oleg Malenkov is dead. And, sadly, so is Yelena."

The news was a gut punch, but Delaqua didn't blink. "When? Where? How?" he said.

"A few days after his unfortunate trip to Mexico, which is, I am sure, what you were planning to ask me about. They went to dinner with friends Thursday night. Oleg's driver dropped them off at home about eleven. When he came to pick Oleg up Friday morning, the two of them were in bed, bullets through their heads. The killer must have disabled the alarm while they were out and was waiting for them to go to sleep. I was called immediately. I made arrangements to ship the bodies to the Novodevichy Cemetery in Moscow that same day."

"Who took Malenkov's place in the organization?" I asked.

Dmitri swiveled in his seat and looked squarely at me. "His brother Fyodor, but if your friend over here thinks he can still hold my affair with Yelena over my head, he is sadly mistaken." He turned back to Delaqua. "Fyodor never liked her, and he won't give a shit who she was fucking."

"Whom," Delaqua said.

Dmitri responded with a dumb stare. "What?"

"You said Fyodor wouldn't give a shit *who* she was fucking. It's *whom*, not who. You Russians got no fucking respect for our mother tongue."

If Delaqua was trying to push Dmitri over the edge, he succeeded wildly.

"Fuck you, *former* Agent Delaqua! You're nobody. You're shit on the bottom of my boot heel. Malenkov's dead. This is our last meeting. Get out."

"Aw, Dmitri," Delaqua said. "After all the good times we've had together . . . The hot fudge sundaes at the Bellvale Farms Creamery in Warwick, the hot dogs at Walter's in Mamaroneck, the Swedish meatballs . . . You're saying it's *over*?"

"*Correctamundo, my friend,*" Dmitri said, mimicking Delaqua flawlessly. "You have no power over me."

"Hmm," Delaqua said, looking at me. "Do you think he's right? He said I have no power, but remember, he's not so great with the English language. I think what he meant to say was that I have no *authority*."

He whipped around, drove his fist into Dmitri's perfect nose, pulled out his Glock, and pressed it to the man's head. "But I've got *this*. This is power," he screamed. "Wouldn't you agree, Dmitri?"

"I'm sorry. I'm sorry," Dmitri said, sobbing into hands that were pressed to his nose and dripping blood. "I'll tell you anything. Everything. Please. I'm sorry."

"Start with the meeting between Malenkov and Joaquín Alboroto in Mexico City last week. Did you book the trip?"

"Yes. Oleg flew down there with two of his lieutenants, Ivan Lipski and Alexei Minkevich."

"We heard it didn't go well."

He shook his head. "No. I had to scramble to book them on a return flight a few hours after they arrived in Mexico."

"What happened?"

"I don't know. I swear."

"You're lying. And don't tell me you're just the guy who arranges transportation. I'll bet Malenkov's plane was barely wheels up out of JFK before you were buried dick deep in his old lady. And when you were done boning her, you rolled over, cuddled up, and got her talking about her hideous husband, picking her brain about what his little business trip was all about. So it's time to make a decision, comrade."

"Anything you want to know. I swear. I swear."

Delaqua lowered the gun, pulled a red bandanna from the pocket of his jeans, and handed it to Dmitri. Then he turned to me. "Doesn't it make you feel good all over when you see two people work out their differences?" he said.

I was in combat as a marine, worked undercover for NYPD, and came face-to-face with a string of whacked-out people in my days at ESU. I've seen crazy. And if I ever write a book about it, Frank Delaqua will get his own chapter.

By now Dmitri had stopped the bleeding and regained some of his composure. "Oleg got a call from Alboroto himself, inviting him to come to Mexico for an important meeting. He assumed it would be a one-on-one—just him and el Carnicero. Yelena said he was looking forward to it, but when he got on the plane and saw the Albanians, he was furious. And when he got to Mexico and saw there were dozens of them, he went ballistic. He drove directly to Alboroto's house and told him he wasn't about to discuss his operation with a bunch of *muzhiks*. And then he flew home."

"Nice try, Dmitri," Delaqua said. "You left something out. He didn't leave Mexico without finding out what Alboroto was about to share with everyone else."

"Yes, yes, of course. And whatever it was, he didn't tell Yelena. All she told me was that Oleg said he would be damned if he let Alboroto tell him how to run his operation."

"It sounds like kind of an over-my-dead-body thing," Delaqua said. "And Alboroto took him up on it."

"But it wasn't just Oleg's and Yelena's dead bodies. That night, Lipski and Minkevich, the two who went to Mexico with him, were also murdered in their homes along with their wives and Lipski's teen-age daughter."

"Alboroto is never subtle when he sends a message. Anything else?"

Dmitri shook his head. "That's all I know."

"That's all you know *now*," Delaqua said. "But you're still travel agent to the stars, so keep tabs on Fyodor and the new regime. My friend here may have some more questions."

Dmitri nodded blankly.

Delaqua opened the car door, and Dmitri pulled the rearview mirror toward him to survey the damage to his nose.

"You really ought to get a doctor to take a look at that honker, comrade. You don't want to lose those boyish good looks. You never know whose wife you're going to have to start banging to keep me happy."

CHAPTER 24

"WE GOOD?" DELAQUA ASKED.

"Tasty as hell," I said, popping a Swedish meatball into my mouth. "Worth the trip to Jersey."

"First of all, you're scarfing them down like an amateur," he said. "Let me show you how it's done."

He rolled one of his meatballs in gravy, cut it in half, dipped it into the mashed potatoes, crowned it with a dollop of lingonberry jam, and held it to his lips. "And second of all, I didn't ask if the food was good. I asked if *we* were good. You and me."

He slid the fork into his mouth and chomped on the savory-sweet concoction while he waited for my answer.

"*First of all*," I said, cutting a meatball in half and mimicking his technique, "thank you for the tutorial. And second of all, yeah, we're good. Why wouldn't we be?"

"You and I have different styles. You never would've handled Dmitri the way I did."

"Oh, that," I said. "You're right. I never would have put the gun to his head. Way too messy. A heart shot would have been much cleaner."

He responded with a throaty laugh. "You're a real asshole, Corcoran. I like that in a cop."

I returned the laugh and let his words sink in, not sure if I was actually a cop any more. Two weeks earlier, I'd been leading one of NYPD's most elite units in a top-secret operation to protect and defend the Statue of Liberty. Now I was in a furniture store, looking out the window at the Jersey Turnpike while getting a lecture from a failed FBI agent on how to eat lunch.

"So let's cut to the chase," Delaqua said. "Who are you working for?"

"They call themselves the Baltic Avenue Group. Private company, deep pockets. Single-minded mission: protect the city of New York—its people, its property, and its thriving economy."

Delaqua grinned. "I thought that was what NYPD was for."

"So did I. But it's amazing how one asshole falling out of a chopper and landing on the Statue of Liberty can cause a seismic shift in how politicians view their police departments. Budgets were cut, critical response units were scrapped, and worst of all, the mantle of leadership was passed from a giant to a narcissistic slug. But the good news is that Trace Baker is running this new unit, and the people who hired him are giving him the resources and the latitude to get the job done."

"And in this case, 'the job' is to stop Alboroto from whatever he's planning next," Delaqua said.

"Exactly."

"Are you hiring?"

"Absolutely."

"How low are your standards?" he said, another forkful of meatball perfectly slathered with potatoes and jam poised at his mouth. "Asking for a friend."

"I'll give it to you straight, Frank. With Ceteño dead, you probably know more about the Alboroto cartel than any cop around. And you're wired into the Russians. But I've seen your report card. Does not work well with others. When things aren't going his way, he makes up his own rules. This unit has a structure: Baker at the top, me in the second slot, and then a team that works together. There's no room for cowboys."

Delaqua sat there in silence for a solid thirty seconds. "That day in the courtroom," he finally said. "When the judge pulled out the Glock 45, that was the second-worst day of my life. Because I knew what was going to happen, and I knew it was my fault. Ten days later, when Alboroto strafed thousands of innocent people to get revenge for what *I* had done, I sat in my cabin, and for the first time in my career, I seriously considered eating my gun. But I didn't. I believe in second chances, Danny, and this is my shot. You take me on, and I promise I won't let you down."

He had a strong jawline and deep-set steel-blue eyes that exuded confidence. There wasn't a hint of desperation about him as he waited for my verdict. I was ready to give it to him, but I had to make sure he understood where I was coming from.

"This isn't the FBI," I said.

He cracked a smile. "Thank God for that."

"Or NYPD. Or any other police force I can think of."

"What's your point, Danny?"

"My point is, you fucked up. You did the wrong thing for all the right reasons, and the repercussions were devastating. So now you're ready to do the right thing. The irony here is that this group, which is still trying to define itself, isn't going to play by the traditional rules of right and wrong. We're operating under the rules of war. Alboroto is a terrorist, a ruthless murderer. I don't plan to track him down, cuff him, read him his rights, and bring him to trial. My goal is to do to him what the Navy SEALs did to Osama bin Laden. I just want to make sure you understand that if you're looking to redeem yourself for your sins by following the path of righteousness, you're talking to the wrong church."

"I appreciate the heads-up, Father Corcoran, but I don't need redemption. Not if I can get justice. You just tell me the rules, and I'll follow them."

"In that case, congratulations," I said. "You're my first hire."

"When do I start?"

"Right now. What do you think is the most important thing Dmitri gave us?" I asked.

"Alboroto is planning something big, and he sent for all the major players in the Northeast to tell them about it."

"Right," I said. "The Russians walked away mad, and they paid the price for it. Do you think they're going to talk to us about what went down?"

"No. The Russians will settle their score with the Mexicans in their own sweet time. The last thing they'd ever do is talk with us."

"Exactly. So the best way to find out what happened at that powwow is to talk to someone who went to Mexico and didn't walk away mad."

"Not gonna happen, Danny. The drug business is all about supply and demand. These guys aren't going to go up against their biggest supplier. They're in lockstep with Alboroto. They won't talk to us."

"One of them will. Mercury Maldonado. You know him?"

"Of course I know Mercury," Delaqua said. "He's the main distributor to every organized Dominican drug crew in New York, New Jersey, and Connecticut. He may have done you a quid pro quo in the past, but after what happened to Malenkov, what makes you think he'll rat out Alboroto?"

"He owes me."

"Look, just because you cut him a break doesn't mean he'll be willing to—"

"I did more than cut him a break," I said. "I saved his daughter's life."

CHAPTER 25

"MERCURY HAS FOUR KIDS," I said. "Three boys and one girl, Dariana. She's the golden child. She's also the one who drives him crazy. Three years ago, she got involved with some dusthead from the streets, an ex-con named Wilfredo Pagán.

"Daddy went ballistic, but Dariana was nineteen, and Maldonado was smart enough to know that if he tried to break up the relationship, she would dig in even harder.

"A few months into it, she comes to her senses, and she dumps him. By text. But then she remembers she left some of her shit at his place, so she waits till he's at work, and asks a friend to go with her. They get to Wilfredo's apartment, but he's not at work. He's all hopped up on PCP. He punches Dariana in the face, grabs a knife, and puts it to her throat. The friend runs for her life. Wilfredo barricades the door and starts screaming he's going to kill her.

"I was in command of the ESU team that was called in. I got him on his cell phone, but his brain was fried, and all he did was tell me, if he can't have her, nobody can, and then he stopped picking up. We managed to get a pinhole camera into the room where he was holding her hostage, and about an hour into it he started praying and asking God to forgive him. He came at her with the knife, and I made the call. We took him out with one shot.

"After it was over, Mercury said he owed me. I told him I was only doing my job, but every year on the anniversary of that date, he makes a donation to the NYPD widows-and-orphans club in my name."

"Giving money to charity is one thing, but do you think he's grateful enough to tell you what Alboroto is going to do next?" Delaqua asked.

"I doubt if he has any idea what's next. Alboroto doesn't share his plans with anybody. Our job is to find out what went down at that meeting in Mexico and figure it out for ourselves. And if anybody who was there will talk, Mercury's our best bet."

"I know his patterns. It should be easy enough for me to track him down," Delaqua said.

"And this will make it even easier." I handed him a card with Kaori's cell phone number. "She's your contact. Whatever you need, just ask."

We walked back down to the parking lot.

"Where are you off to?" Delaqua asked.

"I'm going to drive up to Pearl River and try to sign up my next team member."

"Anyone I know?"

"Chris Redwood. You'd hate him. He's fifteen years younger than us, annoyingly good-looking, picked up a law degree at NYU that he never uses, and can shoot the nut sack off a fruit fly at a hundred yards."

"Sounds easy to hate," Delaqua said, "but with a résumé like that, I'd be surprised if he wasn't already gainfully employed."

"He was. He worked for me. The last time I saw him, we had just lowered Brady Lebeck's remains from the crown of the Statue of Liberty. The next day, Ennis reassigned him to the Bronx tow pound, take it or leave it. He told Ennis to go fuck himself and he left."

"Well, now I hate him a lot less," Delaqua said. "Good luck. Sounds like he'll fit right in."

I hopped on the Jersey Turnpike and headed north. Forty minutes later, I crossed back into New York. Chris's house on Pascack Road was only half a mile over the state line.

"Great to see you, Doc," he said once we'd opened a couple of cold ones in his backyard.

"Right back at you, Sequoia," I said. "You figure out what to do with the rest of your life yet?"

"The rest of my life? Hell, man, I don't even have dinner plans."

"The last I heard, your brother wanted you to come on as a partner in his law firm."

"Oh, that," he said. "That's the one thing I decided not to do."

"I thought you and Victor got along great."

"We do. And the best way to keep it that way is never to go into business together. Look, I'm lucky. Eleven out of sixteen guys on the team took the shit assignments they were offered, because they have mortgages to pay and kids to send to college. I don't have anything like that hanging over my head. I was fourteen years shy of my pension, and I'll be damned if I'm going to spend them as a glorified parking lot attendant. Or a lawyer. Victor and I both went to law school because it made our old man happy. But Pop's gone now, and I need something a lot more challenging to make me happy."

"I might have just what you're looking for," I said.

"I was hoping this was more than a social call," he said. "Tell me about it."

"It's a private company funding a task force of retired cops. The core mission is to protect the city of New York from terror attacks like the one that just hit Central Park."

"You mean you actually get to do what the whole world thinks the NYPD Counterterrorism Bureau is doing?" he said.

"Right. Only we're not part of NYPD. We're not part of anything, so we work outside the normal bureaucratic channels."

"I'm in," he said.

"I'm not finished."

"I don't care. I lost two friends when they bombed the park. They were running that 5K race. Your new outfit is going after the people who did it. I'm in, Doc. Mind, body, heart, and soul."

I smiled. Two hires in less than two hours. I was on a roll.

CHAPTER 26

WHEN I GOT TO THE FIREHOUSE the next morning, there were four new people in the command operations room. Kaori had been on a bit of a hiring jag herself.

"Amazon was having a sale on analysts," she said.

"There are more of them than there are of us," I said. "I hope we can come up with something for them to analyze."

"I know it looks like overkill," she said, "but right now they're training together—team building. Once we're up to speed, any one of them will be able to hold down the fort."

"You're the boss," I said.

And a damn great-looking boss at that. More than I'd realized when I first met her. Maybe it was the fact that she had traded the corporate black blazer for a fitted pink scoop-neck shirt that showed off her well-toned arms.

Frank Delaqua was sitting at a console with one of the analysts. He gave me a thumbs-up and headed my way.

"We got Mercury Maldonado," he said.

"Great news," I said.

"I know, but there's some less-than-great news to go with it. He's in a little town called Cortona."

"Queens?"

"Italy. The Tuscany region, to be specific."

"I thought they make wine there. What kind of drug deal is he putting together in Tuscany?"

"I don't think it's a drug deal. He's there with his whole family. They rented a villa through the end of September."

I looked at Kaori. She was way ahead of me. "I can have you on a plane to Florence today," she said.

"Make it tonight," I said. "I've got a lot of work to do here. I can sleep on the plane and be in Tuscany first thing tomorrow morning."

"Done," she said.

"On second thought," I said, "book two tickets, please."

Delaqua's eyes brightened.

"I'm going to have to get Frank a new identity," Kaori said. "It won't take more than a few hours."

"Frank's not going," I said. "I'll be traveling with the other new guy, Chris Redwood. He should have been here by now."

"He got here an hour ago," Kaori said. "He's upstairs in the print shop getting his new passport. I'll run up there and tell him he's going to be taking it out for a spin tonight." She looked at her watch. "You two should go to the conference room. Kevin Cavanaugh is calling in at seven fifteen."

"Good job finding Maldonado so fast," I said as Delaqua and I headed down the hall.

"It wasn't that big a deal. He pays cash for everything, but his wife loves to shop. She left digital breadcrumbs everywhere. I just tapped into a couple of databases. The technology here is as good as it gets. I'd say we're in the same league as the Bureau."

We got to the conference room, and I stopped just as he was about to open the door. "I know what you're thinking," I said.

"*You* know what *I'm* thinking?" he said, doing a pretty damn good De Niro impression, complete with the actor's trademark crinkly-eyed shit-eating grin.

"Yeah, I do. You're thinking, if you found Maldonado, how come I'm taking Redwood to Italy with me?"

"Never crossed my mind," he said, not nearly as convincing as his De Niro. "But now that you bring it up, why did you pick him over me?"

"Remember Wilfredo Pagán, the guy who took Maldonado's daughter hostage and was about to kill her until we brought him down with one shot?"

"Of course I remember."

"Chris Redwood was the shooter," I said. "Maldonado will be happy to see me. He'll be ecstatic to see Redwood."

"In that case, good call, boss." His face softened, and I knew he meant it.

"I saw that look in your eye when I asked Kaori to book two seats. Sorry I couldn't take you to Italy."

"No problem," he said with a shrug as he opened the door to the conference room. "We'll always have IKEA."

CHAPTER 27

"GOOD TIMING," BAKER SAID as soon as Delaqua and I walked in. "We were just getting started."

He was sitting alone at a large table. Kevin Cavanaugh, the Midtown South cop turned TV true crime reporter, was bigger than life on the wall monitor. It was still the middle of the night in LA, and he was staring bleary-eyed into the camera, his hair and T-shirt both sleep-rumpled.

"Danny, it's good to see you," he said. "I was devastated when I heard. I knew Jávier. He was smart. He knew he needed to get out of there, but fucking Ennis said no. He's the one with Jávier's blood on his hands."

"We can't undo the damage Ennis has done," Baker said. "Our job is to stop Alboroto. Kevin, this is Frank Delaqua. He just joined the team. Let's get him up to speed before you give us an update."

"Frank, welcome aboard," Cavanaugh said. "Two nights ago, I reached out to Alboroto. The man is a narcissist. He wants people to be in awe of his brilliance. And like all narcissists, we know he has grand plans. So I offered him a platform—a face-to-face interview. I thought if I could get him to open up, he might give us a clue to what he's planning next. I know it sounds crazy, but John Miller did it with Osama bin Laden. Sean Penn did it with El Chapo. I figured it's worth a shot."

"It was better than a shot," Baker said. "It was a brilliant mindfuck. Kevin did a one-hour special on the attack on Central Park. I'll spare you the first fifty-nine and a half minutes, but I want you to watch the Hail Mary he throws in the very last play of the game."

He tapped on his iPad, and a second screen lit up with the video seen by millions two nights earlier.

"Ladies and gentlemen, thank you for watching," Cavanaugh said, looking stone-faced at the camera. "Let me close with an apology. A good journalist has to deliver the five "W's" to his audience. Tonight, I told you the who, what, when, and where of the story, but I failed to tell you the why.

"I know Mr. Alboroto lost his wife and son, but does that justify the murders of almost a thousand innocent men, women, and children? Why destroy the natural beauty of a New York icon, a beacon of tranquility for millions of visitors from around the globe? There is only one man who can tell us the why. One man who can tell us if his thirst for revenge is quenched.

"Mr. Alboroto, I'm reaching out to you on behalf of the people of this ravaged city, this shocked nation, and this horrified world. They want to hear from you. I offer you a way to communicate, to tell your side of the story. Unedited. Uncensored. Only your words, straight to the people. I will meet you anywhere. I will come with nothing more than a video camera and a quest for truth. I await your response."

"It *is* a brilliant mindfuck," Delaqua said, "and I bet it worked."

"The newsroom got a call about two a.m. from someone who claimed to be Alboroto's lawyer," Cavanaugh said. "We've logged hundreds of those calls a day, so the first thing we ask for is proof of authenticity. So far, every one of the callers has been a con artist, crackpot, or somebody who likes to fuck with the media. This guy asked for an email address where he could send the proof. Take a look at what he sent."

He played us a forty-five-second film clip. It was everything I'd seen before—cocaine blanketing the park, people gasping, collapsing, dying on the roadway—only this footage had been shot from a GoPro camera aboard the helicopter that decimated the park.

"Our tech people checked it out to see if it could have been faked," Cavanaugh said. "It's authentic. The lawyer called back. He told me to fly to Mexico City, check into the Four Seasons, and wait there until I'm contacted."

"There's something you can do for us while you're waiting," I said.

I filled him in on the meeting Alboroto had arranged for his platinum-tier customers in Mexico City.

"We have no idea what happened at that meeting," I said, "but we just tracked down one of the dealers who was there, and I'm flying to Italy tonight with Chris Redwood to talk to him. As soon as I hear anything, I'll let you know."

"Are you serious?" Cavanaugh said. "A meeting of forty major dealers? This story is already big, but that—shit, man, that's my shot at an Emmy. Fuck Emmy. That's a Pulitzer. Anything else?"

"Yeah, one more thing. Oleg Malenkov, who ran the Russian cartel, locked horns with Alboroto, said fuck you, and flew back to New York. The next day, Oleg, his wife, and his two lieutenants all wound up with a bullet through the head."

"Holy shit," Cavanaugh said. "And I'm flying down to Mexico to meet with this crazy bastard?"

"You'll be fine," I said. "You're Alboroto's connection to his public. He's not going to hurt you."

"Can you guarantee that, Corcoran?"

"Hell, no. The man's a homicidal maniac. But I can guarantee one thing: if he does blow you away, I will personally show up at the Pulitzers and accept the award on your behalf."

CHAPTER 28

REDWOOD AND I LANDED AT PERETOLA AIRPORT in Florence, Italy, the next morning. I was still Tim Randall, and he was now Harold Scott, a lawyer. My lawyer. Kaori created a detailed backstory for our business trip together, but this was Italy, not the Middle East. Nobody asked. Nobody cared.

We rented a car and were on the road by nine o'clock. Cortona was only 120 kilometers away, but we couldn't show up too early. We knew that Mercury's wife, Xiomara, didn't start giving her credit card its daily workout until noon, and it always goes smoother if you talk to a drug dealer when his family's not home. So we opted for the scenic route and stopped at an osteria for a four-star meal in the middle of nowhere.

Cortona is on a hilltop overlooking the blue waters of Lake Trasimeno, and a sprawling green valley dotted with farms, vineyards, and a sea of sunlit red roof tiles.

"Wow. We are definitely not in Kansas any more," Redwood said as we drove through the stone gateway of the walled city. "Mercury thought he was off the grid. He's going to freak when he sees us."

"Not for long," I said. "Most of these dealers never made it through high school, but they can logic a situation out faster than a Harvard

MBA. His first thought will be that NYPD is after him, and then he'll quickly process that they don't have jurisdiction, and then he'll finally decide that if he was in trouble, they wouldn't send the two of us."

And that's pretty much what happened. Mercury opened the vintage chestnut door to his medieval hideaway, and the expression on his face went from shock to cool to genuine joy within seconds.

He spread his arms open wide. "*Buongiorno*, mother fuckers. Come in, come in."

He was dressed in classic New York City streetwear: basketball shorts, a limited-edition Supreme logo T-shirt that had to have to set him back close to two grand, a pricey pair of Gucci slides, and white socks with a Nike swoosh, which he probably picked up in the ten-dollar bin at Modell's.

We followed him through a rustic farmhouse kitchen that was a joyful blend of wood beams, brick walls, marble countertops, and timeworn copper pots. We walked through an archway into a spacious living and dining area.

"I want you to meet someone," he said, pointing to a wooden playpen filled with brightly colored stacking cubes, dozens of cars and trucks, a menagerie of stuffed animals, and, in the center of it all, a happy baby with a full head of thick, dark, curly hair and a smile that showed four perfect white teeth.

"This is Dariana's boy, my grandson Caden," Mercury said. "He's fourteen months old, and if it wasn't for you two . . ." He stopped and reined in any potential display of emotion.

"Congratulations," I said. "How's Dariana doing?"

"She finally got her fucking head screwed on straight. And the baby daddy is a good man. He's a mechanic—fixes jet planes for the Air Force. He's stationed in Korea until . . ."

Caden threw a stuffed elephant out of the playpen, and Mercury tossed his hands up in the air and moaned, "Ay, ay, ay."

The kid laughed. It was clearly a regular routine they had going. Mercury picked up the toy, handed it to his grandson, and said, "So, Caden, do you want to ask them what NYPD is doing in Italy?"

"We're not NYPD," I said.

That got his attention.

"But we were wondering what *you're* doing in Italy."

"My wife," he said. "Years ago, she saw this chick flick about a woman who gets divorced, so she comes to Tuscany and she buys this run-down villa. Ever since then, Xiomara wanted to come here on vacation, so—"

"You don't take *vacations*," I said. "Quickies, maybe. A weekend in Vegas, a few days back home in the DR, but you don't rent a villa six time zones and four thousand miles away from your turf."

"If you're not with NYPD, who you with?" he said.

"Private company. Got no beef with you."

"Good, because I didn't know that crazy Mexican was gonna pelt New York City with a fucking zillion dollars' worth of cocaine."

"But you spent two days with him before it happened," I said.

"It wasn't just me. Alboroto had everybody fly down to . . . oh, fuck, you know that already."

Another stuffed animal came flying out of the playpen and landed at my feet. A rabbit. I picked it up, threw my hands in the air, and croaked out a passable "ay, ay, ay."

The kid loved it.

"Caden," I said, "tell your *abuelo* there's a maniac out there who doesn't think twice about killing innocent men, women, and children. *Children.* Sixty-seven kids died in Central Park. He also killed some Russians who weren't so innocent, and their families who were."

I nuzzled the soft bunny into his nose, and he took it, plopped down, and went back to playing.

"Smart boy," I said to Mercury. "You're a lucky man."

"I can tell you what's going on," he said, "but I can't make any fucking sense of it."

He sat down on the sofa across from Redwood and me and leaned into us. "We get to Mexico, and we get driven out to the desert, and there's food and booze and women. It's like a big party. And then Alboroto, the man himself, stands up, thanks us for coming, and says he wants us to sell off whatever reserves we have, and then he's going to cut off our supply.

"The whole room goes batshit. He holds up his hand, and he says it's only for a while. And someone yells out, 'How are we supposed to make a living?' And he says, 'I'll pay you. I don't want you to look for another supplier, so I will pay you more money to not sell than you'd make selling.'

"I'm thinking he's lost his marbles, but he's serious. 'More money,' he says. 'And no risk. Plus, when we amp up production and we go back into business together, I will give you a guaranteed wholesale price on cocaine for a year, so your profits will go through the roof.'"

"It doesn't make sense," Redwood said. "Alboroto is a major supplier. Why would he pay you *not* to sell?"

"I don't know," Mercury said. "Maybe he blew his wad dumping it all over the city and he doesn't want to lose his best customers, so he's paying us to sit tight, rather than risk us going to the Colombians. All I know is, everyone took the deal except Oleg Malenkov. A few days later, Oleg died of lead poisoning, his brother Fyodor took over, and now the Russians are also on board."

"Fyodor Malenkov is working with the guy who killed his brother?" I said.

"No. He's *not* working with the guy who killed his brother. Alboroto is paying every dealer up and down the Northeast to *not* work. I don't know why Oleg said no, but I guess Fyodor is more like me."

"How's that?"

"Neither of us are the type to walk away from free money."

CHAPTER 29

WE SPENT THE FIRST HOUR of the car ride from Cortona to the airport trying to figure out why Joaquín Alboroto would pay his entire distribution team not to sell drugs. We came up with nothing, so we decided to clear our heads and revisit it over a couple of drinks. And sitting in first class, we didn't have to wait for takeoff before the flight attendant brought us our first round.

"To Italy," Redwood said, lifting his glass. "I've always wanted to visit, and this was everything I dreamed it would be." He checked his watch. "I only hope I can come back someday for another nine hours, twenty-three minutes, and fourteen seconds."

"Who knows, Harold?" I said. "Maybe in your next life, instead of being my lawyer you'll come back as a drug dealer and stay for six weeks."

We drank. But the alcohol did nothing to enlighten us.

"It still doesn't make sense," Redwood said after polishing off his beer.

"It makes sense to Alboroto," I said. "Otherwise, he wouldn't be doing it. Drug dealers don't give away money. In fact, they're very good at figuring out how to milk the most money out of . . ." I stopped.

"You got something?" Redwood said. "I think I just saw a light bulb pop on over your head."

"It's crazy, but let me play it out," I said. "Back in the eighties, the dealers sold powdered coke. A lot of the users would take it home, cook it up with baking soda, and make crack. Then one day, a bunch of dealers got together and came up with this bright idea: instead of selling powder to the crackheads, they could make the crack themselves and sell it for higher margins. That business model is still pretty much in use today."

"Yeah. I think they teach a course in Crackonomics at Harvard Business School," Redwood said, giving me a grin.

I responded by giving him the finger.

"I get it, Danny," he said. "And I admit it was a brilliant marketing strategy, but what does it have to do with Alboroto paying his dealers not to sell cocaine?"

"I'm just spinning wheels here, but what if he's clearing the shelves of coke to make way for another drug—one that's much more profitable?"

"Yeah. Maybe he'll call it 'New Coke.' It worked out real well for the soft-drink geniuses."

I flipped him the finger again and picked up my drink, just as my cell phone vibrated on the tray table. I looked at the caller ID: Bobby Petrocevic.

I'd worked with Bobby at the Four-Four in the Bronx, but I hadn't heard from him in at least two years. It was almost midnight in New York. My mind flashed back to other late-night calls that started with "Sorry, Danny, bad news," and five days later I'm wearing my dress uniform, watching a couple of kids cling to a weeping widow while the bagpipers skirl "Amazing Grace."

I put down my drink and answered the phone.

"Petro," I said. "You calling me out of the blue at this hour of the night can't be good."

"It's not. I'm sorry, Danny. My nephew Tommy is a cop in Bedford. He responded to a call at your sister-in-law Kirsten's house."

My stomach clenched, but before I could utter a word, he said, "She and the kids are okay, but I'm sorry to tell you that your brother-in-law, Phil, is dead."

"Phil? Dead?" I don't know why I sounded so surprised. Phil had graduated from coke to heroin in the past few years, and there was a lot of bad shit out on the streets. "Overdose?" I said.

"No. He was shot."

"What?"

"It was a bloodbath, Danny."

"Jesus . . . You said Kirsten and the kids are okay?"

"Yeah, the kids weren't even home when it happened," Petrocevic said. "Bedford PD got a 911 call. Shots fired. When they got there, Phil was dead on the couch."

"What have you got on the shooter?"

Petrocevic hesitated. "That's the thing, Danny. When the cops arrived, Kirsten was lying on the floor, covered with blood, with a gun in her hand."

"No," I said.

"She was in bad shape, pretty doped up on heroin. They had to give her Narcan to bring her around."

"There's no way Kirsten could shoot Phil," I said.

"That's the thing, Danny. They asked her what happened. She said she didn't know. They had no choice. The Westchester DA is charging her with murder."

CHAPTER 30

REDWOOD HAD HEARD ENOUGH from my side of the conversation to put most of the pieces together. Keeping my voice to a whisper, I filled him in on the particulars.

Then I sent an email to Trace Baker describing our meeting with Mercury Maldonado. I included the wild theories and half-baked scenarios that Redwood and I had explored, but admitted that nothing about Alboroto's decision to pay his dealers not to sell cocaine made any sense. I also told him that I had a family emergency and I'd be out of touch for a while.

He answered within minutes.

> Great job. I'll pass it on to the team.
> It might not make sense now, but it's
> exactly the kind of intel Cavanaugh
> needs. What family emergency? Details.

I wrote back that my sister-in-law was in jail for a murder I knew she didn't commit, and I gave him the bare-bones specifics I'd gotten from Bobby Petrocevic.

His response was swift and crystal clear.

You are not in this alone. Whatever we can
do, we will. Anything. Just ask.

The flight attendant announced that we were about to take off, and
instructed the passengers to stow their phones and laptops.

I stared at Baker's words on my screen. *Anything. Just ask.*

It wasn't a hollow offer. I knew how deeply he meant it. I swal-
lowed my self-reliance. I asked.

For the first hour of the flight, neither of us said a word. I stared
out the window, picked at my food, and tried to replay the phone
call from Bobby Petrocevic in my head.

*Phil was dead. Kirsten was doped up on heroin, lying on the floor covered
with blood, a gun in her hand. The DA is charging her with murder.*

But the kids were okay. The kids were okay. The kids were okay.

Finally, Redwood broke the silence. "Anything I can do?"

"I don't think there's anything either of us can do," I said. "At least
not until we're back in New York."

"You're wrong," he said. "There's one thing you can do. Get some
sleep. You're going to need it."

"I don't know if I can—"

He turned off my overhead light. "Try."

I tipped my seat back, closed my eyes, and thought about the
hell that Phil had put Kirsten through. Yes, she had suffered. Yes, she
resented him. Yes, she complained, often to me. But she never would
kill him. She never would . . .

The next thing I knew, we touched down at JFK. Somehow, my
mind had stopped spinning, and I'd managed to sleep for five hours.

Redwood hopped a cab back to the city, and I rented a car and
headed north. An hour later, I pulled into the Bedford Police Department parking lot in Bedford Hills, New York.

I walked in, approached the officer at the front desk, and smiled
politely. "Good morning, Sergeant Aubrey," I said. "I'd like to speak to
Kirsten Grissom. She's my sister-in-law."

Aubrey was the kind of cop you might endearingly refer to as a grizzled old fuck—seen it all, well past retirement age, but he couldn't quit because, as he would tell anyone who'd listen, "If I stayed home all day, either my old lady would kill me, or I'd kill her."

He gave me a steely-eyed stare. I expected it. I had just asked the unaskable. There's an unwritten rule that says nobody is allowed to see a homicide defendant before her arraignment, except her attorney. I might look innocent, but once I was alone in a cell with Kirsten, I could kill her, give her something to kill herself, slip her a weapon, help her craft an alibi—the list goes on.

"Can I see some identification, please?" Aubrey said.

I handed him my driver's license and my NYPD Retired ID card.

He took his time, his eyes darting back and forth between me, my ID, and the top sheet on his clipboard. When he was sure he got it right, his face softened and he said, "Captain Corcoran, we've been expecting you. Wait right here, and I'll have an officer escort you to the holding cell."

I had the feeling this was a first for him, and he was handling it very well. "Thank you," I said.

"One thing, sir," he said. "Judge Edwards gave you twenty minutes. I'll have to hold you to that."

"Understood," I said.

"You a friend of Judge Edwards?" he asked.

"Friend of a friend."

He stifled a smirk. Sergeant Aubrey was well aware that there was a good-old-boy network of cops, lawyers, politicians, and one-percenters. I had no idea who Judge Edwards was, but he was clearly part of that tight fraternity of people in power.

Aubrey held up the clipboard so I could see the signed paperwork. "Edwards has been on the bench twenty-five years," he said. "You know how many of these he's signed before this?"

"No, sir," I said.

"None. I showed it to my lieutenant. He said, 'That's not a court order. It's a freakin' miracle.'"

I nodded and mentally added another bullet point to the long list of Trace Baker's outstanding attributes: freakin' miracle worker.

CHAPTER 31

KIRSTEN, LIKE HER SISTER DEIRDRE, has a natural, wholesome beauty about her. She can look as heart-stopping in a pair of cutoffs and a T-shirt as she does in a designer dress, ready for a night on the town.

But she couldn't pull off the unisex Tyvek coveralls provided to her by the county. She was sitting on a pee-stained wafer-thin mattress that lay on a narrow shelf that passed for a bed. Her face was drawn, her hair lifeless, eyes red and fraught with defeat.

As soon as I entered her cell, she wrapped her arms around me.

"Ma'am," the guard said. "No contact. Please."

She backed off, sobbing. "I didn't do it. I couldn't do it. I wouldn't do it. As much as I hated him, he was the father of my children. They'll be devastated when they find out that he's dead. Do you think I would do that to them?"

"I know you wouldn't. Where are they now?"

"They went on an overnight with about thirty other kids from the church. They'll be back at noon. I was supposed to pick them up."

"I'll get them. Just tell me where."

"It's okay. The police called Phil's sister Jo Ann. I'm sure she's devastated, and she probably hates me, but I know she'll take care of them. They'll be okay . . ." She started sobbing again. "No, they won't. How can two kids be okay when they find out their father's dead and their mother's in jail?"

I led her to the bed and sat her down. "They didn't give me a lot of time, so try to focus and tell me what happened."

"That's just it, Danny. I don't know what happened. One minute, he was alive, and then the next thing I knew, he was dead, and I was arrested."

"That's okay. We'll figure out what happened, but right now I want you to think back to yesterday and just tell me everything you remember."

"Okay. I finished work, came home, picked up the kids, and dropped them off at the bus."

"What bus?"

"That's the overnight. They signed up for one of those trips where they get to sleep over at the American Museum of Natural History. I dropped them off at about 5:45, and I waited till the bus left at about ten after six. Then I went out to dinner."

"With Phil?"

She hesitated. "No. I went with one of the other parents who dropped their kids off."

I could see where this was going, and I knew enough to tread lightly.

"Where did you have dinner?"

"A little Japanese place in Wilton. I forget the name."

"It must be good."

"It's okay."

"I would have thought it's better than okay if you're driving all the way to Wilton, Connecticut."

She lowered her head.

"Kirsten, you know I'm a cop. I've spent my life interviewing people who are trying to hide things. I know how to get them to give up their deepest, darkest secrets, even when they don't want to. My job is to trap them, catch them in a lie. This is different. I'm here to help you. But you've got to trust me."

"Danny, I do, I do. It's just that Phil is dead, and if it comes out that I was having an affair . . ."

"You're charged with murder," I said. "It *will* come out, and the prosecution will use it against you. The people who are trying to prove you're innocent can't afford to be blindsided. Decide who you trust, and tell them."

"His name is Gordon Joliet. He's a widower with two daughters about the same age as Ryan and Jake."

"What does he do?"

"Oh, God. Is that important?"

"I wouldn't ask if it weren't."

"He's the principal at the middle school."

"So the boys know him," I said.

"Everybody knows him. If he gets dragged into this mess, it could ruin his career."

I didn't give a rat's ass about Gordon's career, but I wasn't about to share that with her. "How long has it been going on?"

"Two years."

"Did Phil know?"

She shook her head. "Gordon and I have been very careful, but I finally got tired of sneaking around. Three weeks ago, I met with a divorce lawyer to give me some guidance, and last night I was going to tell Phil I'm leaving him."

"You were going to tell him, or you told him?" I said.

"I . . . I don't know. It's all messed up in my head." She closed her eyes. "I can picture myself saying good night to Gordon and driving home. I went into the house, and Phil was just sitting there on the sofa. Not moving."

"Dead?"

Her eyes opened. "No. He was alive, but the look on his face was . . ." She struggled, but she couldn't find the words.

"You're doing real good," I said. "This is a big help. Keep going. Tell me about the look on his face. Was it anger?"

"Oh, no. It was fear. He looked at me. He couldn't speak, but I could see that he was petrified. And that's the last thing I remember. Everything is a blank after that. I must have blacked out."

I cringed. I could just hear the prosecutor saying, "So your husband was looking at you, and he was petrified. The police state that the gun that killed him was in your hand when they arrived. Was your husband in fear for his life because you were pointing the gun at him?"

The defense counsel would object, the judge would sustain the objection, and the prosecutor would withdraw the question. But the damage would have been done. Another seed of doubt about Kirsten's innocence would have been planted in the jury's collective psyche. Add to that her two-year affair, the fact that she hired a divorce lawyer, and the physical evidence found at the scene, and the case against her was getting stronger by the minute. She told Phil the marriage was over. He said the hell it is. She shot him.

"Tell me what happened when you came out of the blackout," I said.

"I was on the floor. My heart was racing, I was woozy, and I looked around and there was Phil on the couch, slumped over, covered in blood. The blood was everywhere—on the furniture, on the floor, all over me. And then I started vomiting."

"The police report says you were under the influence of heroin."

"That's insane. Phil is the drug addict. I would never do heroin."

"The cops said they had to bring you back with Narcan. That induces vomiting." There was a fresh Band-Aid on her arm. "Did they take a blood sample?"

"Yes. But that's the least of it. When I woke up there were two cops standing over me. As soon as I stopped vomiting, they pushed me back down and handcuffed me. Then they dragged me into a police car with the neighbors watching. They took mug shots and fingerprints. They made me take off my clothes, and they gave me this hideous thing to wear. Then they locked me up in this fucking cell. It's been a nightmare, Danny, but I swear I didn't do anything."

"I believe you," I said. But at this juncture, I doubted that a jury would.

The guard outside the cell door gave me a hand signal to wrap it up.

"What happens now?" she said.

"You'll be arraigned. The judge will set bail. Do you have a lawyer?"

"Yes. Marjorie Becker. The last time Phil got in a jam, I called my father and asked him for a good criminal lawyer. Marjorie was at the top of his list."

"How did she do, working for Phil?"

"She never met him. He wanted a man. She's my lawyer now. I like her. She was here last night."

"Did you tell her everything you told me?"

"Some. But not *everything*."

"You're going to have to fix that," I said.

"Captain Corcoran." It was the guard. He opened the cell door.

I looked at my watch. "I thought I had twenty minutes."

"I'm sorry, sir, but we just got a call. Mrs. Grissom is being arraigned. We have to transport her to the courthouse."

"Give me a few more seconds," I said.

Kirsten stood up, tears streaming down her face, and threw her arms around me. I turned toward the guard to apologize for breaking the no-contact rule, but he had quickly shifted his body the other way and pretended to tie his shoe.

"I can't believe this is happening," Kirsten said.

"I'll be in court with you," I said. "I'll talk to your lawyer as soon as it's over. I'm here for you. Whatever it takes."

"I didn't kill him, Danny. I swear."

"I know you didn't," I said.

Even more important, I knew who did.

CHAPTER 32

JUDGE SOLOMON HAD BEEN RIGHT. Marjorie Becker was a top-notch lawyer. She had a keen analytical mind, excellent people skills, and was as tenacious as a Rottweiler on a T-bone. But like most good lawyers, she hated losing.

"*Merde!*" she thundered as soon as she shut the door to her office behind us. She plopped down in her desk chair and flashed me an engaging smile. "Pardon my French."

"I'm a cop," I said. "We don't exactly say 'oh, fudge' when the *merde* hits the fan."

The smile grew brighter, and her honey-brown eyes let me know she appreciated my brand of humor.

Marjorie Becker was not at all what I'd expected. I had a great-aunt named Marjorie, so when Kirsten told me her lawyer's name, I conjured up silver hair in a bun, furniture wrapped in plastic, and a cut-glass bowl full of individually wrapped butterscotch candies.

This Marjorie was nobody's great-aunt. She was in her late thirties, with thick chestnut hair, a trim athletic body, a killer smile, and an inherent sex appeal that even her appropriately understated courtroom attire couldn't hide.

"I really thought we had a shot," she said.

"We did," I said. "But you were blindsided."

Becker had known it wouldn't be easy to get Kirsten released on bail, but she brought her A game to the arraignment. She told the judge that Kirsten was a pillar of the community, a member of the local church, and was ready to turn over her passport, put the family home up to make bail, snap an electronic bracelet on her ankle, and anything else the court asked for that would allow her to be free to care for her kids.

Judge Stevens looked receptive.

And then the prosecutor dropped a bombshell. After the murder, the police searched the house and found an envelope that contained three passports. One was Kirsten's, and the other two belonged to her sons, Ryan and Jake. The envelope also contained fifty thousand dollars in cash and three confirmation numbers on Delta Airlines, which turned out to be one-way trips from JFK to Vancouver, British Columbia.

When Kirsten heard that, she screamed. "That's a lie! I would never do that to my children."

Marjorie practically propelled herself out of her chair. "Your Honor, this is a put-up job. Somebody planted that."

The judge leaned forward and growled. "Counselor, are you accusing the Bedford Police Department of falsifying evidence?"

"No, Your Honor. But my client is not a flight risk."

The gavel came down hard. "Bail is denied. The defendant is remanded to Westchester County Jail."

Kirsten was immediately handcuffed, and her legs shackled. As two officers led her toward the holding cell in the rear of the courthouse, she turned to me and mouthed the words I'd heard her say in her cell: *I didn't do it.*

"She didn't do it," I said to Marjorie as she grabbed two bottles of water from the mini fridge behind her desk.

"I know," she said, handing me one of the bottles.

"Alboroto did," I said. I thought it might shock her. It didn't.

"I was afraid you'd say that," she said.

"Really? I'd have thought you'd be happy to hear that I believe your client is innocent and that I can tell you the real killer."

"I'd be happier if it were a drug dealer Phil ripped off, or a husband whose wife he banged, or a client whose money he stole. You know, someone who's likely to trip up, someone I could point to so I could at least create reasonable doubt. But how do I go up against the cartel? Look at the team of lawyers they hired to defend Sebastián Alb . . ." Her voice trailed off. "I'm sorry. Sore point."

"Yeah, and it's a point that the district attorney will do his best to get in front of the jury," I said. "You stand up and tell them that Kirsten is not a murderer, and the prosecutor will come back at them with 'neither was her father until he opened fire and killed two innocent people in his courtroom.' You can object as loud as you want, but so what? It'll be indelibly etched in the jury's minds."

"Do you have any proof it was Alboroto?"

"No. Not yet."

"The murder weapon belonged to Judge Solomon," Becker said. "Kirsten said he gave it to her years ago for protection. She told him she didn't want it, but he insisted. She says she put it in a drawer, never fired it, and doesn't even know how to load it."

"That sounds right," I said. "Kirsten's never been a gun person. She's much more peace, love, and granola."

"Then explain this," she said, picking up a folder from her desk and handing it to me. "The medical examiner is still working on the autopsy, but they sent me these preliminary photos of Phil once they had him cleaned up and on the slab."

I rifled through the pictures. Phil had taken four bullets to the chest. They were clustered in a perfect shot group. The fifth bullet hit him in the neck, causing the hemorrhage that covered Kirsten in blood.

"Damn," I said. "You can't get any more accurate than this. Alboroto doesn't go cut-rate when he hires a hit man."

"You and I can see that, but there's no way I can convince a jury that Kirsten is totally incapable of this kind of precision."

She finished her bottle of water and tossed it at the wastebasket. It bounced off the rim onto the floor. "Not my day," she said.

"Judge Solomon said you were a good criminal attorney. He didn't say anything about your ability to sink an easy layup."

She laughed. "Thanks. But even a good lawyer can be buried by circumstantial evidence. Kirsten called the cops twice in the past nine months because Phil got physical with her when he was whacked out on drugs. No arrest was made, but it's on record that there's a history of domestic abuse. Motive. She's been having an affair for two years, and she retained a divorce lawyer. More motive.

"There was no sign of forced entry. The cops found her with the murder weapon in her hand. She tested positive for heroin. She says she didn't do it, but her mind is foggy, and she can't even come up with a *bad* cover story. And 'I don't remember' is not a defense."

"And now you know why Alboroto's hit man didn't kill her when he killed Phil," I said. "It's not enough for him to destroy the city of New York—he wants to destroy whatever is left of the judge's family. Instead of putting a bullet in the back of her head, he wants her to spend the next fifty years living in a cage for something she didn't do. He's not only making the daughter pay for the sins of the father, but he wants to completely destroy the family's good name and their legacy."

"I need help, Captain Corcoran."

"Danny."

"I need help, Danny. I'm not sure I can convince the jury that Kirsten is innocent. I need you to help me find the person who did it. But you said you can't prove that the cartel is behind this."

"Right. But I'm just getting started."

CHAPTER 33

I SPENT THE NEXT THREE HOURS with Marjorie, going through the police reports and trying to hammer out a defense strategy. We were still groping for a game plan when she sat back from the table and said, "I know you're a smart cop, so don't take this the wrong way, Danny, but right about now you're pretty useless."

She was right. I could barely think. The gunfight in Mexico, tracking down Delaqua, the overnight to Italy—it all had caught up with me.

I apologized, mumbled some cliché about burning the candle at both ends, made it back to my apartment alive, and slept for the next sixteen hours.

The next morning, I was back in the firehouse. Redwood was at his desk, poring over the intel alerts that our analysts had compiled overnight. Delaqua, Baker, and I were in the conference room, waiting for an eight a.m. teleconference with Cavanaugh. We had ten minutes to kill, so I filled them in on the latest with Kirsten.

"No question," Delaqua said. "Alboroto set it up. Kill Phil and frame Kirsten. The problem is, how do we prove it?"

"I appreciate the offer, Frank," I said, "but I don't mean to turn this into a *we* thing. I shouldn't have to drag you guys into my problems."

"You're right, Danny," Baker said. "Our mission is primary. But it looks like your problems are about to crash headlong into our problems, so like it or not, you're stuck with us."

I gave him a grateful nod. "I've done worse," I said.

The center screen on the wall popped on, and Cavanaugh's image came alive. "*Hola, amigos. Saludos de México,*" he said.

"*Hola,* my ass," Baker said. "You're pretty chipper. Either you woke up in bed this morning with a beautiful Mexican woman, or you've got something on Alboroto."

"Sadly—or happily, depending on your perspective—it's the latter," Cavanaugh said. "The man's been dicking me around. I've been here for two days waiting for him to reach out, and I haven't heard a word. It's a typical power play, but it's not a smart tactic when you're dealing with an investigative reporter. He thinks I'm sitting on my hands, but what he doesn't realize is, he's given me plenty of time to ask questions."

"What have you got?" Baker said.

"You know me, Trace. I'm as Irish as they come. But that's on my father's side. My mother is from Spain. I still have first cousins in Barcelona. I don't look like I speak the language, so when I sit in the cafés or walk around the marketplace, I come off like your average clueless American tourist. I listen. I pick up a lot."

"And what did you pick up that's got you smiling?" Baker asked.

"There's trouble in paradise. Alboroto is so obsessed with his campaign to punish New York City for the death of his wife and son that he's not focused on his day-to-day business. His cash in reserve is being drained to pay the dealers not to sell drugs, but his people down here aren't doing much work, so they're not getting paid. I decided to go looking for a disgruntled employee who is hurting for money, and negotiate for a little quid-pro-rat-out-your-boss-quo.

"It wasn't as easy as I thought, because I'm a gringo and because they all know the penalty for defectors. But I finally found this guy Santiago. Four days ago, he's told to drive to the airport and pick up a couple of Americans. Three of Alboroto's goons go with him, so when the Americans get in the van, they assume the three guys are passengers and they're all going to their hotel. But no. He drives them to a compound in the desert, drops them off, and leaves."

"What do you make of it?"

"Santiago thinks they're being held for ransom. They came to Mexico on their own, but once they got in that van, Alboroto was planning the rest of their trip."

"Who are they?" I said.

"Santiago couldn't give me a name. He was told, when he picked them up at the airport, to hold up a sign that said 'UNAM,' which stands for 'Universidad Nacional Autónoma de México.' It's a top-tier school, one of the best universities in all of Latin America. I had no idea how to track these people down, so I called your two Federale buddies, Vadillo and Bolano. They don't have any reports on missing Americans, but they'll let me know if they get something."

"Don't hold your breath," Delaqua said.

Cavanaugh's face tightened up. "How's that, Frank?" he said, not trying to hide his disdain.

"I think your CI knew you were willing to pay for something juicy," Delaqua said, "but 'Hey, Alboroto is smuggling drugs' isn't worth a hell of a lot, so he cooked up this little kidnapped-American-couple story and gave you your money's worth. I know Alboroto, and extorting ransom money isn't his style."

"And getting suckered by informants isn't my style," Cavanaugh snapped. "Bottom line on my report: a couple of Americans have gone missing. Alboroto took them. I don't know why, but I could use a little help digging into it, rather than just shitting on the intel because it doesn't line up with your preconceived notions of what he does or doesn't do."

Delaqua held up a hand. "Hey, take it easy, pal."

"No, I'm not done, *pal.* If I called you two weeks ago and told you my CI thinks Alboroto is planning to drop two tons of cocaine on New York City, what would you have said then? 'Don't hold your breath'?"

Delaqua had always been a loner, one of those cops who trusted his own judgment over anyone else's. It had been his downfall at the FBI, and I had warned him that day at IKEA when I hired him. We're a team that works together. There's no room for cowboys. Kevin Cavanaugh just took my little lecture and beat him over the head with it.

"I'm sorry, Kevin," Delaqua said. "Old habits. You need help? That's what I'm here for."

Before Cavanaugh could respond, the door to the conference room flew open and Redwood burst in.

"The city is under attack," he said. "Looters. Thousands of them. They're hitting hospitals, pharmacies, clinics—wherever there are drugs."

He grabbed a remote from the table, and a bank of nine screens came alive. Each was tuned to a different channel, and each channel was broadcasting live from a different location—Lincoln Hospital in the Bronx, Metropolitan Hospital in Spanish Harlem, a CVS Pharmacy in Times Square.

Redwood muted all but the local ABC station. A reporter was on the street about two blocks from a building I knew all too well. We picked her up in midsentence.

"… NYPD Property Office on Pearson Place in Queens. We heard gunfire when we got here, Bill, so my cameraman and I are two blocks away."

"Property office," the anchorman said from off camera. "Can you tell us what's in the building, Michelle?"

"This is where the police store all the evidence they've seized in connection with a crime, Bill. It's a giant warehouse full of anything and everything imaginable, but anyone who has ever walked past it recognizes the overwhelming smell of marijuana coming from the building. I don't have any details, but I would venture that there are millions and millions of dollars' worth of pot, cocaine, heroin, and other drugs inside, and as you can see by those cars and vans and U-Hauls parked in front, a lot of it is going out the door."

A volley of gunfire erupted. The reporter crouched low as the camera followed her to a safer spot behind a Con Edison truck.

Redwood muted the sound. "It's Alboroto," he said. "I don't know how he orchestrated this, but now we know why he cut off the city's drug supply. We've just entered phase two of his siege against New York."

CHAPTER 34

JOAQUÍN ALBOROTO WAS A MASTER STRATEGIST, and his latest maneuver bordered on genius.

We estimated that he catered to about half a million addicts across the tri-state area. These were not the people who might do some blow at a party. These were the hard-core users, the ones with a daily drug habit, who couldn't quit even when they tried. And whether they were crashing in a crack house in the Bronx, driving a delivery truck through Brooklyn, or managing a multibillion-dollar hedge fund on Wall Street, they all had one thing in common.

They needed Alboroto. Desperately.

Cutting off their supply was a stake through the heart.

But that was only the first domino he toppled. The wheels of the drug trade can't turn without the thousands of pushers, enforcers, and other traffickers who work the streets. He made them suffer as well.

Many of them were teenage entrepreneurs who realized they could make more money selling crack in a day than they could flipping burgers for a month. And as soon as they made it, they spent it. Their newfound wealth defined them. It bought shoes, clothes, cars, jewelry, electronics, and most of all, it bought respect.

They lived for the moment, never thinking about tomorrow, because they were sure that when tomorrow came there would be more drugs in the pipeline.

And when it all dried up, they went from riches to rags overnight.

Alboroto knew the culture. He knew that they, too, would be desperate. But they were hustlers, not businessmen. They wouldn't know how to solve the problem he had created. He had to solve it for them.

He sent in *los Siete*—the Seven—his own personal undercover squad, his eyes and ears in the marketplace, who reported back to him with qualitative research like a team of clandestine focus-group moderators.

They never had any contact with Mercury Maldonado or anyone at the top of the drug hierarchy org chart. They were *gente de la calle*—street people—who had spent years gaining the trust of middle management. And as the shortage grew more dire by the day, they spread the seed, one dealer at a time.

"Fuck the supply chain. There's plenty of product in this city. And you don't have to pay for it. It's ours for the taking."

And so, in the predawn hours on that morning in late August, more than a thousand do-or-die bangers, most of them armed, unwittingly followed the plan sown in the twisted mind of a man obsessed with revenge. They fanned out across the city and ransacked hundreds of locations known to store drugs.

The NYPD Property Clerk's Office in Queens, with its sixty thousand square feet of coke, crack, heroin, meth, pot, and pills, was the hardest hit. Most of the gunfire we'd heard on TV turned out to be gang-on-gang fighting over the spoils. The people inside the Property Clerk's Office were basically that: clerks—a mix of civilians and cops who were assigned to light duty and were no longer armed.

With precision timing, the looters plundered hospitals, carrying off morphine, oxycodone, methadone, and other narcotics that turned out to be lethal in the hands of many of the junkies, who gobbled them down hoping for blessed relief from the interminable drought.

Gangs who were late to the party went to war with those who had stocked up early. Bands of middle schoolers went after the dregs, breaking into doctors' offices, animal hospitals, and mom-and-pop pharmacies.

In less than twenty-four hours, the drug economy was booming again, the police were outnumbered, and shootouts left hundreds of young gangbangers and collateral bystanders dead.

Within a week, there was nothing left to steal, nothing left to fight over, no smack, crack, meth, blow, or even weed to get high on. A city filled with addicts was suffering the agony of withdrawal.

Suicides skyrocketed. Buildings sealed off their rooftops to discourage jumpers, pedestrians were banned from bridges, and once again the morgues were overwhelmed, the funeral parlors and cemeteries backlogged, and a fleet of refrigerated trucks was called in to store the dead.

For those of us in law enforcement across the country and beyond, it was a wrenching blow to realize that the only thing worse than a city riddled with drugs is a city filled with desperate addicts.

But through it all, the politicians pounded their chests and sounded their horns.

"This is the drug-free city I promised you," Mayor Richardson preened as he campaigned for reelection. "Working in close concert with Police Commissioner Ennis and his team, we have successfully cut off the drug supply to these five boroughs.

"I know there is some *unrest* as those poor souls caught up in the scourge of the drug culture withdraw from a life of self-destruction, but we will provide them with the medical help they need, and I promise you that we are going to emerge from this test of our fortitude as the safest city on the planet. And for peace-loving people everywhere, New York City will be nirvana."

"Nirvana?" Delaqua screamed as we sat in the conference room and watched the crowing politico take credit for the devastating effects of Alboroto's second onslaught. "New York will be hell. Alboroto isn't finished, you gaping fucking asshole!"

It wasn't a knee-jerk reaction on Delaqua's part. It wasn't even an educated guess. We knew for a hard fact that Alboroto wasn't finished. Because ten minutes after the attack on the Property Clerk's Office in Queens began, there was a knock on the door of Kevin Cavanaugh's hotel room in Mexico City.

Señor Alboroto was ready for his interview.

CHAPTER 35

Two hours after alboroto summoned him, Cavanaugh was returned safely to his hotel room. He called us immediately.

"How'd it go?" Baker asked.

"I knew it wouldn't be an in-depth interview. In fact, it barely qualifies as an interview at all. A guy like Alboroto isn't about to sit in front of the camera and answer probing questions from some asshole gringo like me. He had a statement to make, and I'm just the guy he picked to be his conduit to America and the world."

"You're also the only reporter who gave him a legitimate platform," I said. "He could rant all he wants on social media, but you offered him national exposure on a major American network. That's got to count for something in his book. I'll bet he didn't *treat* you like an asshole gringo."

Cavanaugh smiled. "You're right. The trip to his compound was downright pleasant. I was treated like visiting royalty. No blindfolds, no strong-arm tactics, just the usual precautions you'd expect when you're popping in on one of the most ruthless madmen on the planet.

"They searched me and Hank, my cameraman, scanned the equipment for bugs, tracking devices, and God knows what else, and laid out the ground rules, which were pretty simple. We roll camera, start the interview, and as soon as *el Jefe* raises his hand, Hank cuts the roll, the session is over, and Elvis will leave the building."

"Tell us about the compound," Baker said.

"Oh, man, we've all seen the drone pictures, but when you're up close and personal, stopped by armed guards at three checkpoints along a winding driveway, you realize it's a fucking fortress.

"Y'know, ever since this whole clusterfuck started, I've been getting emails from viewers asking why the mayor of New York doesn't just call the president and ask him to send in the Air Force and bomb the shit out of the place. My stock answer is that if the United States starts dropping thirty-thousand-pound bunker busters on a private citizen of a foreign country, the government of said country will see that as an act of war and respond with some planes and bombs of its own.

"But now I have a simpler answer. Alboroto has radar, antiaircraft guns, and a giant steel vault he can hole up in that's seven stories underground. You could carpet bomb the entire compound and you still wouldn't kill the bastard."

"How'd the interview go?"

"Bin Laden was filmed in a cave," Cavanaugh said. "But I knew I'd get a completely different show. The room we shot in was a cross between the grand ballroom of a French chateau and the lobby of a Vegas hotel. Not my taste at all, but it dripped with fuck-you money. You all know Alboroto's backstory: peasant kid, left school, worked in a butcher shop. He was dirt poor, so now he wears his wealth like a badge of honor. He had us set up the camera in front of a fireplace. It was a cozy little spot—tasteful hacienda furnishings, portraits of his dead wife and his scumbag son hanging in a place of honor, lots of framed family pictures all over the place. Homey as all hell. I mean, we were shooting a film, and it was like he had somebody design a set for the billionaire-Mexican-drug-lord version of *The Brady Bunch*."

Baker cracked a faint smile. "All right, let's see what you shot."

"Nothing's edited," Cavanaugh said. "I had Hank upload the raw footage to my laptop so I could share it with you." He tapped on his keyboard, and a wide shot of him and Alboroto popped up on our screen in New York.

"Ideally, we should have had two cameras, one pointing at each of us. But with a single camera we had to set up dead center, and Hank panned left or right depending on who was talking. But fair warning— he didn't let me do a hell of lot of talking."

The video rolled, and Cavanaugh began. "Señor Alboroto, you knowingly strafed Central Park with cocaine that killed hundreds of innocent men, women, and chil—"

"Don't talk to me about innocence," Alboroto said, cutting him off. "My son was innocent. My wife was innocent. Your justice system *knowingly* put them to death. *Vive por la espada, muere por la espada, señor Cavanaugh.* Live by the sword; die by the sword."

"Sir, I just received news from New York that you purposely cut off the supply of cocaine, which incited your vast network of drug dealers to loot hospitals and pharmacies, depriving people awaiting surgery of anesthetics, and the chronically ill of much-needed medication. The mayor and the police commissioner have vowed to protect our citizens from any further—"

Alboroto burst into a fit of laughter.

"I'm sorry, sir," Cavanaugh said. "But you find that funny?"

"I find it very funny that an intelligent man like yourself believes what your corrupt politicians and your incompetent police force tell you. They don't control New York City. *I* do. I give, and I take away. And you see what happens when I take away."

"But your actions must have cost you untold millions of dollars. You're a businessman. Surely, you want your product back in the marketplace."

"The whole world is a marketplace, Señor Cavanaugh. The people of New York need me more than I need them. And you can tell your mayor that they need me more than they need *him*."

"I'm going to have to disagree with you on that, sir. Some New Yorkers may *need* you, but right now the city is in chaos, and most of the people are afraid of you. They've described you as brutal, barbaric, ruthless. How do you respond?"

"Those are not the words of the people. That sounds to me like the hollow voice of the politicians and the police. Instead of condemning me, Mayor Richardson would do better for his citizens if he apologized for the murders of my wife and son."

"You don't really expect the mayor to apologize, do you?"

Alboroto sat there, fingers of both hands touching each other. The camera moved in slowly. "My family was mowed down in cold blood," he said. "Executed. If I were anyone else, the mayor would have been kneeling at their funerals, extending his condolences, taking the blame for the damage his city inflicted on our lives, compensating me for my loss."

The camera stayed trained on Alboroto, and Cavanaugh's voice came from offscreen. "Sir, surely you know that the United States—and that includes the city of New York—does not negotiate with terrorists."

"I am not a terrorist. The city drew first blood. They attacked my family." He paused, his face softened, and the camera moved in closer. "Imagine the last moments of my son's life. Having all charges against him dropped in a court of law, and then moments later watching the judge open fire on him, killing his innocent mother and then turning his wrath on Sebastián. Who is the terrorist in that scenario, Mr. Cavanaugh?"

He raised his hand. The interview was over.

"One more question," Cavanaugh said. "Please."

"One more," Alboroto said.

The camera panned over to Cavanaugh. He turned away from Alboroto and looked squarely into the lens. "Four days ago, I made a promise to you, my viewers, to bring you *both* sides of the brutal attack on New York. And now you've heard from the man who openly takes credit for it all. I have a hundred more questions, but he has granted me only one more, so my final question is the one I'm sure is on the mind of every New Yorker watching this."

He turned to Alboroto. "Señor Alboroto, if your demands for an apology are not met, what next?"

The camera panned back to Alboroto and slowly drifted in. "You are wrong, Señor Cavanaugh," he said. "Dead wrong."

He leaned forward, and the camera reciprocated until his face filled the screen. The easy smile that he offered up several times during the interview was gone, replaced by a hateful malignance that seeped from every pore.

"My demands *will* be met. I *will* get an apology from the mayor of New York. The only question you should be asking is, how much suffering does he want to bring down upon his city before I finally get one?"

CHAPTER 36

TEN HOURS AFTER THE LOOTING BEGAN, and just in time to go live on the six o'clock news, the mayor held a press conference to reassure the electorate that the rioters had been quelled and peace had been restored to the city. It was far from the truth, but then, he was smart enough to know that you can't win the hearts and minds of the voters by bringing them bad news.

Several shovelfuls of bullshit later, he brought on his six-foot wooden dummy Ennis the Menace, and without moving his lips, the mayor made his own words came out of the police commissioner's mouth.

"This city is committed to waging a war against drugs, and the disturbances that occurred this morning are irrefutable proof that we are winning that war."

"Disturbances?" Delaqua yelled at the giant monitor.

The dummy continued. "Many of our fellow New Yorkers, our friends and neighbors, are in the throes of withdrawal, and I am pleased to announce that the mayor has provided us with the resources necessary to help them get through this most difficult time. He has created a new unit to monitor and assist with their transition to a drug-free life, which will be the new norm in New York.

"Not only has our strategy to defeat the influx of poison from the evil hands of the murderous cartels been successful, but it should set the precedent for other cities to do the same. Never again, Mr. Alboroto, will you rule over the people of this city. Thank you, Mayor Richardson, for your vision, your commitment, and your leadership."

Trace Baker muted the TV. "That was brilliant," he said. "The only thing missing is the mayor wrapping it up at the end with 'This is Lloyd Richardson, and I approved this message.'"

"What do you think he'll say when he hears Alboroto demand an apology?" Redwood asked.

"I'm not sure how he'll spin it," Baker said, "but I guarantee it will end up with him and Ennis doing a victory dance."

Which is exactly what happened.

Cavanaugh's interview with Alboroto aired three days later. By that point, some of the far-reaching effects of the drug shortage began to kick in.

Many of the street addicts bought one-way bus tickets to Miami, Detroit, or DC, where drugs were still plentiful. Pushers with nothing to push found new sources of income, like credit-card scams. Mercury Maldonado and the rest of the upper-echelon distributors remained out of town, or at least out of the spotlight.

And in a city barren of drugs, the statistics for drug-related crimes inevitably plummeted. The mayor and his hapless five-star stooge heaped themselves with praise as they took credit. With a little more than two months till the election, the mayor's lead in the polls kept climbing.

I was absolutely confident that an apology to Alboroto would not be forthcoming, so my team and I spent most of our waking hours brainstorming what he would do next. And then one morning, I got a call from Mexico City.

"Captain Corcoran, this is Sergeant Inés Bolano. How are you?"

"Up to my ass in dumb politicians who think they've defeated the cartel and deserve to be reelected for another four years. But then, you must have the same thing."

She laughed. "Just the opposite. We have smart politicians who know they can't beat him, so they get on his payroll and share in the victory."

"To what do I owe the pleasure?" I said.

"First, let me apologize for not getting to you sooner, but when your colleague Kevin Cavanaugh gave us a tip on a possible kidnapping, my unit got called to help out with some craziness that blew up at the prison. It took us several days before Detective Vadillo and I could get to the security footage at the airport. But I have good news. We've identified the two Americans that the informant says he picked up. They are Mark and Jenna Gardner, a husband and wife from Herndon, Virginia."

"What can you tell me about them?"

"Practically nothing. That's why I'm calling. They flew first class from Washington, DC, on United, with a stop in Houston. When they went through immigration, they said they were here for business and pleasure. The agent asked the nature of their business, and they said they were guest lecturers at the university. We called the school, but nobody has heard of them. Then we called the Hacienda Peña Pobre, the hotel they claimed to be staying at, but there was no reservation in their name. Nobody has called to report them missing, but they haven't left the country. We were hoping you could do some digging on your end—find out who they are and why they came to Mexico."

"Absolutely. Email me copies of the paperwork from passport control, plus any video footage you think might help. Thanks. I don't know where this is going, but any information that leads to Alboroto is a big help."

As soon as I hung up, I could feel the adrenaline rush. I had been sitting on my hands for days on end, and now I had something to do. I could have assigned it to Delaqua. But he had pissed all over the intel, convinced that kidnapping wasn't in Alboroto's playbook. I knew it was a long shot, but a lead is a lead, and if Alboroto had taught me anything, it's that he had thrown away his playbook the minute the bullets started flying in Judge Solomon's courtroom.

I called Marina Whitney in Washington, DC, filled her in on my conversation with Sergeant Bolano, and asked her to get me anything and everything on Mark and Jenna Gardner.

"Piece of cake," she said.

"I know," I said. "And for that I apologize."

"What are you talking about?"

"Come on, Marina. I've got a zillion dollars' worth of tech power and half a dozen analysts, any one of whom could pull profiles on this couple, put it in a neatly bound case folder, and have it on my desk in twenty minutes. Asking you to do it is like giving Michelangelo a roller and asking him to help me paint the ceiling."

"Twenty minutes?" she said. "Sweetheart, as soon as you gave me Mark and Jenna's names, I started a deep dive. And by the time you got through flattering me by comparing me to a dead white guy, I can tell you that Mark is an ophthalmologist and Jenna is a biochemist. They both work at Ocumax Labs in Reston, Virginia. They have no kids, two horses, and as far as I can tell, no red flags on their financials."

"You're amazing."

"Give me another minute, and I can have it neatly bound for you."

"Don't bother. I'm jumping on the next train to Washington, renting a car, and driving out to Reston to talk to somebody up the food chain at Ocumax Labs."

"You want me to book you a room for the night?"

"Talk about overqualified. Now you're a travel agent? Great. Put me in the Intercontinental."

"Sorry. It's booked solid."

"The Hilton's fine."

"Huge fire last night. Burned to the ground," she said.

"Oh, really. Funny how it didn't make the news."

"In fact, every hotel in the city is slammed. Nothing available. Oh, wait, I found you a cozy little bed-and-breakfast in Bethesda."

"It wouldn't be close to your place, would it?"

"Extremely close."

"I appreciate the invitation, but I don't think Troy would be too happy to see me padding around in my boxers tomorrow morning."

"There is no Troy."

"Since when?"

"Since I found out he was a manipulative, narcissistic political ass-kisser."

"I hate to break the news to you, but you're living in the mecca for manipulative, narcissistic political ass-kissers."

"Yeah, but Troy was banging his assistant," she said.

"I'm sorry."

"Don't be. Oh, look, reservations just confirmed your room. And good news. Not only do you get breakfast, but you won't even be needing boxers. See you tonight."

She hung up, and I sat back in my chair. Now I was really glad I hadn't assigned this one to Delaqua.

CHAPTER 37

THREE YEARS AGO, BOTH MARINA WHITNEY and I were featured speakers at a two-day hostage-negotiation seminar. When the first day was over and a hundred cops all headed for the bar, she didn't want to be one of the few white shirts in a sea of blue, so she invited me to join her for dinner.

We had worked together in the past, and it had always been purely professional, but that night it was just the two of us, sharing a bottle of wine, feeling good that the day had gone so well, and happy to talk about anything but police work.

She knew I was still recovering from Deirdre's death, and over coffee she confided in me that her own marriage had imploded when her college professor husband got caught trading good grades for sex.

I shook my head, groping for the right words. "I'm sorry" was the best I could do.

"Thanks, but you know what they say: 'every cloud . . .'"

"Wow," I said. "I can't imagine finding a silver lining in that."

"You would if you were a woman on the wrong side of forty-five and you had a husband ten years your junior who barely showed any interest in you for over a year. I blamed myself for Troy's lack of desire, but then I found out he was giving these girls the fuck-or-fail option, and I decided, okay, I can't compete with a bunch of twenty-year-olds, but maybe I'm not as unattractive as I thought."

"Damn it, Marina," I said. "Why do women do that to themselves? You're plenty attractive. I guarantee you that when the wound heals over and you're ready for another relationship, guys will be lining up."

"Thanks for the pep talk, Coach, but I'm not looking for a relationship. I'm looking for an arrangement. My self-esteem may have gone to shit, but my sex drive is on point."

I didn't say a word. I didn't have to. When a woman tells a man she's horny, she has no problem reading his body language.

"Just to be clear," she said, "I'm talking no strings, no emotional attachments. Just pure, simple, unadulterated, and, hopefully, spectacular sex. Are you interested?"

She had caught me completely off guard, and she knew it. She let a finger twirl through a thick jet-black ringlet of hair that hung below her shoulder. Her lips parted, and the soft lighting in the restaurant played off her perfect white teeth and tawny brown skin. Her eyes, dark and full of mischief, locked on mine as she awaited my response.

"Me?" I finally said.

"Yeah, you. Damn it, Corcoran, why do guys do that to themselves? You're plenty attractive," she said, giving me a taste of my own bullshit.

"Friends with benefits?" I asked.

"Friendship is optional," she said. "As long as the sex is good, I'll be happy to think of you as my totally insignificant other."

The sex was better than good. And that evening in Marina's home in Bethesda, it was better than ever. Sometimes it's torrid; sometimes it's tender. This time it was both. We hadn't been together for six months, because of what Marina had labeled the "failed Troy experiment," and as we stood in the shower after our marathon reunion, I wrapped my arms around her and said, "I missed this."

It was a cover-up. The truth was, I had missed *her*, but admitting that would be a flagrant violation of the rules, so I kept it to myself.

Marina hated to cook, but she was a whiz at catering. "Tell me about your visit to Ocumax Labs," she said as she opened take-out containers of onion soup, duck confit, Lyonnaise potatoes, and haricots verts. "What was your cover story?"

"Freelance journalist doing a piece on married couples who work side by side," I said. "Ocumax is a small company, so the director of communications almost wet himself when I told him I was writing it for *Bloomberg Businessweek*."

She gave me an appreciative nod. "What'd you find out?"

"The company is still a small cog in the zillion-dollar vision-care industry, but they're growing fast because they know how to think outside the box."

"Too bad you're not really writing the story. You're making them sound good."

"They're on the premium end of over-the-counter products, but a good deal of the focus is on the surgical and pharmaceutical end. Mark Gardner is an ophthalmologist. Every damn job description in that business starts with 'O P T,' but Mark is top of the food chain: an eye surgeon. He's thirty-seven, graduated from Duke Medical School, easygoing, well liked. His wife, Jenna, is a biochemist. Married ten years, no kids. They have separate roles in the company, but they're both on the same task force to come up with a medication that could reverse macular degeneration. If they did that, Ocumax Labs would go from obscurity to household name overnight, and the stock would go to the moon."

"Why did they go to Mexico?"

"They were invited to speak at a university in Mexico City. Somebody at the school called them, sent them first-class tickets, booked the hotel, made all the arrangements. As far as the people at Ocumax know, the Gardners are speaking at a symposium for eye doctors and then taking a few days' vacation time for themselves. But that's bullshit. The Federales checked. The university never heard of them."

"And Alboroto's crew picked them up at the airport," Marina said. "So why do you think he sent for them?"

"Maybe the fucker's going blind," I said. "That's the thing about macular degeneration—it doesn't care who you are. But if you're Joaquín Alboroto, you kidnap the people who are at the forefront of a cure, and lock them up in your compound till they crack the code."

"That would explain why there are no ransom demands," she said. "He doesn't need money. He needs *them*."

"It's the best theory I could come up with so far," I said, "but that's all it is—a theory. I could be dead wrong."

"There's only one way to know for sure," Marina said. "Get your ass down to Mexico, find the Gardners, and ask them."

"I like the way you delegate, Captain, but the last time my ass was in Mexico, a bunch of hopheads with AK-47s tried to shoot it off, whereas your ass spends the whole day sitting at a giant console pushing buttons."

"I know it sounds easy, but yesterday I managed to infiltrate the entire West Coast missile defense system for eight minutes and eleven seconds before anyone even noticed the breach. The command staff of the cyberterrorism division didn't know whether to shit or pin a medal on me. And just because you're boots on the ground and I'm not doesn't mean I don't get my daily dose of disaster. This morning, we ran out of whole milk and I had to take my hazelnut cappuccino with two percent."

A rush of joy surged through my body, and I couldn't stop it from spreading across my face. It was all I could do to keep from saying, "Can we rethink this no-emotional-attachments shit?"

Instead, I went with "What's for dessert?"

"Two choices," she said. "The restaurant sent some bananas Foster crème brûlée."

"What's the second choice?" I said.

"It's being served in the bedroom," she said, tossing me a heart-stopping smile and heading toward the stairs.

"Crème brûlée is highly overrated," I said, and I followed her like a puppy dog who has just found his new home and never wants to leave.

CHAPTER 38

THE NEXT MORNING, I caught the first flight back to New York. By the time I got there, I had several more viable theories on why Alboroto might have kidnapped the two scientists. And once I filled in the team on what I'd learned at Ocumax Labs, we came up with a dozen more. They all had one thing in common. We agreed that men like Alboroto don't do anything unless it's to their own benefit, and by midafternoon, three of us were on a flight to Mexico City.

I was still rare-books dealer Timothy Randall, and Redwood was still my attorney, Harold Scott. Delaqua, sitting two rows behind us, was Dr. Eric Sandoval, a psychologist.

"Great cover," Redwood whispered to me over a drink. "Most shrinks are crazier than their patients, and if anybody can pull off crazy, it's our boy Frank."

He laughed. I didn't. "I know," I said. "He's been obsessed with bringing down Alboroto for years. He's more use to us in the field than sitting around the office in New York. But keep an eye on him. He has a history of going rogue."

As soon as we cleared immigration and customs, I scanned the terminal for a driver holding up a sign that said "Randall." Instead, I caught sight of a familiar face. It was Kevin Cavanaugh.

He didn't approach us. He just nodded, and we followed him to the parking lot.

"We got something," he said as soon as the four of us were in the SUV. "The Federales didn't want to go public that we were looking for Mark and Jenna Gardner, so they put out an alert at the investigative level. Thirty-six detectives, all vetted—as best you can vet any cop in Mexico—so there's a good chance it won't leak to Alboroto that we even know about the scientists.

"One of the detectives was also working a jewelry store robbery. The owner was killed, so he was canvassing the pawnshops hoping to get a hit on some of the stolen merchandise. There's an envelope in the glove compartment. Open it up and take a look at what he found."

I pulled out the envelope. Inside was an 8" x 10" picture of two gold wedding rings, each engraved *Jenna and Mark Forever.*

"Fuck," I said, and handed the picture to Redwood.

"Not a good sign," he said, passing it to Delaqua.

Delaqua shook his head and said, "We're too late."

"We don't know that," Cavanaugh said. "Sergeant Bolano called me. They just collared the guy who hocked the rings. She said they would wait for us before they start talking to him."

Thirty minutes later we were at the police station, and I got a warm reception from three veterans of the safe-house gun battle: Inés Bolano, Luis Vadillo, and the man who knelt beside me and prayed over my fallen comrade's body, Domingo Ordóñez.

I introduced them to Redwood and Delaqua, and they led us to the observation room. It was dark, but an oversize two-way mirror on the far wall gave us a perfect view of the interrogation room. On the other side, unable to see anything but his own reflection in the mirror, was a large man, at least six feet four, with big beefy hands, and dark eyes that were haunted by fear. He paced the small space like a caged animal, looking up, down, and side to side.

"His name is Eliezer Galdós," Ordóñez said. "He is second-generation cartel. His father was Armando Galdós, another big oaf who worked body removal, first for Quintana and then for Alboroto. *Como padre, como hijo.* Like father, like son. But Junior is not as smart as his father, and trust me, his *papá* was not hired for his brains. This is the first time Eliezer has ever been picked up, and look at him."

"He's scared shitless," I said. "You'll break him. It should be fun to watch."

"Why sit back here and watch?" Ordóñez said, grinning at his two partners. "Why don't you come in there with me?"

The Federales had proved themselves to be team players, but this was over the top. "You're kidding, right?" I said.

He shook his head. "I'm dead serious, amigo."

"You're good with me going in the box with him? I was NYPD, but I'm not a cop any more."

"But you're American," Ordóñez said. "I don't need a cop. I need a prop."

I followed him into the interrogation room. He pointed at a chair on the far side of the table, and Galdós immediately sat down. Ordóñez and I sat opposite him, our backs to the mirror, two cameras covering both sides of the interview.

"I'm Detective Ordóñez," he said, his voice calm and congenial. "I knew your father. He was on the wrong side of the law ever since he was big enough to carry a three-hundred-pound body. He was a hard worker, loyal to the cartel. And he never got in trouble. You know why?"

It was a rhetorical question, but the big man shook his head in wonder.

"He cleaned up the cartel's mess," Ordóñez said, "but he never took the mess with him. Your *papá* was a magician. They paid him to make things disappear, and he did it well. But you . . . He wouldn't be so proud of you, would he?"

Ordóñez reached into his pocket and removed the two gold wedding rings. He let one fall to the metal tabletop. It danced around and clattered to a stop. He dropped the second one. It landed on its side and rolled onto Galdós's lap.

Galdós sat there, his mouth turned down, quivering, embarrassed to have brought shame to his father. He retrieved the ring and put it on the table.

"I'm curious, Eliezer," Ordóñez said. "When did the rules change?"

Galdós was blindsided. "What rules?"

"Alboroto's rule. If there is any jewelry on the body, it has to be removed and melted down so it can't be traced back to the cartel."

Galdós lowered his head.

"Look at me!" Ordóñez yelled.

Galdós's head snapped up.

Ordóñez stood up, agitated now. He seemed genuinely angry at the big man for fucking up such an uncomplicated job. "You see this guy?" he said, pointing at me. "He's a crazy American from New York. Mean as fuck. He wants to put out the word that you pawned those rings."

Galdós shook his head.

Ordóñez mellowed. "I said *por favor, no, señor.* I said if you do that, Alboroto will find out in minutes, and how long after that before someone is hauling poor Eliezer's body parts in garbage bags? Your father would be devastated. I tried to defend you, Eliezer. I told him the cartel is hemorrhaging cash. They're not paying their people a living wage any more, are they?"

Galdós grabbed on to the lifeline. "*No, señor, no.*"

"So you stole a few gold rings to feed your wife and kids, didn't you?"

"*Sí.* I took them," Galdós said, eyes wide, as if he were hoping a confession would grant him exoneration.

"But this American doesn't give a shit about your wife and kids. He doesn't care if you live or die," Ordóñez said, his voice getting louder and more urgent. "He doesn't care if your father spends the rest of his days hating himself for not teaching you how to be a *real* magician!"

Silence.

Ordóñez didn't move. He stood there letting Galdós's unsophisticated thought process do the rest of the job.

Finally, Ordóñez spoke. It was barely a whisper. "So I thought maybe you could help me change his mind."

Galdós nodded vigorously. "*Sí, claro.*"

"He only has one simple question," Ordóñez said. "Answer him like your life depended on it."

Ordóñez turned to me. This was why he brought me into the room.

"Where are Mark and Jenna Gardner?" I said.

Galdós looked at me pleadingly, hoping he could convince me not to give up his dirty little secret to the cartel.

"They are dead, señor," he said. "I fed them to the sharks."

CHAPTER 39

ORDÓÑEZ CROSSED HIMSELF and slowly sat back down in his chair. He leaned across the table and whispered, "You didn't kill them, did you, Eliezer?"

"Never," Galdós said. "It's a sin."

"Then who committed the sin?"

He shrugged. "Maybe Del Pozo. Maybe Lavandera. *¿Quién sabe?* They don't tell me. I don't want to know."

"Tell the American what you *do* know. Everything."

"I sat in the *laboratorio* all day and watched them work. They were afraid. The woman would sometimes stop and cry. She said they would give me money if I helped them escape. But I kept silent. I would bring them food, but many times she didn't eat."

"They were working in the laboratory for Alboroto," Ordóñez said.

"*Sí.*"

"What were they doing for him?"

Galdós buried his head in his hands. This was yet another question that demanded he reveal more about the man who could snuff out the lives of his entire family in an instant.

"*Por favor, señor,* why do you need to know these things? It's over. *Terminado.*"

Again Ordóñez looked in my direction and passed the baton.

"Nothing is over till I tell you it's over," I growled. "What were the scientists doing in the lab for Alboroto?"

"He's crazy now," Galdós said. "First, he says he want to kill the people of New York, and then he changes his mind, and he attacks the Estavillas."

"The Estavilla cartel?" Ordóñez said, giving me context. "How could he attack them? They're history. He's the one who crippled their business. More than three hundred of them are in prison, and nobody wants to work for Manuel Estavilla, because Alboroto kills the new recruits as soon as they sign up."

"*Sí.* They're in prison. But they are not dead. I told you he was crazy. That's why he had the gringos make the poison."

"What poison?" Ordóñez demanded.

"I don't know. Poison. They make it, and they mix it with the coca, and then Alboroto sends it to the Penitenciaría Santa Martha."

Ordóñez sat back in his chair and exhaled heavily. "Stay in your seat, Eliezer," he said.

Then he stood and gestured for me to follow him out the door.

As soon as we got to the viewing room, a staccato stream of rapid Spanish erupted between Ordóñez and the other two cops.

"What's going on?" I said when they finally settled down.

"Remember when I called you?" Inés Bolano said. "I apologized for the delay because there was a problem at the prison. Thirty Federales were called in to deal with the situation at the Penitenciaría Santa Martha."

"What . . . situation?"

"At the morning count, twenty prisoners wouldn't come out of their cells. They complained of dizziness and nausea, and some said they couldn't see. By that night, we had transported hundreds of them to hospitals throughout the city. Over half of them are blind."

Delaqua jumped in. "Did you get a sample of—"

I cut him off. "Let her finish."

"At first, we didn't know what happened," Bolano said. "But then we searched the cells of the victims. Not everyone had disposed of the packaging. We found dozens of empty bags and had them analyzed. Galdós was telling the truth. The lab confirmed that the cocaine was poisoned."

"With what?" I asked.

"Methanol."

"Inés, with all due respect to your lab," I said, "methanol is liquid; cocaine is powder. You try to mix them together, and all you'll wind up with is lumpy coca."

"Not if you kidnap two scientists who know how to convert liquid molecules into dry granular particles."

She'd said it in perfect English, and yet I had trouble processing it.

Ordóñez read my baffled look. "We had difficulty making sense of it ourselves," he said. "Water into wine, we understand. But liquid into powder? It seemed impossible."

"But we found out that it's been done successfully in the past," Bolano added. "With ethyl alcohol—ethanol."

"Booze," Delaqua said.

She smiled. "*Pues sí.* Tequila, rum, vodka. Scientists have figured out how to turn a bottle of booze into a bag of powder."

"Why do I expect there's not a big demand for that at happy hour?" Delaqua said.

"But what happens if you convert *methanol* into powder?" I asked.

"Chaos. Madness," Ordóñez responded. "Suddenly, you have the power to make the world go blind."

"Alboroto didn't want the Estavillas to die," Bolano said. "He laced the cocaine with methanol, and it left most of his enemies sightless."

"We arrested the guards who were paid to bring it in and distribute it," Ordóñez said. "There were seven of them. They said they didn't know it was poisoned. They were just mules for Alboroto."

"You know what this means, don't you?" I said.

"I'm afraid I do," he said.

"Alboroto wouldn't kidnap and kill two Americans just to get even with a rival gang that he's already essentially destroyed," I said.

"No, señor," he said. "I think he has a bigger target."

"Much bigger," I said. "The Estavilla cartel was only his beta test."

CHAPTER 40

By the time the four of us got to Cavanaugh's hotel room, it was one a.m. in New York. I hit my speed dial for Trace Baker, and he picked up on the first ring.

"The Gardners are dead," I said. "Alboroto conned them into flying to Mexico because they worked for an ocular compounding laboratory, and he needed them to doctor his next batch of cocaine so that most of those using it would go blind."

"Blind?" Baker said. "Is that possible?"

"Alboroto must have asked himself the same question, so he smuggled a shipment into a prison, and now hundreds of men from a rival cartel will be spending the rest of their lives in darkness. I'm here with Cavanaugh, Redwood, and Delaqua, and we're all betting it was a trial run for his next attack on New York."

"Jesus," he breathed. "You've got to stop it before it gets here."

"We're on it," I said. "Alboroto's got a lab out in the desert. The Federales know where it is, but they never had a green light to hit it."

"Why the fuck not?"

"Boss, this is Mexico. The bad guys pay the good guys to look the other way. But now we have three dead Americans: the Gardners and Jávier Ceteño. Even the cops who are on the take don't want the heat of the US government to come down on them. The Federales are gearing up to hit the lab at dawn."

"Are you invited to the show?"

As soon as he asked the question, all eyes turned to me, waiting for the answer. I'd had a private conversation with Ordóñez, and I hadn't yet shared the disappointing news with the rest of the team.

"We're invited, but we've got spectator status only."

As soon as he heard the news, Delaqua shook his fist in the air, furious at the gods who would keep him from a final showdown with the man he had been hunting for years.

"The team leader was adamant, Trace," I said. "This may be our fight, but this is definitely not our turf. He knows how much this means to us, so he agreed to let us observe. Delaqua, Redwood, and I will be in the rear with the gear, but only the Federales get to engage the enemy."

"I'm sorry to hear that," Baker said, "but right now we can't argue with the Mexicans. We need them. This city is still reeling from the aftermath of Central Park, and it will be for a long time to come. I can't even begin to conceive of the permanent damage to our entire way of life if Alboroto does to the people of New York what he did to those inmates. Good luck, gentlemen. Be safe. *Vaya con Dios.*"

As soon as I hung up, Delaqua exploded. "We're not in it? Did you tell Ordóñez that we didn't come to this fucking hellhole to be fucking spectators?"

"Actually, Frank, I did," I said. "Although maybe not in those exact words."

"I don't get it, Danny," Redwood said. "We're all trained. Tactical is in our DNA. And God knows we've got skin in the game. Ceteño was one of our own."

"Chris, Frank, I am in violent agreement," I said. "I want in as much as you do. But Ordóñez was clear. The unit that's going in has been training together for something like this for years. The last thing they need is three gringos with a score to settle getting in their way."

"Excuse me for counting," Cavanaugh said, "but when did there get to be three of us? If anybody should be embedded, it's me. I'm a journalist, for Christ's sake. Since when did I get to be Rosie the fucking Riveter, dutifully doing my bit on the home front?"

"You're not *a* journalist," I said. "You're *our* journalist. You're our connection to the head of the cartel. I don't know if he trusts you, but he's willing to talk to you, and that's much more valuable to this operation than having a fourth American observer tagging along in the ass end of the assault team."

"Easy for you to say," Cavanaugh snapped. "You're going."

"I'm going, too," Delaqua said, "but for all the good it'll do, I may as well stay home and do some riveting."

"Guys," I said, "this discussion is over. We've got a briefing at 0330, which gives us less than four hours to sleep. The Mexicans made the call. I know how much you want to be part of the action, but it's not happening. We're lucky they're letting us watch."

CHAPTER 41

ORDÓÑEZ WAS RIGHT. His combat unit was a finely tuned machine. As he briefed them for the operation, I could see that every single one of them had their own individual set of skills, but there were no individuals. They were ingrained with a sense of teamwork that can only come from years of training. It was a classic example of the whole being greater than the sum of its parts, and adding three strangers into the mix might throw them out of sync.

Each unit had been given its own specific mission, and finally, just before we rolled out, we all gathered in the ops room for one last look at the big picture. Ordóñez opened with a satellite image of the target: a twenty-thousand-square-foot fortress surrounded by a stone wall. There were five separate structures inside the stronghold, and he used a laser beam to point out each one.

"This is where the coca is processed," he said, focusing the red dot on the largest rectangle on the screen. He moved the pointer to a U-shaped box. "And this is where they do the packaging. At this hour, both buildings should be quiet. Guards, but no workers.

"The bulk of the crew will be here, in the bunkhouse," he said, highlighting a gray square. "We don't know how many packagers and transporters were brought in for this operation, but they can cram as many as sixty men into this shit can. We do know that most of them will be asleep, they're not likely to be armed, and they'll drop to the ground as soon as we show up."

He moved the laser. "This bigger, more elegant building is the honeymoon suite, where Señor Alboroto stays when he comes to visit."

"Please tell us that you invited him," someone called out, and the room laughed.

"No, but I'm hoping the state can provide him with some different accommodations in the near future," Ordóñez said. He moved the red dot to the last spot on the map. "And finally, the garage and the loading dock. It's huge. There's room for half a dozen eighteen-wheelers and a convoy of smaller trucks."

"Like Amazon for junkies," another voice observed.

Another round of laughter, and Ordóñez put down the laser pointer. "We will be coming in with the sun at our backs. Armored vehicles first. They'll breach the perimeter and take out the guards. Once we're inside, there will be a security team of fifteen or more men who will try to put up a fight. Alpha and Bravo squads will take them out while the remaining teams sweep the buildings. On my command, two choppers will fly in for air support or emergency evacuation. Bringing up the rear will be the mobile armory to make sure you don't run out of ammunition. Inside the vehicle will be medical personnel and three American observers. Gentlemen, stand up and show your faces so we don't shoot you."

Delaqua, Redwood, and I stood up, looked around, and then sat back down.

"Any questions?" Ordóñez asked.

The room remained silent.

"Good." He gestured to one of the Federales in the front row. "Sergeant Gonçalvez."

The man stood up, and everyone in the room followed. Gonçalvez bowed his head and began to pray. *"Nuestra señora de Guadalupe . . ."*

I didn't know what they were saying, but I didn't need a translation. It was a solemn moment and a powerful reminder that we were all marching into a life-or-death struggle with one of the deadliest criminal forces in the world.

When the prayer was over, Ordóñez yelled, "*¡Vámonos!*" and we filed outside and loaded up in our vehicles.

Ours was a twenty-foot-long Mercedes Sprinter. Every luxury feature designed for the van had been ripped out. Creature comforts gave way to function, and the vehicle was now one part arsenal and one part field hospital. The three of us, along with two tactical EMTs, were relegated to fold-down jump seats along each side. The rest of the Sprinter was filled with weaponry and the emergency equipment needed to sustain the lives of those who fell during combat.

We introduced ourselves to the medics, Ricardo Adanza and Isabella Royos, who both spoke English.

And then the caravan began to snake its way through a fifty-mile stretch of Mexican desert. Thirty-six brave men and women determined to put an end to the reign of the boy butcher who had grown up to be one of the most evil men on the planet.

CHAPTER 42

THE CARAVAN WAS SIXTEEN VEHICLES LONG, most of them armored. Not ours. We hung back a mile from the lead SUV.

Nobody said a word. Redwood and the male EMT nodded off. Isabella, the other EMT, kept busy with her cell phone. Delaqua sat motionless, eyes surveying every inch of the van. He reminded me of a sniper hunkered down in the jungle, willing to wait as long as it takes until he's ready to squeeze the trigger. On the outside, he seemed at peace, but I knew that deep down he was seething with the knowledge that he wouldn't get a chance.

Our driver, Juan, the youngest member of the elite task force, kept us updated on the ETA. He had just yelled "two miles out" when we heard the gunfire, and the radio crackled in urgent Spanish.

"¡Dios mío!" Juan blurted out.

"What's going on?" Delaqua demanded. "In English."

"The compound is no more," he stammered. "It's burned to the ground. It's a trap. Ordóñez says they must have known we were coming. We're aborting the—"

The blast must have killed him instantly. It came from directly under the driver's seat, tore through metal, rubber, and flesh, and flipped the van onto its right side. The left side, where I had been sitting, was now up in the air, and suddenly I was hanging there, held in by only my safety harness.

The inside of the Sprinter filled with thick smoke, and my face was pelted with swirls of stinging sand, broken glass, and flying debris from the medical cabinet.

I struggled to unbuckle my harness, failed, and finally managed to cut the restraints and drop straight down onto Redwood's chest.

"IED," he said, choking on the unbreathable air. "You okay?"

Before I could answer, Delaqua began screaming, "Load up! Load up! Load up!"

The side panel where the gun cabinet was mounted had now become the floor of the van, and Delaqua was pulling FX-05 Fire Serpents from the rack.

We each grabbed a gun and stuffed our vest pouches with magazines and grenades.

Ricardo was moaning in pain, his chest oozing blood. His partner was searching through the rubble, looking for something to stop the bleeding.

"Isabella, we've got to get out of here," I said.

"You go," she said. "I'm not leaving him."

There's no arguing with a warrior. Redwood kicked the back doors hard. The left one flew up, but because the hinges were now at the roofline, gravity brought it crashing back down. But the right one slammed to the ground, and the three of us spilled out onto the ground, firing as we scrambled for cover behind an outcropping of red rocks.

We could hear guns and grenades going off a mile down the road, at the front of the convoy. But we were in no position to help. We had our own problems. Two, maybe three, automatic weapons were firing at us, and the bullets were whizzing by at a fast clip, keeping us pinned.

Alboroto must have beefed up the quality of his army since our last encounter. This unit was much better trained than the thugs on drugs we had fought off at the safe house. A handful of them had hung back, waited for the last vehicle, set off the IED, and effectively turned our

Sprinter into a roadblock, trapping the rest of the convoy between us and the burned-out shell of the drug operation.

"Doc!" Redwood yelled, pointing at the van. "It's Isabella. She's trying to get out."

The EMT was flat on her belly, just peering out of the open panel door. I held up my hand, telling her to wait, and then turned to Delaqua and Redwood.

"Light 'em up," I yelled.

They laid down a volley of suppressive fire, and I signaled the medic to start running. Then I opened fire, and between the three of us, we unloaded hundreds of rounds, keeping the enemy at bay while Isabella, a large duffel bag over her shoulder, ran toward us and managed to dive to the ground behind our shelter.

"Ricardo is stable," she said. "For now." She dumped the duffel and poured out as much of the mobile arsenal's weaponry as she could carry.

Ordóñez's voice erupted from her radio.

"*Apoyo aéreo. Aquí en dos minutos.*"

"Air support," Isabella said. "Two minutes out."

Redwood pulled a grenade launcher from the new cache of weapons. "Just what the doc ordered," he said, giving a nod to the medic. "Thanks."

He loaded it up and zeroed in on the enemy's position. "It's about to get loud," he said.

Loud and deadly. One of the attackers flew up in the air, enveloped in a red mist, his body shredded by the concussion. Two more, also injured, stood up, threw their rifles to the ground, and started screaming, "*No más, no más. ¡Me rindo! ¡Me rindo!*"

"My Spanish is a little rusty," Redwood said, looking at Isabella, "but I think they're calling it quits. Tell 'em to hit the dirt."

"*Bajar, bajar,*" she ordered, and the two of them spread themselves facedown on the ground.

Redwood and Delaqua fanned out behind them and scanned the area for more of their team.

"Clear," Delaqua barked.

"Incoming!" Redwood yelled, pointing skyward.

It was not yet dawn, but the two Sikorsky Black Hawks were close enough to see and hear. Isabella pulled out her flashlight, flipped to a green lens, and waved it left to right, letting the spotter know that we were friendlies and had it under control.

Seconds after they roared past us, we heard the whine of rockets being launched. Then came the deafening stutter of the M230 chain gun that was mounted under the fuselage of the lead chopper as it pumped more than six hundred 30mm rounds a minute into the dazed and quickly disintegrating enemy force below.

As the sound of resistance tapered off, Delaqua ran to where Isabella and I were standing, our weapons trained on the prisoners.

"On your knees!" he yelled, kicking them.

Isabella translated. The smaller of the two scrambled to follow the order. His partner sneered and brought himself up slowly, defiantly.

Delaqua held the barrel of his gun inches from the big one's chest.

"Ask him where the poisoned cocaine is," Delaqua said. "The shit that's going to New York City."

Isabella translated. The man looked up at Delaqua and laughed.

"You think this is funny?" Delaqua said. He raised his gun, put it to his eye, and looked down the barrel.

In all my years in law enforcement, it's been drilled into me that my job is to bring criminals to justice. Juries decide guilt or innocence. Judges dole out punishment within the confines of the law. Judge Solomon had gone too far. And now Frank Delaqua was teetering on the edge. But I shared his desperation. We were three anonymous vigilantes on the verge of crossing that ethical line to prevent hundreds of thousands of New Yorkers from going blind.

"Tell him he has one last chance, or I will send him straight to hell," Delaqua said to Isabella.

She did.

Eyes full of hate, the man spat on the ground. "*Chinga tu madre,*" he said.

Cops have been cursed out in just about every language there is.

None of us needed a translation. We'd all heard that one. But Delaqua turned to Isabella. "He told me to go fuck my mother, right?" he said, grinning.

She nodded apologetically.

"Thought so," he said, taking two steps back. "Just wanted to make sure."

He squeezed the trigger, and a three-shot burst blew the man's heart through a gaping hole in his back. His horrified partner shrieked as rivulets of fresh warm blood streamed into his eyes and mouth.

Delaqua turned toward the second prisoner and put the rifle to the man's head. "Now you," he said. "How do you feel about my mother?"

CHAPTER 43

A DARK, WET STAIN BLOSSOMED on the front on the man's pants, and he knelt there trembling uncontrollably.

"*Tsk, tsk, tsk,*" Delaqua said, smiling sympathetically, shifting from cold-blooded murderer to new best friend. "*¿Como se llama?*"

"Gustavo," the man said. "I speak English. I have a wife and four children, señor. I will tell you everything I know. I swear."

As soon as she knew we no longer required a translator, Isabella leaned toward me and whispered. "My team needs me."

I nodded, thanked her, and she took off quietly.

"Gustavo," Delaqua said, "did you hear the question I asked your late friend?"

"*Sí, claro.* Yes. My job was to protect the factory. Many hours, every day. I see much," he said.

"So you saw them making the cocaine."

"Yes."

"How much?"

Gustavo shrugged, then quickly realized that "I don't know" was not an acceptable answer. "The workers can produce maybe forty kilos an hour. They worked Monday, Tuesday . . ." He closed his eyes to do the math, muttering numbers in Spanish and still trembling.

"Relax," Delaqua said. "You're doing great. Keep it up and you'll have dinner with your wife and kids tonight."

Gustavo opened his eyes. "Maybe a thousand kilos," he said.

"All riddled with methanol?"

"Riddled? Methanol?" Gustavo said, wanting to help, but scared that he didn't understand what Delaqua wanted from him.

"Poisoned! Like the shit that made the prisoners blind," Delaqua said, leveling his gun at the man's chest.

"Sí. *Veneno*. Poison. They tell us not to go near it. All the workers wear special clothes. Like *astronautas*. Is very poison."

"And you saw them shipping it?"

"Yes."

"How many truckloads?"

"One."

"Bullshit!" The old Delaqua came back without warning. "Don't fucking lie to me, *pendejo*. Alboroto doesn't put all his eggs in one fucking basket. He would never put all that shit in one truck. The man hedges his bets. Now, try again. How many trucks?"

"Señor, I swear. One truck. No eggs. Just coca. Truck is very, very big—plenty room."

"What happens when the shipment gets to the seaport in Veracruz?"

"*La grúa* picks it up . . ."

"Who is *la grúa*?" Delaqua demanded.

"No, no, no. Is not person. La grúa. La grúa." He raised his right arm, spread his fingers wide, clamped them around his left wrist, and lifted it up in the air. "La grúa takes the box with the coca from the big truck and puts it on boat."

"It's a crane," I said. "He's putting the coke on a container ship."

"*Sí, sí*," Gustavo said, grateful for my help. "Container ship."

"When did the truck leave?" Delaqua asked.

"Yesterday. Early in the morning. Maybe six. The driver takes the coca to Veracruz. We send the workers home, but the guards—we stay. And then—I swear this is true, señor—last night they tell us to burn everything."

"Who told you?"

"Rugerio. He is the only one of us who speaks to Señor Alboroto."

"And where can I find this Rugerio now?"

Gustavo pointed at the bloody body on the ground.

Delaqua looked at me and grinned. "Oops." Then he turned back to Gustavo. "So this shitbag tells you to torch the place. So now there is nothing to guard."

Gustavo didn't answer.

"But they told you we were coming, and they paid you extra to stick around and kill us, didn't they?" Delaqua said.

"No. Just *la policía*. I would never hurt Americans."

"You blew up our fucking van, and you tried to mow us down with automatic—"

"Frank," I said. I had let him run with it, but now he was veering off target. "Get back to the container ship."

"Right. So they take the cocaine to Veracruz. Which ship do they load it on?"

"I don't know, señor. I swear."

"Then who knows? And don't say Rugerio, or you're joining him. Who knows what ship the drugs are on?"

Gustavo was trembling again. "*El Portugués.*"

Delaqua lowered his gun and turned to look at me. I recognized the look of defeat in his eyes. We had just hit a brick wall. He reset his scowl and turned back to Gustavo. "El Portugués is running the drugs to the US?" he asked.

"He is the only man Alboroto would trust for a shipment so big," Gustavo said, still trying to be helpful. "He only calls in el Portugués when—"

"Get DOWN!" It was Redwood. Delaqua and I both dived for cover as a single gunshot exploded through Gustavo's head.

Redwood caught the flash of the muzzle, fired his grenade launcher, and in a split second the man who had silenced Gustavo was just as dead.

"Let's get out of here," I said.

"One of the drawbacks of the job," Delaqua said, taking one last look at Gustavo. "You don't talk, your enemies kill you. You do talk, your boss kills you."

"Who the fuck is el Portugués?" Redwood asked as we started walking.

"Don't answer," I said. "No more talking within earshot of the Mexicans. Whatever you know, save it till we get back."

We headed west, and five minutes later we caught up with Ordóñez.

"We were compromised," he said, telling us what we already knew. "I'm sorry, but someone in our organization must have tipped Alboroto off. They were waiting for us. We had eight casualties. We took out twenty-three of them. The rest fled when the choppers arrived."

"They torched their entire operation," Delaqua said, surveying the charred ruins.

"No," Ordóñez said. "They merely conceded one location. They have others. More are being built as we speak. Isabella told me you were interrogating one of them."

"Yes," I said. "But one of his own men killed him before we could get any information."

Ordóñez nodded. "Unfortunate," he said.

He knew I was lying. But he didn't call me on it. He'd just lost eight comrades because someone had leaked the details of his operation. At this point, he could no longer expect me to tell him the truth.

CHAPTER 44

ORDÓÑEZ OFFERED US A RIDE BACK to the city on one of the choppers. We grabbed it, as happy to get away from the Federales as they were to see us leave.

As soon as we got to Cavanaugh's room, I asked Delaqua to brief us on el Portugués.

"His real name is Fortunato da Costa." Delaqua said. "At least, it was, but he shed that identity years ago. He was born in Portugal in the late sixties, got a job working on a merchant marine ship when he was fourteen and fell in love with the sea. By the time he was nineteen, he graduated to assistant navigator on a Norwegian oil taker. But then he got a job opportunity he couldn't turn down."

"Doing what?" I asked.

"Running blood diamonds out of Angola. Smuggling has always been a logistical nightmare. If you wanted to get something from one place to another, you had to rely on so many people along the way. El Portugués streamlined the entire process. He handles it all. One-stop shopping. Today he's the undisputed king of illegal maritime transport—smuggler to the stars who can afford him, like Alboroto. He knows the trade waterways like you know your way from your bedroom to your bathroom, and he can ship anything—drugs, guns, human traffic—from any port in the world and it will arrive at its destination undetected. That, in a nutshell, is the legend of el Portugués."

"I never heard of him," I said. "None of us did."

"You were NYPD," Delaqua said. "You'd sure as hell know him if you were Homeland, or ICE, or Interpol. For them, he's the Holy Grail. The man is a phantom, never been arrested. *Never*. The Bureau has been looking for him for years, Danny. I don't know how we're going to find him in the next few—"

"Fuck finding el Portugués," I said, cutting him off.

Delaqua stood there staring at me. "Did I hear you right?"

"You did. You just said he's a phantom who's been eluding the law for years. Even if we could find him in few days, which I doubt, why should we waste valuable time hunting for the shipper when we should be looking for the shipment?"

Redwood was the first to slowly nod his head in agreement. I kept going.

"I finally understand why Alboroto paid his dealers to stop selling cocaine," I said. "Because at this point, people in New York will be crawling out of their skin waiting for their next fix. And I'm not talking about crack-house junkies. I'm talking regular people—teachers, lawyers, bus drivers, doormen, stay-at-home moms. A thousand kilos of methanol-laced cocaine is enough to leave a million of them blind. Forget el Portugués. Our mission is to find that container and destroy what's inside before that happens."

"How?" Cavanaugh asked.

"For starters, we've got something el Portugués didn't count on. Gustavo told us when the truck left the lab and where it's going."

"How do you know if he was telling the truth, or just feeding you what you needed to hear?"

"I don't. But he was negotiating for his life, and at that moment, he was more afraid of Delaqua than he was of Alboroto. It felt like a solid lead, and for now it's the best one we have, so I called Marina as soon as we landed. She's hacking into the surveillance system at the port of Veracruz."

"Danny, do you know how many containers go through a major port like that every year?" Cavanaugh said.

"Actually, I do. Close to two million. Marina looked it up."

"And she's going to find one box out of the thousands and thousands that roll in every day?"

"If anyone can, it's Marina," I said.

My phone rang. "Talk about perfect timing," I said, tapping the speaker button. "What have you got?"

"Danny? Is that you?" It was a woman, but it wasn't Marina.

"Who's this?" I said.

"It's Marjorie. Marjorie Becker. Kirsten's lawyer."

I took the phone off speaker and put it to my ear. "How you doing, Marjorie? Is everything okay? I'm a little busy here. Can I call you back?"

"Danny, it's Kirsten . . ."

I felt my chest tighten. "What is it?"

"She's in the hospital."

"What happened?"

"This morning, a guard found her hanging in her cell."

CHAPTER 45

"SHE'S OKAY," MARJORIE ADDED QUICKLY. "Pretty banged up, but by the grace of God, she's alive. I'm at her bedside right now."

Cavanaugh's room had a terrace, and I stepped outside to get some privacy. "What happened?" I said.

"I don't know yet. I just got to the hospital. She asked me to call you so she can fill the two of us in together."

"Put her on FaceTime," I said. "And don't take no for an answer."

It took at least thirty seconds, but finally, Kirsten's face popped up on my phone. Even on the small screen, I could see the swelling around both eyes and the multiple contusions.

"Hey, Danny," she said. "I may be overreacting, but I don't think I'm cut out for jail."

"Jeez, Kirsten. I am so sorry," I said. "Who did this to you?"

"Four women. Lupe, Gisele, Paloma, Celia, but their names don't mean anything. They were paid to do it."

"Who hired them?" I said, knowing the answer before I asked.

"I'd bet my last nickel it was Alboroto."

"Take me through it."

"It was this morning after breakfast. There are thirty-four women in the pod. Most of them were downstairs playing cards or watching

TV, but I've been keeping to myself. I was in my cell reading, and the four of them walked in. Lupe was the leader of the pack. She made a couple of remarks like 'Why you keep to yourself, bitch? We not good enough for you?' I knew what was coming next, so I yelled for the guards."

"But there were probably a few more women downstairs distracting them," I said.

"I guess. Then the TV started blasting loud enough to drown me out, and I figured they're getting ready to beat the shit out of me, but I'm not going down without a fight. So I came out swinging, just like my dad taught the three of us when we were kids. I tagged one of them real good right in the nose. There was blood everywhere, but then two of them dragged me down. One of them shoved a wet sock in my mouth, and then this rolled up bedsheet comes around from behind, and just before it's pulled tight, I manage to dig my fingers between the fabric and my neck, and I'm clawing at it trying to suck in air. Then three of them yank me up hard. My feet leave the floor, and I'm hanging from the rail on the top bunk."

She angled the phone so I could see the ligature marks around her throat.

"Damn," I said.

"Wait," she said, giving me a fat-lipped smile. "It gets better. I can see Lupe, and she's got a cell phone, and she's filming me choking to death, and she says, 'You gonna be a Mexican movie star, bitch.' That can only mean one thing, Danny: Alboroto ordered the hit as payback for what my father did, and he wanted video proof that I was dead."

"You're right, and I owe you an apology," I said. "I knew you didn't kill Phil. And the way you were found, in a heroin stupor with the murder weapon in your hand, I knew Alboroto had to be behind it. I didn't say anything to you, because I didn't want you to worry. I figured if he didn't kill you that night, his plan was to make you spend the rest of your life in prison. I was wrong. First, he wanted you to suffer the shame of being arrested for murder. Then he recruited those women to finish the job. I'm sorry. I should have said something."

"Don't apologize. You've always protected me from the uglier realities of life. And just in case I had any doubt about who recruited Lupe, when it was over I found out that her brother is down there in Mexico working for the cartel."

"I'm really glad I'm standing here looking at you, because if someone else were telling me this story, I'd be willing to bet you're not going to come out of this alive. How'd you manage to do it?"

"I don't know, but I kept thinking about my two boys and how they just lost their father, and they can't lose me. I was thrashing and flailing around—about to black out from lack of oxygen—when Lupe moved toward me to get a close-up with her camera, and I mustered up one last kick. I put everything I had left into it, and I caught her square under the chin. Her head snaps back, the blood comes spurting out of her mouth, and I could see that she bit down hard on her tongue, and a big chunk of it was hanging by a thread. The last thing I remember is, she's screaming, gurgling blood, and the other three women are getting the hell out of the cell in a big hurry.

"The next thing I know, I was on the ground, in a shitload of pain. A guard heard Lupe screaming, ran upstairs, and saw me hanging there unconscious. He didn't have time to lower me gently, so he cut the sheet, and I hit the floor hard and broke an ankle and a wrist."

"Thank God you're all right," I said. "Look, Kirsten, I'm in Mexico. It's about noon. I can catch a plane and be in New York by tonight. Tomorrow morning at the latest."

"No, no, no, and no," Kirsten said. "I don't know what you're doing in Mexico, but I'm sure it has something to do with bringing down Alboroto. That's more important than holding my hand. There's nothing you can do here, so promise me you'll stay where you are. I'll be fine. Tell him, Marjorie."

"She's right, Danny," Marjorie said. "I spoke to Judge Stevens and demanded that she be put in protective custody. I told him that the same man who has been terrorizing New York orchestrated Kirsten's attempted murder. The judge agreed. She's under guard here in the hospital. When she goes back to jail, he's putting her in solitary."

"Solitary?" I said. "Isn't that a bit much? Why didn't he just beef up security?"

"Probably because he doesn't want Judge Solomon's daughter murdered on his watch. I'm the only one who can see her. Not her kids, not her boyfriend, not you, not anybody. So whatever you're doing in Mexico, stay there and get it done."

"Okay," I said. "But I need you to do two things for me. First, if anything changes, call me. Day, night, whenever."

"Easy enough," Marjorie said. "What else?"

"The night Phil was killed, the cops showed up in a big hurry. In fact, Kirsten might have OD'd on heroin, but they got there in time to bring her back with Narcan."

"Right," she said.

"How did they get to the crime scene so fast?"

"I asked the same question," she said. "The investigating detective said a Good Samaritan called 911 to say he heard shots coming from the house."

"Did they get his name?"

"No, so I subpoenaed the phone number. It turned out to be a burner. It was purchased at a gas station in Schenectady six months ago. They have video surveillance, but it's been recorded over a dozen times since then. The buyer paid cash, so there's no subscriber information, and listen to this: that 911 call was the only one ever made on that phone."

"How convenient that a Good Samaritan with a throwaway phone just happened to be passing by when Phil was shot," I said. "Text me the number."

"Will do, Danny, but I tried everything. That phone is a dead end."

"Maybe so, but I have a good friend who has been known to raise the dead."

CHAPTER 46

I DON'T USUALLY JUMP TO CONCLUSIONS, but in this case, it was impossible not to. Nobody walks around the quiet streets of suburban Bedford, New York, with an untraceable burner phone, makes an anonymous call to report a shooting, and then never uses that phone again.

No. Whoever made that 911 call was either the killer or working with the killer. I went back inside and told the others what had happened to Kirsten and about my conversation with Marjorie.

"I know you hate the idea of your sister-in-law being in solitary," Redwood said, "but at least she's safe there. Alboroto paid those four women to kill her, and if she went back into the general population, he'd pay four more to take their place."

"He also paid to have your brother-in-law killed," Delaqua said. "And the anonymous 911 caller set her up to take the rap. No question about it."

"No question," I said. "But no proof. Once Marina is done trying to track down that container truck, I'm hoping she can work her geek magic and help me find the shooter."

Twenty minutes later, the call we were waiting for came through. I hit the speaker. "Marina, you have the four of us," I said. "What have you got?"

"I narrowed the search down to three ships that left Puerto de Veracruz for the New York area yesterday," she said. "But one was a RORO headed for Newark."

"A what?" I said.

"Sorry—cargo jargon. There are half a dozen US and foreign car manufacturing plants in Mexico, cranking out about a million cars and trucks a year. For the most part, they don't use containers. They export their vehicles on these giant car ferries. The stern drops down, and the cars—thousands of them—get driven up the ramp one at a time. Roll on, roll off. RORO. I eliminated it and focused on the other two ships."

"The no-RORO boats," Delaqua said, hoping for a laugh. He didn't get one.

"These are the ones where the cranes move the containers from the truck to the ship. It's called a LOLO—lift on, lift off," Marina said. "I knew the drugs had to be on one of those two ships, so I tapped into their surveillance cameras. The first thought that went through my head when I looked at the wide shot was 'what a clusterfuck,' but then I realized, no, it's more like organized chaos. The trucks come through the front gate, get assigned to a lane, and then sit there inching up, waiting their turn to offload."

"Needle in a haystack," Redwood said.

"Exactly," Marina said. "So I tried to narrow it down based on your saying the shipment left Alboroto's place at six a.m. It's about a six-hour drive, so I backed the footage up to eleven a.m. and watched the trucks coming and going. And then at 12:42, we got lucky. One truck pulled in, and a guy with a white shirt and tie steps out of the gatehouse, signals to the driver, and waves him out of the pack."

"Special treatment," I said.

"Very special. It was the only truck that didn't have to wait. Then it was a simple matter of following it from camera to camera. Ten minutes after the driver came through the front gate, his load was picked up by a crane and deposited into the hold of the *Elvira Mendola*, bound for New York."

"It's a decoy," Delaqua said. "Guys like el Portugués don't make it that easy for cops to spot what they're trying to hide."

"I thought exactly the same thing," Marina said. "But then I thought el Portugués doesn't have to worry about the cops in Mexico. Everybody who has to be paid to look the other way has been well taken care of. Even so, I decided to track the truck from its point of origin. I knew the markings on the container, so I checked the traffic camera system along the entire route from the lab to the seaport. The earliest sighting is when the truck got on a toll road six miles from the lab. The manifest said it was carrying upholstery fabric, but there isn't a textile mill within fifty miles of that location. I picked it up on dozens of other cameras until it got to the loading dock.

"So far, it looks like container number 022390 is the one we're looking for, but I decided to put it through one last test. The tare weight is marked on the outside. The box weighs 8,776 pounds empty. When the crane lifted it onto the ship it weighed it at 10,776 pounds. That means the cargo inside weighed 2,287 pounds, and that's damn close to the thousand-kilo number your informant gave you. Bottom line: if it's a decoy, it's a pretty elaborate one."

"You're right," I said. "It sounds like you zeroed in on the real deal. What can you tell us about the ship it's on—the *Elvira Mendola*?"

"It's been in service for eighteen years, and she's one of twenty ships owned by the Mendola Shipping Company. They're totally legit."

"FedEx is legit," Delaqua said, "but people use it all the time to traffic illegal shit from one place to another. When I was in the FBI, we broke up a ring of—"

"Frank," Marina said. "I can only imagine what the FBI did to keep America safe, but *we* can't stop a ship and search it. And if we went to a judge and asked for a warrant, he'd throw us in jail. I hate to break it to you, but Mendola Shipping and FedEx are law-abiding entities. We, by contrast, are decidedly not."

Frank's jaw tightened. Having blown up his career by lying to a federal judge to get a warrant illegally, I'm sure he was seething inside at the veiled reference. But he knew that this round was over, and Marina had won.

"Whatever," he said, sitting back in his chair and folding his arms across his chest. "What else have you got?"

"The ship is due to dock in New York in four days. It's stopping in Miami along the way. I downloaded the stowage plan. There are two thousand, two hundred and thirty-nine containers on board, and I can give you the exact location of the one we want."

"Great job, Marina," I said. "Thank you."

"Anytime," she said. "Let me get back to my day job, and I'll talk to you later."

She hung up, and the four of us sat there letting the news sink in. Finally, Cavanaugh broke the silence. "We have three days to figure out what to do when that ship gets to New York."

"I figured that one out already, Kevin," I said. "Nothing. We have no authority, no jurisdiction; we can't do a damn thing. And we're certainly not going to call Police Commissioner Martin K. Ennis and ask him to take it from there. The only thing we can do is keep the drugs from ever *getting* to the city."

"And how do we do that?" he said.

"I have an idea. Let's see if I can make it happen."

I tapped a button on my speed dial and put my phone on speaker.

Kaori Piper picked up on the first ring. "Danny," she said. "Are you guys okay?"

"We're all fine, but there's a thousand kilos of deadly cocaine on its way to New York, and I need your help to stop it."

"Name it," she said.

"I need a submarine."

Kaori didn't hesitate. "When, where, and how big?" she said.

Cavanaugh, Redwood, and Delaqua all went wide-eyed. It's the kind of reaction you'd expect from three guys who spent their careers jumping through hoops just to requisition a ream of copy paper.

CHAPTER 47

IT WAS NOT YOUR GRANDFATHER'S SUBMARINE. In fact, it was unlike any submarine I'd ever seen. Her name was *Emily G*, and she was a sleek, Darth Vader–black forty-five-foot speedboat that could zip along the top of the water at thirty knots. But once the occupants were safely tucked inside the dry chamber, all the pilot had to do was flip a few switches, and she could dive twelve hundred feet and travel three hundred miles without ever surfacing.

"It's called a multipurpose subsea vehicle," our pilot, Captain Jim Charles, told us, "but I like to think of it as the kind of watercraft Dr. Frankenstein would have built if he hadn't been so preoccupied with dead bodies."

The line was probably a standard part of his orientation speech, but he delivered it so deadpan that both Redwood and I responded with the genuine laughs he was expecting.

"How much does one of these beauties cost?" Redwood asked.

"They start at about nine million," Captain Jim said, "but that's bare bones. The owner wanted a lithium polymer battery which is another four million, plus a few other bells, whistles, and creature comforts, so all in, this one would run you about thirty-six million, give or take a mil."

I nodded as if "give or take a mil" were something I heard every day.

The *owner* that our captain referred to had chosen to remain anonymous. All Kaori could tell us was that "he or she was a good friend of the Baltic Avenue Group" and that "he or she was proud to donate the vessel, the fuel, and the pilot in pursuit of our mission."

"He or *she?*" Redwood said after Kaori had briefed us. "I'm sorry, but if ever there was a rich-boy toy, this is it."

It was one thing for our benefactor's identity to be kept a closely guarded secret, but since our lives were in the hands of the congenial fellow with the Frankenstein joke, we told Kaori that we needed to know more.

"Fair enough," she said. "Jim Charles isn't his real name, but he did spend thirty years in the navy, sixteen of them commanding a submarine. He was awarded the Navy Cross three times for extraordinary heroism in combat, two Silver Stars for gallantry in action against an enemy of the United States, and—"

I held up my hand. "He'll do," I said.

The plan was simple. Captain Jim would maneuver as close as possible to the container ship; then Redwood and I would leave the sub on a diver-propulsion device—the same underwater motorized vehicle the marines used for amphibious missions. We would board the ship, find the container, and rig it with incendiary bombs that wouldn't go off until the drugs got to their final destination point on land. Whoever opened the box would be killed instantly, and the contents would be consumed by fire.

Perfect plan. There was only one hiccup. Actually, it was more like a one hundred-thousand-ton hiccup. The *Elvira Mendola* was moving at about eighteen knots. As fast as *Emily G* was on top of the water, she could only plod along at six knots when she went into stealth mode. And the diver-propulsion device was even slower than that.

"That shouldn't be a problem," Kaori said.

And it wasn't. Not with Marina Whitney able to access the Department of Defense's global armament network and bring the big ship to a standstill.

At two a.m., approximately sixty hours after the *Elvira Mendola* left the seaport at Veracruz, she was about ten miles off the coast of Florida on her way to Miami.

Redwood and I, dressed in tactical wet suits, were aboard the sub as it hovered thirty feet below the Gulf of Mexico, three miles off Longboat Key.

Trace Baker and Kaori were in New York, monitoring the feed from the GoPro cameras mounted to our helmets.

And Delaqua, our spotter, was in an Airbnb on the fourteenth floor of a luxury beach condo, a pair of high-powered computerized night-vision binoculars trained on the horizon.

In truth, I didn't need a spotter, but Delaqua was too much of a loose cannon to risk letting him board the ship. The civilians on the crew weren't the bad guys, but that might not stop him from killing them if things went south.

When the ship was five miles west of our position, I signaled Marina. And then, in an act that could put her in prison for life if she were caught, she tapped in a code that initiated an electromagnetic pulse aimed directly at the *Elvira Mendola*'s coordinates.

Within seconds, Delaqua radioed. "Visual confirmation: target has gone black."

Marina had successfully disabled the ship's computer system. Everything went down: engines, navigation, autopilot, communications—everything.

Less than ten seconds later, Delaqua radioed again. "Backup lighting is activated."

The auxiliary battery had kicked in. It was enough to power the emergency lighting system, but for about the next forty minutes the entire ship would be dark while the computers reset. Marina told us the *Elvira Mendola* had been in service for eighteen years. At her age, the captain wouldn't suspect sabotage. He would enter the event in great detail in the ship's log, but in his head, he would probably sum it up in two words: *shit happens.*

"She's decelerating," Captain Jim said. "Speed down to sixteen knots, fifteen, fourteen."

We had calculated that with her computer system down, the ship's momentum would carry her about five miles. We were close. She coasted for 4.7 miles before she came to a dead stop.

Captain Jim turned away from his console and looked up at us.

"Gentlemen," he said, the congenial smile ever present, "the *Elvira Mendola* is now ready for boarding."

CHAPTER 48

WE SURFACED. I opened the hatch and scanned the skyline. Mother Nature was on our side, hiding the moon behind a thick layer of low-hanging clouds. To the east, a few lights still flickered on Longboat Key and in Sarasota. To the west, there was nothing but sweet, sweet darkness.

Redwood and I slipped into the water, grabbed on to the diver-propulsion vehicle, and made our way to the stranded ship.

The *Elvira Mendola* had no radar, no sonar, and limited visibility, so our pilot was able to get us close enough to the target that we could reach it in less than ten minutes. We knew the exact location of the container we were looking for, so we moved through the water until we were directly below it.

Redwood moored our DPV to the hull by magnet, and I fired a grappling-hook gun to the main deck forty-five feet overhead. It held tight, and the two of us climbed up and silently slipped aboard.

The cargo area had no emergency lighting, no security cameras, no crew standing guard. It was pitch black. But with night-vision goggles, we could make everything out perfectly.

Alboroto's container had been placed in the fourth slot of a nine-box stack. We climbed up the steel support beams that ran the width of the deck to separate the containers and make every one accessible.

"Zero, two, two, three, nine, zero," Redwood said, reading the numbers off the front of a forty-foot container.

"Bingo," I said. "Break the seal."

Each container is sealed at the point of origin—sometimes with a padlock, but more often than not with a slightly more sophisticated version of a twist tie. In theory, it's the shipper's way of ensuring that everything inside has been kept locked until it was delivered to the buyer. But it's basically window dressing. The shipping industry loses billions of dollars' worth of cargo every year, but most of it is lost or stolen in big chunks—piracy, disasters at sea, or entire containers simply disappearing. Very little of the loss comes from petty pilferage by a crew member breaking the seal and copping a Samsung flat-screen for the kids.

Still, we knew the protocol, and it was simple enough for Marina to get a picture of the seal while the box was being loaded, and for Kaori to produce a duplicate for us.

"Got it," Redwood said, clipping the low-tech plastic security device.

"Don't move," a voice said.

It took me half a heartbeat to realize it was Delaqua.

"Repeat, do not move. One of the access doors opened just long enough for me to catch a glimpse of the emergency lighting. Whoever it was flipped on a flashlight, pointed it at the deck, and made his way to a stack twenty feet from your location."

A cigarette lighter sparked.

"Got him," I whispered into my face mask, too low for anyone beyond arm's length to hear. "Smoke break."

The radio went silent. Redwood and I flattened our bodies against the container, and I was grateful that our black wet suits could get lost against the deep, dark barn red of the metal walls.

And then we waited. It took our visitor a full eight minutes to finish his smoke while I stood frozen, hoping the cigarette would take at least that many minutes off the fucker's life.

He must have grown accustomed to the dark, because he didn't turn his flashlight back on, but I could hear him leave.

"Access door just reopened," Delaqua said half a minute later. "He's inside. All clear."

"You guys have a picture?" I asked, as Redwood slowly moved the bolt and opened the door to the modern-day Trojan horse that a revenge-obsessed madman was delivering to the gates of New York.

Affirmative responses from Baker, Kaori, and Delaqua.

"Yes," Marina said, "but the clock is ticking. You have to wire the box and be off the ship in twelve minutes just to be on the safe side. As soon as those computers reset, the captain is going to be hauling ass to make up for lost time. If you try to jump ship then, those props can turn you into chum."

Redwood opened the door.

"Shit," I said.

"What the fuck is that?" Baker said.

"Rubble," I said. "No cocaine. Just rocks and charred wood. Lots of it. I'm guessing it's about a thousand kilos of what was left of the lab Alboroto burned down."

"Do you have the right box? Are you sure that one's his?"

Redwood shined a light on the other end of the giant metal cavern. A large poster-size photo was taped to the far wall. We moved in closer to get a better look.

It was a picture of my late father-in-law, Judge Harvey Solomon, dressed in his judicial robes, a somber look on his face as he posed for his official photo. The picture was black and white. Except for his hands. They had been Photoshopped. Both were now blood red.

"We are so fucked," Redwood said.

"Copy that," I said.

"What do we do now?"

The answer came to me immediately, maybe because deep down I knew there was only one possible solution.

"There is still one person who knows where the drugs are," I said.

"El Portugués," Redwood said. "And the whole world has been looking for him for twenty years."

"I know," I said. "But we have to find him in the next forty-eight hours."

CHAPTER 49

SIX HOURS AFTER EL PORTUGUÉS HAD LEFT us holding our dicks in our hands, Redwood, Delaqua, and I were back in the firehouse in Staten Island, drinking coffee, chugging Red Bull, and conducting postmortems with Trace Baker.

Marina, who had flown up from Washington in the middle of the night, stepped into the conference room, and I watched Delaqua give her a quick glance and then, liking what he saw, a slow, lingering appraisal.

I knew she had spent the past four hours *accessing* even the most inaccessible databases in the known universe, but she still managed to look fantastic—her coal-black hair cascading to her shoulders in thick spiraling curls, her skin a vibrant bronze, and her perfectly tailored safe-for-work pants and sweater moving with her body in a let's-see-what-happens-after-work rhythm.

Delaqua stood up and introduced himself. They shook hands, and Marina sat down between Baker and me.

"Did you get any sleep?" I said.

"It's hard to sleep when you're kicking yourself all night," she said.

"It's not your fault," I said. "Gustavo swore they loaded the truck with cocaine. Snitches lie, Marina. It goes with the territory."

"Gustavo didn't lie," she said, opening her laptop. "The other day, the best I could do was pick up the truck on the local traffic cams and track it to the seaport. This morning, I managed to hack into the DEA's eye in the sky, which keeps tabs on Alboroto's operations. Take a look at these screenshots."

She tapped a few keys, and a black-and-white satellite image popped up on the wall screen. She had enhanced the original so that we had a grainy but unmistakable picture of truck number 022390 backed into the loading dock.

"They had already burned the place down. Here are a few shots of the crew filling the truck with wreckage to give it the weight it needed to make it convincing," she said, throwing more photos on the wall.

"So it was a decoy," Delaqua said.

He had warned her when the truck was moved to the front of the line that it was all part of el Portugués's shell game. And now he was playing gotcha. I tried not to crack a smile. *No wonder FBI guys can't get laid. Way to impress the girls, pal.*

"I'm sorry, Frank," Marina said, smiling at him. "What did you say?" The woman takes no prisoners. She made him repeat his dumb-ass remark.

"Umm . . . I said, I guess the truck we were following was a ruse . . . a decoy," he said, the cockiness sucked right out of him.

"Yes and no." She pulled up another image. "Look at this."

A forklift was loading a large crate onto the back of the truck.

"After they filled it with remnants of the fire, they loaded five crates into the container," she said. "I'd say each crate had two hundred kilos of cocaine inside. After the last one went in, the forklift stayed on the truck. So technically when it left the lab, it wasn't a decoy. It was the real deal."

"Well, there was no coke and no forklift in there when we opened it," Redwood said.

"That's because el Portugués transferred the cocaine when the truck was en route to the seaport. There are at least a dozen blind spots along the way. Using the forklift, it would take him less than two minutes to make the switch."

"And while the first truck got flagged and pulled out of the pack, truck *número dos* got on the queue at Veracruz and blended into the pack," I said.

"If it even went to Veracruz," Marina said. "It could have gone to Tampico, about six hours away. So we not only don't know what ship it sailed on, we don't even know which port it sailed from. Bottom line, the coke is totally off our radar."

"So I guess Frank was right about one thing," I said, looking at Delaqua. "El Portugués is a master. We're not going to find him."

"The hell we're not," she said. She looked at us defiantly and gave us a killer smile.

"Now that I've got your undivided attention," she said, "let me give you my thinking. Start with the attack on Central Park. The helicopter pilot livestreamed the whole thing on his GoPro camera, correct?"

I nodded. "Alboroto's lawyer sent Kevin Cavanaugh some of the footage to prove he was legitimate."

"And when those women tried to kill Kirsten, they were shooting a video and telling her she was going to be a Mexican movie star," Marina said.

"Alboroto doesn't trust anyone," I said. "He wants visual confirmation that the job is done."

"Exactly!" Marina said, her adrenaline pumping. "So I figured whoever killed Oleg Malenkov and the rest of the Russians probably wore a GoPro and livestreamed everything so Alboroto could watch the murders in real time. All I had to do is go to the cell phone records and see who's uploading a ton of data."

She stopped abruptly. "Oh, shit, wait," she said. "I didn't know the time of death. So I decided to narrow it down to a manageable window between midnight and four a.m. But it's Brooklyn, so even in the middle of the night there are about eight thousand phones in use in a half-mile radius. I might be able to figure it out if I had a week, but I don't.

"And then I remembered Phil, Danny's brother-in-law. None of us believe that Kirsten shot him. It was Alboroto—an eye for an eye—and if ever he'd want to watch a hit in real time, it would be this one. The good news is that thanks to the Good Samaritan's 911 call, we know exactly what time the shooting occurred. And the phone traffic in middle-class suburban Bedford isn't nearly as busy as the Russian neighborhood in Brooklyn. So I pulled up all cell phone usage within a five-mile radius of Kirsten's house for fifteen minutes on either side of the 911 call. I got six hundred and four unique cell phones."

"That's still a shitload of possible suspects," I said.

"Yes, but only one of those suspects was livestreaming video at the approximate time of the murder."

"Livestreaming on the internet?" I asked.

"No. To a single device." She paused. "In Mexico."

"Holy shit," Redwood said.

"Thanks. But I'm not done. Once I had a phone number, I ran it to see if the same cell phone was in Brooklyn on the night the Russians were whacked. It was. And between 1:37 and 2:56 a.m., it livestreamed the festivities to Mexico."

"Let me guess," I said. "He was streaming it from another burner phone."

"No. It was an iPhone, purchased at a Verizon store on 3rd Avenue in Manhattan two days before the Russian hit. The buyer paid cash, but he still needed to give up a name and address to complete the sale."

I stood up. "That's fucking brilliant," I said. "You realize, if we can find this guy, he can lead us to el Portugués. What's his name?"

"Baker," she said. "Trace Baker."

CHAPTER 50

Baker held out his arms. "Go ahead. Cuff me," he said in his best 1940s movie gangster voice. "And I would have gotten away with it, too, if it weren't for you meddling kids."

Cop humor.

"On the other hand," he said, lowering his arms, "it's also possible that the real killer is some asshole who stole my identity, and he's still out there."

"Not only is he still out there," Marina said, "I can tell you exactly where he is."

She threw a Google map up on the wall. A little green dot was pulsating near the center of the screen, close to the Connecticut Turnpike. "Right now he's at 20 Railroad Avenue in Greenwich."

Redwood stood up. "Let's go get him."

"Relax," Marina said. "He's coming to us. It's the Metro North Station. It's now 8:36. The next train to New York will be there in three minutes. Let's see if he gets on it."

Five minutes later the green dot started to move south. "He's on train 6311," Marina said. "It arrives at Grand Central Terminal in an hour and five minutes. We can get there in half an hour. If he gets off before then, we can still track him."

Rush-hour traffic was heavy, and without lights and sirens the half hour turned into forty-five minutes, but we still managed to get to Grand Central with twenty minutes to spare.

Delaqua stayed in the car while Marina, Redwood, and I entered the terminal. She took up a dead-center position under the iconic four-sided clock above the information booth. Redwood stood at the edge of the Graybar passage, ready to follow our target if he headed east toward Lexington Avenue. I found a spot under the west balcony, covering the street exits to both Vanderbilt Avenue and 42nd Street, as well as the passage to the subways.

At 9:34, Marina talked into her earpiece and gave us the good news. Train 6311 had just left the 125th Street station in Harlem, the last stop before Grand Central. Our target was still on board.

Ten minutes later, he arrived, exited the train, and entered the main concourse.

On her screen, he was one lone green dot. But from my point of view, he was indistinguishable from the hordes of commuters who crisscrossed the main concourse. It was like trying to find one specific Ping-Pong ball in a pool of thousands.

"He's heading west," Marina said, and I knew that Redwood would be racing across the terminal, to cover the stairs to Vanderbilt Avenue, while I waited on the main level, hoping our target didn't plan to enter the giant underground maze known as the New York City subway system.

"He's under the flag, headed south toward 42nd Street," Marina said.

The pool of Ping-Pong balls had thinned out. There were fewer than fifty people exiting the main concourse.

"He's passing through the Jackie Onassis Foyer," Marina said.

The clump of commuters got even thinner. Now we were down to about twenty.

"He's on 42nd Street. He turned west toward Madison."

I exited the terminal, Redwood behind me, Marina coming up fast on the two of us. One by one, people began to break off from the pack of twenty, either entering office buildings or crossing Forty-Second and heading south.

"He turned right on Madison," Marina said.

My original cluster of Ping-Pong balls was now down to four. One woman, three men.

"He's crossing Madison," Marina said.

One of the four had turned left at the crosswalk on 43rd and was making his way to the other side of the avenue.

"Got him," I said. "Male, tall, red hair, green shirt, khaki pants, black knapsack."

Delaqua, who had been slowly tailing us in the chase car, sped past, hung a left on Forty-Third, and pulled in front of a FedEx truck in a no-standing zone about halfway up the block.

Green Shirt was walking at a normal pace. When he was twenty feet from the car, Marina barreled past him—just another rude New Yorker yakking on her cell phone. Then she stopped dead in her tracks.

"Jesus, lady," he yelled. "Watch where you're—"

Redwood was right behind him, jammed a needle into his butt, and shot a double dose of GHB into his bloodstream. Gamma hydroxybutyrate, better known as "fantasy," is a fast-acting date rape drug. Within seconds, the big man's central nervous system began shutting down.

Redwood and I each latched on to one of his hands in case he had a gun. Then we hooked ourselves under his armpits and walked him to the car, where Marina was waiting with the back door open. No one on the street gave us a second look. Redwood shoved him to the middle of the back seat and slid in next to him. By the time I came around to the other side, his hands and ankles were secured with flex cuffs, his head slumped to his chest. I grabbed him by his mop of red hair and pulled his head back so I could get a look at his face.

"Jesus," I said. "I can't fucking believe it."

"You recognize him?" Delaqua said, making a left on 5th Avenue.

"Damn right," I said.

"Me, too," Redwood said.

Marina, sitting in the front seat, turned around, got a look at him, and immediately let out an "oh, shit."

"His name is Jason Harding," I said. "He's a dirty cop turned media whore who trashes the department every chance he gets."

"Looks like Mr. Harding's got himself a side hustle working as a hit man for Alboroto," Delaqua said.

"Not any more," I said. "Starting now, he's working for us. And the first thing he's going to do is help us track down el Portugués."

CHAPTER 51

"Harding?" baker said when i told him who we were bringing in. "Jason Fucking Blowharding goes from dirty cop to contract killer for the cartel? It almost makes sense."

"It made a lot of sense to Alboroto," I said. "Think about it. He has a list of people he wants dead in the city. Harding is a retired cop who knows the system, has a permit to carry a gun, and if he gets caught, why should Alboroto give a shit? Harding is totally expendable."

"Kudos to you and your team for getting him off the street," Baker said. "But how does it help us stop that shipment of coke from getting into the city?"

"That's where you come in," I said.

"Name it," Baker said.

"I need you to set up a face-to-face between Fyodor Malenkov and me."

"Just you and Malenkov?" Baker said. "You sure you don't want me to include the pope or the queen of England? Danny, even in normal times, getting an audience with the head of the Russian mafia in the US is not an easy ask. And seeing as how his brother just got whacked in his own bed, he's probably not eager to invite people over for a chat."

"So then, you can do it," I said.

"Not elegantly and definitely not directly, but I can get you two degrees of separation from Malenkov, and we'll see how it plays out."

Twenty-five minutes later, I walked into the conference room, and a familiar voice with a thick Jewish accent boomed out at me.

"*Boychik!* I haven't seen you since we talked that jumper down at the Bronx Zoo."

I looked up at the monitor. The man on the screen had a thick mane of silver hair, a neatly trimmed beard, and blue eyes that brightened when the glare bounced off his glasses. Moshe Wolf was the most insightful psychologist ever to carry an NYPD shield. *We* hadn't talked down the jumper. *He* had.

The man's boyfriend had dumped him, so he broke into the aviary, climbed fifty feet to the top of the cage, and was threatening to jump.

"Your boyfriend hurt you, so now you're going to hurt these birds?" Moshe said. "How many do you think you'll kill when you come crashing down on their nests? You've already scared the poor things half to death."

Moshe glanced over at the ESU team. They picked up on his cue and started cawing and squawking. It was hard to keep a straight face, especially when one of them began clucking like a chicken. But it worked. Moshe Wolf had a gift for getting inside people's heads. He had retired to Israel two years ago.

"So, Danny, what can I do for you?" he asked.

I told him about Alboroto's plan to permanently blind as many as a million New Yorkers. Then I took him through the wild-goose chase that led us to an empty container aboard the *Elvira Mendola*. And now our last hope for keeping the cocaine from getting into the hands of a drug-deprived city was to find an enigma who went by the name of el Portugués.

"I'm sorry, Danny," Moshe said, "but I never heard of him."

"Did you ever hear of Fyodor Malenkov?"

"Who hasn't? He's one of the most corrupt people in New York City, not counting the ones who were duly elected to public office. I heard his brother just met an untimely death, and Fyodor is now in charge of the Russian cartel."

"I thought that was still a well-guarded secret."

"Danny, just because I'm in Israel doesn't mean I don't keep up with my roots. I make it my business to know what's going on in Brooklyn."

"I guess you still have friends there."

"My friends, I don't have to keep tabs on," he said. "I still have enemies there. Them, I watch like a hawk. What do you want with Fyodor Malenkov?"

"I want to have a one-on-one sit-down with him."

"You're not a cop any more, Danny."

"I'm hoping that will work in my favor."

"There's only one reason you're asking for a meeting with Malenkov. He has something you want."

"Correct."

"The man is not a giver. First question he'll ask is, what's in it for him?"

"I got that."

"What could you possibly have that Fyodor Malenkov wants?"

I told him.

He said something in Hebrew. I didn't understand it, but the inflection had all the characteristics of someone blurting out "holy shit."

"So, knowing that, Moshe, do you think you can broker a meeting with him?"

"Not from Tel Aviv. Plus, it's not like Malenkov and I are friends. But I know some people in Russia. They might be able to help."

Baker wrote three letters on a piece of paper and slipped it to me. KGB.

"I need all the help I can get," I said. "How long do you think it will take?"

"Normally, longer than you'd want to wait. But you've got a bombshell here. What's your direct line?"

I gave him my cell number.

"Give me an hour," he said. "Maybe two."

Forty-eight minutes later, my phone rang.

"Corcoran," I said, putting the phone on speaker so Baker and the rest of the team could listen.

"*Danny* Corcoran?"

"Yes."

"Where are you now?" It wasn't Moshe. It was a man with a different foreign accent.

"I'm on Staten Island."

He turned his head away from the phone and started barking orders in what sounded like Russian. A good sign.

"We'll pick you up," he said.

"Where?"

"A tanning salon on Page Avenue near Richmond Valley Road. Come alone. No tail, no guns, no phones, no electronics. We will search you. If we find anything, the meeting is off. Anything. Understood?"

Baker waved his hand at me. He wasn't happy with the deal.

"Understood," I said.

Baker drew a finger across his throat, telling me to end the call.

"How long?" the Russian said.

"I can be there in thirty minutes."

The caller hung up.

"Alone?" Baker said. "No GPS? I don't like it."

Of course he didn't like it. Baker was a dyed-in-the-wool law-and-order guy. But we weren't the law. And there certainly was no order.

"This is too risky," Baker said. "I don't think you should go."

"Too late now," I said. "They're expecting me. You should have said something."

CHAPTER 52

"I'LL DRIVE YOU TO THE DROP POINT," Baker said.

"Redwood can do it," I said. "You're the boss."

"Not that anyone would know after the shit you just pulled. Get in the car."

"Sure. Do I get to ride in the back seat?"

"Don't press your luck, Doc."

We climbed into the Audi Q7, and I gave him a rundown on Jason Harding, including the session I'd just had with him while I was waiting for Moshe Wolf to call me back.

"So let's see," Baker said. "You tracked Harding's phone without a warrant, shot him full of GHB, kidnapped him, didn't give him a chance to lawyer up, and interrogated him while he was still coming out of a drug stupor."

"Well said. Will you put that in the eulogy if the Russians slit my throat?"

"Not funny, Danny. You're going in there unarmed and without any backup."

"My choice, Trace. I've got one shot to win over Malenkov. If you were still commissioner, you'd never let me do it, because you had to go by the book. But this isn't NYPD. This is a fledgling counterterrorism unit, and we're making up the book as we go along. Alboroto is going balls out to destroy this city. We've got to go balls out to stop him."

He responded with a short, low guttural sound. I knew it well. It was his grunt of acceptance, not approval.

For the next twenty minutes, we waxed nostalgic about the old days and how remote our past lives felt right now. When we were a quarter of a mile from the intersection of Page Avenue and Richmond Valley Road, he stopped the car and shook his head.

"Don't worry, Coach," I said, getting out of the car. "I got this."

"Be safe," he said.

He made a U-turn and drove back to the firehouse.

I walked north until I saw the tanning salon in a strip mall.

Malenkov's top-of-the-line Range Rover stood out in a sea of working-girl and soccer-mom Toyotas, Hondas, and Chevys. I walked over to an empty handicapped parking space and spread my arms, hoping they would interpret it as the universal sign for "Look, guys, no weapons."

The back door of the Rover opened, and my date for the afternoon lumbered toward me. He was big and ugly, with a jagged scar that started at his left ear and disappeared under his shirt collar. He gestured me toward the car, and I got in. Two more goons were in front. As soon as my silent escort got in and closed the door, we started moving.

The air reeked of cigarettes, coffee, and man sweat. If they had blindfolded me, the smell would have fooled me into thinking I was inside a plumber's van instead of a luxury SUV that cost somewhere in the neighborhood of $150,000.

The big man searched me. Thoroughly. I was always getting tossed when I worked undercover, but most guys are uncomfortable patting another man down, so they tend to tap your arms, legs, ankles, and let it go at that. Early on, I learned that if I wore Thunderwear—a nearly undetectable holster that fits snugly against my crotch—I could conceal a handgun even if I was wearing nothing but a Speedo.

But Scarface had no problem reaching down between my legs and squeezing my balls. When he was done, the man in front gave him a metal-detecting wand and an electronic GPS scanner. I had been told to show up clean, and I was glad I had.

We took the Outerbridge Crossing into New Jersey and got on the turnpike north. Nobody spoke except for the passenger in the front seat, who was on the radio with his team of spotters, who were making sure we weren't being followed on the ground or in the air. And yet they had no problem letting me see where we were going. They knew I could easily retrace the route, but they also knew that if Malenkov decided my information was a waste of his time, I wouldn't get out alive. If he liked it, we'd strike a deal, and I'd be too dirty to even think about giving him up.

A dozen foul-smelling cigarettes into the ride, we exited the Palisades Interstate Parkway at Alpine, New Jersey, where a starter mansion goes for about four mil.

This one had to go for at least twice that. But I knew it wasn't Malenkov's home. He lived in the same Brooklyn neighborhood as his late brother, which meant that this place was just one of the cartel's dozens of properties around the world—kind of an Airbnb for Russian mob royalty.

We stopped at the gatehouse, and I'm not sure why the guards scanned the car, but they did. Finding nothing, they opened the gate, and we proceeded up a winding driveway that was thick with oak trees, pines, and security cameras.

There were six more guards in front of the mansion—four human, two canine. I was ordered out of the car and was frisked, wanded, and sniffed until I passed inspection. The front door of the fortress opened, and my traveling companions escorted me to a modest, tastefully furnished den.

"Sit," one of them ordered, pointing at the hard-backed chair positioned in front of a massive mahogany desk that screamed "Supreme Leader."

I sat. And, of course, I waited.

Twenty minutes later, the door opened, and Fyodor Malenkov walked in. He was in his late sixties but still in excellent shape—tall and gaunt, with a thick, sinewy neck that can only come from a lifetime of exercise. He was wearing the official Russian tuxedo: a custom-fitted sweatsuit—this one maroon with black piping.

He took a seat behind the desk, picked up a bottle of vodka, poured two shots, and handed me one.

"I'm sorry for the loss of your brother," I said, raising my glass. "The man who had him murdered also killed a friend who was like a brother to me."

I drank. He looked at me with a menacing dead stare that men of his power cultivate. "So now I'm supposed to think the enemy of my enemy is my friend," he said, and downed his drink.

"I'm not your friend," I said, "but we both have a common interest. Vengeance."

"Cops don't want vengeance," he said, pouring two more shots. "They want justice."

"I'm not a cop," I said. "A cop would never have gotten into the back of that Rover unarmed, with no backup, and tell you there's a thousand kilos of coke coming into this city and every gram of it is laced with methanol."

He didn't drink his second glass. I had his attention. Showtime.

"Your brother Oleg had the right instincts," I said. "He wasn't going to let the Mexicans tell him how to run his operation. And for that, Alboroto had him killed. And now he's playing you for a sucker. He's three thousand miles away, but about twenty-four hours after that shipment hits the streets, your workers, your customers—*you*, if you touch it—will probably go blind. Not only will you be out of business, but you'll spend the rest of your life trying to protect yourself and your family from the thousands of people who hold you responsible."

He put the glass down, leaned back, and clasped his hands over his chest. "What do you want from me?"

"I can stop this shipment," I said. "But only if I can find the man who orchestrated it: el Portugués."

One corner of Malenkov's upper lip curled in an ugly sneer. "And what makes you think I would give him up?"

"Because whatever relationship you might have had with him in the past, that's over. He's working for Alboroto now, and he knows that when the cocaine gets to New York, your entire organization will become collateral damage. It's a big ask, but I don't come empty-handed. Help me find el Portugués, and I will tell you who killed your brother, his wife, his two lieutenants, and their families."

"I know who killed them," Malenkov said.

"No. You know who *had* them killed. Alboroto *paid* someone to bring this grief down upon you and your family."

"Who did he pay?"

"His name is Jason Harding. He was a cop. He's the one who pulled the trigger. Seven times."

"And how do you know he did it?"

I raised the second shot of vodka to my lips, tossed it back, set the glass down hard, and leaned across the desk.

"Because he told me."

CHAPTER 53

DEIRDRE AND I HAD BEEN TOGETHER for about a month when we had our first argument. I won. Well, maybe I didn't technically win, but she simply let it go, and it just went away. I forget what the squabble was about, but I'll never forget what she said to me later that night.

"You should have been a lawyer, Corcoran. You close well."

"I appreciate the thought," I said, "but why waste my God-given talent hoping to persuade a jury? The real challenge is trying to convince a perp that the best thing he can do for himself is confess and take fifteen to twenty years."

"On the other hand," she said, "you totally suck at taking compliments."

That single moment in my relationship with my late wife suddenly popped into my head as I sat across the desk from Malenkov and studied his body language, his face, his eyes, his hands.

I had just made him a tantalizing offer. His brother's killer on a silver platter. All he had to do was rat out a fellow criminal. His instincts would tell him no—honor among thieves, and all that bullshit. I hoped I'd sandbagged that credo when I told him that el Portugués was now in bed with Alboroto.

I waited.

And then Malenkov blinked.

"You have proof of this confession?" he said.

"Yes, sir. I can show it to you."

"Let me see it," he said.

"I was told not to bring anything," I said, "but you can access it on your computer." I gave him the URL and the password, and he typed it into his laptop.

A close-up of Jason Harding's face filled the screen.

Before Malenkov could start the video, one of the guards standing behind him said something in Russian. Malenkov responded, and the two spoke for about a minute.

"This man Harding did business with my brother," Malenkov said. "He was in Narcotics, and Oleg paid him a lot of money to look the other way."

"Loyalty was never Harding's strong suit," I said.

Malenkov clicked on the video. I had edited it so that it started with Harding trying to bully his way out of a bad situation.

"You think you can get away with this, Corcoran?" he said. "You fucking drug me, kidnap me, and tie me up? I've got rights."

"Rights?" I said. "You think you're in the justice system? I didn't arrest you, asshole. I knocked you out with a dose of liquid ecstasy and brought you here. It's not exactly standard police work, and this is definitely not a police station. Are you tracking with me so far, Harding?"

"Fuck you. What do you want?"

"There's a bounty on your head," I said.

That threw him. He opened his mouth, but his brain wouldn't allow him to construct a complete sentence.

"What are you . . . Who . . . ?"

"You think you're the only ex-cop who works for Alboroto?" I said. "He wants you dead, and I could use the money."

"Dead? Why? I did everything he asked."

"But you fucked up, Harding. You left a witness at Malenkov's house."

"Bullshit."

"Did you check to see if there was anyone else in the house after you put a bullet through Oleg Malenkov's head?"

"You mean the wife?"

"No, asshole. The wife was part of the contract. Did you even think to look in the maid's room?"

I could see the fear in his eyes as he frantically flashed back and tried to reconstruct the murders.

"Don't bother trying to come up with an answer," I said, "because I know you didn't. So now Alboroto thinks this woman can identify you, and that's something he can't live with. Correction—it's something *you* can't live with."

"No, bro, please, you've got to tell him he's wrong. Nobody was in the house, and even if there was, they could never have seen me."

"Break it down for me," I said. "From the time you got to Brooklyn till the time you left."

"I got to Brooklyn about nine o'clock that night. I parked about eight blocks away from Malenkov's house and walked the rest of the way. I had the alarm codes, so getting in was easy."

"How did you get the alarm codes?" I said.

"Alboroto gave them all to me."

"All?" I said.

"The code for Malenkov's house and the ones for the other two Russian guys—I forget their names."

"You murdered two men and their families, and you can't remember their names?" I said.

"Fuck them," Harding said. "It's a job. I sleep nights."

"What did you do once you got into Malenkov's house?"

"I went upstairs to the master bedroom."

"That's probably where the maid saw you."

"Impossible. It was pitch black, and I put on my infrared goggles. I never turned on a light. Nobody fucking saw me."

"So you're in the bedroom," I said. "Where did you hide?"

"The wife's closet. It's the size of a goddam football stadium. I bury myself all the way in the back with the winter clothes, and I wait. About eleven o'clock, I hear them come in. They come straight upstairs. The TV goes on, and I can hear the water running in the bathroom. Finally, about 11:45, the TV goes off, and there's enough of a crack under the door to the closet that I can tell the lights are off. I give it another hour, and about one o'clock, I open the closet door, and they're both asleep. She's on her side, looking away from me. He's on his back, wearing this breathing contraption over his face."

"Oleg had sleep apnea," Malenkov said, hitting the pause button. "He didn't tell anybody, because he was embarrassed about wearing the mask. He said it made him look old and weak."

I nodded, grateful that Harding had given up a detail that only the killer could have known. Malenkov clicked the mouse, and Harding continued.

"I wanted to use a small caliber. It's all I needed at point-blank range. But Alboroto didn't just want them dead. He wanted them annihilated. So I brought an HK USP .45-cal. Shot them each through the head once. Made a fucking mess, but it's got a built-in suppressor, so it was pretty quiet. And that was that. I picked up the shells, went down the stairs in the dark—no maid, no witnesses, nobody. I bypassed the alarm and walked a few blocks to the next two houses. They were already sleeping, so I was done by three a.m. and I drove home. I don't know who this maid is, but you can tell Albor—"

Malenkov slammed the laptop shut.

"There's more," I said.

He held up a hand and shook his head. He'd seen enough. "There was no maid," he said.

"No," I said. "The only way I could get him to confess was to convince him that he was next on Alboroto's hit list, and that I could call off the dogs."

"You're a smart cop."

"I was. Now I'm just a private citizen working for an organization that wants to make Alboroto pay for what he's done to New York, and stop him from doing any more damage. But I can't do it without your help, and I'm running out of time."

"I don't know where el Portugués is, Mr. Corcoran, but I can connect you to the one person who does."

"Thank you."

"The information comes with a price," he said.

"Yes. You would like me to connect you to Jason Harding."

"You're a smart private citizen. Where is he?"

"Under lock and key. Give me a phone, and I can have him here in forty-five minutes."

He nodded, picked up the bottle of vodka, poured us each another round, and began speaking in Russian. The guards were enjoying it and started snickering. When he was done, he clinked my glass, and we both drank.

I had no idea what he said or what we were drinking to, but there was one thing I was sure of.

Deirdre was right. I closed well.

CHAPTER 54

MALENKOV CAPPED THE VODKA BOTTLE, and the brief celebration ended abruptly. "Give him a clean phone," he said to one of the two hulks who were standing guard.

One of them opened a wooden box that was sitting on Malenkov's desk. It had at least a dozen cell phones inside, and he reached in and handed me one.

"You said you could have Harding here in forty-five minutes," Malenkov said. "Make it happen." He handed me a Post-It note with our exact address written on it.

I opened the phone and dialed a number. "Please leave a message," a recorded female voice said.

I could picture the entire team sitting in the conference room, waiting to hear one of the four coded messages we had worked out.

I gave them the one they were hoping for. "I need an Uber," I said, then carefully read the address on the Post-It and hung up.

The guard who had handed me the phone took it from me, wrapped it in a handkerchief, put it on the floor, and stomped it with the heel of his boot. He then picked it up, unwrapped it, and dumped the crushed remains into a wastebasket.

"And now we wait," Malenkov said, getting up from his desk.

Of course we would wait. He didn't trust me any more than I trusted him, and he wouldn't make good on his end of the deal until I produced Harding. He left the room.

Phone Crusher and his equally menacing counterpart, whom I decided to christen Bone Crusher, stayed behind.

I sat calmly, the picture of confidence on the outside, but inside I was in fear for my life. When I worked undercover in Narcotics, the most terrifying moments for me came *after* a drug deal was done and I had to turn my back on a roomful of heartless killers, walk out the door, and pray that one of them wouldn't put a bullet through the back of my skull.

That dread was coursing through me now. If Malenkov had given my two babysitters orders to waste me, it would be near impossible to stop them. And when Redwood and Delaqua arrived at the compound, they, too, would be murdered. Harding, on the other hand, would get to live and spend the remaining days of his wretched life wishing he were dead.

Time dragged. I thought about Deirdre and wondered if we really would reunite on the other side. And then I thought about Kirsten and how I would have failed her. No, I decided, I had too much unfinished business to go down without a fight, and as soon as one of the guards reached for his weapon, I would rush them both and—

Malenkov came back. He said something in Russian, and one of the guards picked up a remote, and the feed from four security cameras popped up on a wall monitor.

I watched as the front gate to the estate opened and Trace Baker's Audi pulled in and stopped. The front and rear doors on the driver's side opened, and both Delaqua and Redwood got out of the car. Two guards took their place, and the car made its way toward the house.

"Your people will wait at the gate," Malenkov said. "When we're done, you take the car, pick them up, and never come back."

I watched as the Audi pulled up to the front door, and the guards brought Harding out. His hands were tied behind his back, and I couldn't see his eyes, but I could imagine the fear. They walked him into the house and closed the door. I knew it was the last time that I—or anyone else outside Malenkov's organization—would see him.

Malenkov nodded, and Phone Crusher turned the monitor off. Then he waved a hand, and the two Crusher brothers left the room.

"You've kept your end of the agreement," Malenkov said. "Now I'll keep mine."

He handed me another Post-It note. On the top, in block letters, it said "BEATRIZ." Below that was an address in Newark.

"Back in the day, el Portugués was willing to do business in person," Malenkov said. "He only would meet with the top people in the organization. Oleg and I had separate businesses to run, but we both knew we could depend on him. The meetings were usually face-to-face, and they were always cordial. And then one day, some punks—low-level assholes from an Albanian gang in the Bronx—found out who he was and kidnapped him. They knew there was a shipment of coke from Colombia that was going to one of the Italian families in New York. They said they'd kill him if he didn't give them the location of the drugs. He gave it up immediately."

"And now the Italians wanted to kill him," I said. "So he went underground."

"No," Malenkov said. "El Portugués had a spotless reputation to maintain. I knew him. He would die before he betrayed a client. Instead of telling them where the drugs were, he gave them the address of a Mafia warehouse in Brooklyn that was heavily guarded night and day. As soon as those idiot Albanian kids cut through the fence, they were caught, and all but two were killed. The remaining two were offered a deal. First one to give up where the rest of the gang was would live. They both yelled out the same address. The Italians shot them, drove to the Bronx, wiped out the rest of the gang, and saved el Portugués in the process. After that, he dropped off the face of the earth. The only way you can contact him now is to go through Beatriz."

"I'm guessing that's his wife or his girlfriend," I said.

Malenkov stood up. The meeting was over.

"No," he said, grinning. "It's his eighty-five-year-old mother."

CHAPTER 55

BAKER'S AUDI WAS WAITING FOR ME OUTSIDE, the motor idling, my old buddy Scarface looming over the driver's-side door, ready to send me packing.

"Go straight, get your friends, and no stops on the way," he said.

Another time, another place, and I might have said something like, "I'm flattered that you even think I have the balls to stop." But I'd decided early on that my bons mots were completely lost on Neanderthals.

I picked up Delaqua and Redwood, and the three of us drove out the front gate. Alive.

I programmed the address Malenkov had given me into the GPS, and rattled off a quick summary of what I'd found out.

"His mother?" Delaqua said, "The Bureau sent someone to Jersey to question her a few years ago. The agent came back and said she had dementia."

"She seems to have had a miraculous recovery," I said.

I called Ernie Greco, our senior analyst, and asked him to get us whatever he could find on Beatriz's house, the neighborhood, and anything else that might give us a clue about what we were heading into.

"It's not a house. It's a Catholic church," Ernie said, typing as he talked. "The Church of Saint Damasus."

"Saint who?" Delaqua said.

"Damasus. He was a Portuguese pope. No surprise. It's in the Iron-bound section of Newark, which has a heavy Portuguese population, and they hold a mass in Portuguese once a day. There are no 911 calls from or about the church in more than a decade, which is pretty amazing, considering that it's in a dicey part of town."

"What about their financials?" I said.

"Way ahead of you, Danny. Their balance sheet is in the green—way in the green. In fact, it's off the charts compared to the rest of the diocese." A pause, and then his voice got more animated. "Holy moly!"

"What have you got?" I said.

"You know what they say, follow the money. And it looks like a ton of it is being spent on this church. They filed a dozen construction permits in the past ten years. A lot of big-ticket items: new roof, new flooring, new elevator in the rectory, an industrial-strength facelift, and they totally upgraded the plumbing and electric. This is not collection-plate money, guys. We're talking tens of millions of dollars."

"I think I can guess where the money is coming from," I said. "What do you have on this woman Beatriz? Malenkov only gave us the address of the church. Does she live there?"

"Four priests live in the rectory. No women," he said. "I've got a roster of all their congregants. Six of them have the first name Beatriz. Can you give me a last name?"

"Try da Costa," Delaqua said.

"Got her," Ernie said. "She's eighty-five, lives in a one-bedroom apartment on Oliver Street two blocks from the church. Pays six hundred and forty-two dollars a month, which is a good chunk of her Social Security. She's not exactly a major benefactor. Last year, she donated ten bucks a week to the church, plus another fifty each at Christmas and Easter. She has less than six grand in a savings account, and another fourteen hundred in checking at the Lusitania Savings Bank on Pulaski Street in Newark."

"Check the Cayman Islands," Delaqua said.

Greco laughed. "I'm good, guys, but there are still some things I can't hack."

I thanked him and asked him to keep digging.

"That's crazy," Delaqua said as soon as I hung up. "I can't believe this man who's been smuggling guns, drugs, and blood diamonds all his life is using the money he makes to do God's work."

"Somebody is footing the bill for those renovations," I said, "and right now he's the leading candidate."

Thirty-five minutes later we drove down a quiet tree-lined street and parked in front of an imposing Gothic Revival church.

"Sweet Jesus," Redwood said.

In cop parlance, the subject did not fit the profile of the neighborhood. It was jaw-dropping. A century of industrial grime had recently been acid washed from the facade, and the towering limestone spires and statues of saints were immaculate, returned to their virgin state. Massive stained-glass windows sparkled in the midday sun.

"Should we send for backup, or do you think the three of us can take her down?" Redwood said.

"As much as I would like to meet the woman who spawned the man who has managed to elude police on four continents," Delaqua said, "I think three of us are two too many to interview one old lady. I'm too nasty and short-tempered, and . . ." He turned to Redwood and groped for the right word. "Chris, you're too . . ."

"Young and good looking?" Redwood said.

"That's not what I was thinking, but sure."

"Good call," I said, getting out of the car.

I had already made the decision to tell them I was going in alone, and I was glad that Frank beat me to it. He was learning.

CHAPTER 56

I ENTERED THE CHURCH through a pair of massive bronze doors. The inside was even grander than I had expected. Intricate mosaics on the walls, hand-forged iron chandeliers suspended above rows of polished oak pews, scores of ornate candlesticks, and on the ceiling, a museum-worthy fresco encircled by a wreath of gold leaf.

A priest was standing at the pink-veined marble altar, changing the numbers on the hymn board. As soon as he heard me come in, he stopped what he was doing, and walked down the aisle to greet me.

He was short, with thinning white hair, ears that were a little too big for his head, and a warm, toothy smile and an outstretched hand. "I'm Father Adriano," he said. "Welcome to Saint Damasus. I don't believe I've seen you here before."

"This is my first time," I said, not offering up my name. "What a beautiful church you have, Father. I saw on the cornerstone that it was built in 1892. The restoration is magnificent."

"A labor of love. It's too bad they couldn't refurbish an old priest," he said with a laugh. "How can I help you?"

"I'm here to meet with one of your parishioners."

"Ah, yes. Beatriz," he said. "She told me she was expecting a friend. She's tending the flowers in the memorial garden. Come. It's in back."

He escorted me outside and called out to a woman who was cutting spikes of purplish-blue flowers from a large plant. She waved a thank-you, and as Father Adriano quietly slipped away, Beatriz walked toward me.

I had envisioned a frail, gray, wrinkled octogenarian, but she was a robust woman with a carefully braided bun of black hair, skin that had a healthy glow, and a spring in her step that belied her age.

"I'm Danny Corcoran," I said. "Thank you for meeting with me."

"You can thank Fyodor," she said. "He told me you were a man of your word. How can I help you?"

"I need to get a message to your son."

"I can pass it on for you. Do you mind walking and talking? I still have some work to do. You can help. It will make you feel good."

There was a patch of land beyond the lush, well-tended garden, and as is the custom of many Old World churches, it had been designated as a graveyard.

Beatriz had filled a basket with large sprays of the flowers she had been cutting. "Lavender," she said. "It's the national flower of Portugal. My mother taught me all about them when I was a little girl. They are symbols of purity, devotion, and grace. And the fragrance is a gift from God that can heal your body and calm your soul."

She handed me a sprig, and I inhaled. It didn't calm my soul, but I thanked her all the same.

We began walking among the headstones, and I helped her place a small bunch of the mystical flowers on each grave. "What message would you like me to give to my son?" she said.

"I need him to do something I am sure he has never done in his life," I said. "I want him to stop one of his shipments from getting to its destination."

She turned and looked at me stone-faced.

"You saw what happened in Central Park two weeks ago," I said. "Over a thousand innocent people died, and the death toll hasn't ended."

She crossed herself. "Terrible," she said, "but how does that concern my son? He had nothing to do with it."

"I know. But Alboroto isn't done punishing New York, and he's using your son to help him do it."

"Punishing?" she said. "That's a harsh term. Alboroto is a businessman. He sells drugs. He doesn't force anyone to buy them. People do it of their own free will. He controls the drug trade, so ten days ago, he took all the cocaine off the market. When he finally brings it back, I'm sure he will make it much more costly for people to buy. But that's business, not punishment."

She began walking again, gently setting sprigs of lavender on each grave. And that's when I realized she had no idea what Alboroto had planned.

"Beatriz," I said. "Alboroto is not going to charge more. In fact, I would venture a guess that he will charge *less*. The city is drug starved, and he wants to flood the market again."

"So then the people will be happy," she said.

"For a few hours. Maybe a day. But then, one by one, their happiness will turn to horror. The cocaine you're helping Alboroto bring into New York is laced with methanol. And anyone who comes in contact with it will likely go blind."

She stopped, set down the basket, and put a hand to her mouth. I pressed harder.

"Beatriz, I don't know you, but I know that at heart you and your son are good people. How many millions of dollars have the two of you donated to restore and revitalize this church?"

"The money may be tainted, but it can still do God's work," she said.

"How do you think God will feel when a million people lose their sight? Not just the hard-core junkies, but also the casual users who find it hard to say no when someone offers them a line at a party, or when a friend at school convinces them to try it for the first time."

"My son and I knew nothing about this," she said, picking up her basket and moving on to the final row of graves. "Nothing."

"I believe you," I said. "Because you're right: marketing drugs is a business. But Alboroto has turned it into an act of vengeance so satanic that he had to keep it from you because neither you nor your son could ever be part of such evil."

I paused to let her process the potential devastation. She avoided my gaze and kept her eyes on the lush green mounds at her feet.

"But now you *do* know," I said. "And all I ask is that you take responsibility and help me stop the madness before it happens. I need to find that shipment before it's distributed. I promise, if I can meet your son I will not give up his identity. I will not compromise his safety. I will not betray your trust. Please . . . Beatriz, where is he?"

She stopped and set down her basket again. "My son is right here," she said as she gently spread the remaining lavender against a pure-white headstone.

The name carved into the marble was Fortunato da Costa. The date of his death was over eight years ago.

The eighty-five-year-old woman who knelt at his graveside wasn't a messenger. She was el Portugués.

CHAPTER 57

BEATRIZ KNELT AT THE GRAVE IN PRAYER for several minutes, head bowed, a strand of well-worn rosary beads in her hands. When she was finished, I extended my arm and helped her to her feet.

"I'm deeply sorry for your loss," I said.

"Thank you," she said. "Let's go to my apartment, where we can talk in private. I'll make us all a pot of tea."

"Us *all*?"

"You, me, and your two friends in the Audi."

She'd played me. "You installed security cameras outside," I said.

"State-of-the-art," she replied, and turned toward the church, not waiting for my reaction.

Ten minutes later, Delaqua, Redwood, and I sat at Beatriz's kitchen table and watched her mix milk, cinnamon, nutmeg, and honey in a saucepan and heat it. She poured fresh, hot black tea into four mugs and topped each one off with the sweet, creamy concoction.

"*Chá com leite.* Portuguese milk tea," she said. She followed up with a tray of pastries. "*Caramujo* and *douradinho.* Homemade. Enjoy."

Chris Redwood didn't need a second invitation. He dug in. Delaqua, on the other hand, sat quietly with a look in his eyes that I can best describe as starstruck. For decades, law enforcement agencies around the world had tried and failed to hunt down el Portugués. And now, here in a nondescript kitchen in Newark, New Jersey, sat disgraced former Special Agent Frank Delaqua, blithely sipping tea with the legend's mother. Take that, FBI.

Beatriz sat down and joined us. "Twelve years ago, Fortunato was diagnosed with a terminal illness," she said. "The doctors gave him eighteen months at most. He did what so many people do when they come to grips with their mortality. He took stock of his life."

She paused and sipped her tea. Her grief was palpable.

"He knew the business he was in," she said. "He may not have hurt people directly, but he helped others inflict pain, and now he wanted to make amends. He built five schools in Angola. Anonymously. It was costly, but he had always lived simply, and his earnings were wired to foreign banks, so he had the means."

She closed her eyes, went back in time, and smiled when she reopened them. "I believe that act of kindness not only brought him peace, but it helped keep him alive beyond the doctor's predictions. And then, ten years ago, the roof caved in."

None of this was information we needed, but we knew that it was what Beatriz needed to share with us. As frustrating as it was, we sat there in silence.

"It was January," she said. "The year of all those storms. Part of the church roof collapsed under the weight of the snow. The city ordered us to close the building until we had a new roof. The lowest bidder wanted eight hundred and fifty thousand dollars. The church didn't have that kind of money. But my son did. He gave them a million dollars, again anonymously. It made him feel so good to be helping people he knew and loved that he kept donating more. By the time he died, his bank accounts were almost dried up, and I knew that the only way I could continue restoring Saint Damasus was to become el Portugués."

"And you did an incredible job," Delaqua said. I knew he meant it.

"I never liked Alboroto," she said, switching gears effortlessly. "He's a bully. But this job was so important to him, and he was willing to pay so much that I couldn't say no. And after ten years, the renovation is almost complete, which meant that when it was over, el Portugués could finally retire. Would you like some more tea?"

"No, thanks," I said. "Please, go on."

"The plan was simple. Load a thousand kilos of cocaine onto the container truck at the lab and write that down on the manifest. Then add an equal amount of weight so we could offload the drugs at a blind spot along the route. When the container was weighed at Veracruz, it would still be a thousand kilos."

"But the drugs would be on a different container truck," I said.

"No. I told him to buy five new Mercedes G-Class SUVs at the factory in Mexico, remove the floor plates, and put a compartment in each one that would hold two hundred kilos."

"Damn!" Redwood blurted out.

Her eyes smiled at him. She knew a compliment when she heard one.

"Five Mercedes G's?" he said. "That's like a hundred grand a pop."

"A hundred and fifty," she said. "That doesn't stop a man like Alboroto."

"So the Mercedeses are waiting at some mountain pass, and the container truck unloads so fast that you'd never know he stopped," Redwood said, excited to finally unravel the solution to the puzzle. "Now the coke is in the G wagons, and they just drive to Veracruz and get on one of those roll-on/roll-off ships with thousands of other new cars right out of the factories. Am I right?"

"Almost. I knew you'd be following the truck to Veracruz, so I rerouted the cars to Tampico," she said, a hint of pride in her voice. "They arrived in Newark at ten o'clock this morning."

"Where are they going?" I asked.

"Five cars, five different distribution points. Manhattan, Brooklyn, Long Island, Jersey, and Connecticut."

"Can you give us specific locations? They have a six-hour head start. The drugs could be on the street by now."

"They're not," she said. "Alboroto never takes the coke directly to a cartel warehouse. When a shipment arrives, he moves it to a parking lot somewhere—the airport, a truck stop, the market at Hunts

Point—and then he watches it for twenty-four hours to make sure the cops weren't tipped off. If they have it under surveillance, he'll know. Only when he's positive it's safe does he bring it to the warehouse to be broken down and distributed."

"That's nuts," Delaqua said. "All those cokeheads out there dying to get their noses powdered, and he's just leaving a hundred million dollars' worth of blow sitting around a public parking lot?"

"Not this time," Beatriz said. "A car carrier picked up all five of them when they docked, and delivered them to a car dealer in Manhasset."

"Which one?" I said."

"Shelter Rock Motors, just off Northern Boulevard. It's one of the cartel's money-laundering fronts, but with this much product, Alboroto wants it under lock and key. If the guards decide the Feds or the DEA aren't watching them, the trucks will hit the road when the dealership opens in the morning."

"You're sure he won't move them out tonight?" I asked.

"Positive. He put me on a tight schedule because it absolutely had to be ready to go to market tomorrow."

"What so special about tomorrow?" I asked.

"It would have been his wife's sixtieth birthday."

CHAPTER 58

As soon as we got on the road, I called Trace. "And I thought I'd seen it all," he said when I told him about Beatriz.

"She gave us the VINs on the five cars, and I've memorized the last six digits of each. We're on the way to Manhasset. If any of them are there, we'll hit it tonight. I'll need a dozen more bodies."

"Done."

I dropped Delaqua and Redwood at a Hertz office, drove to the dealership, and parked Baker's Q7 in full view of the sales force inside. A saleswoman pounced on me as soon as I walked in. "Hi, I'm Kristy Kennedy."

"Tim Randall."

"And what brings you to Shelter Rock today, Tim?"

"I'm interested in the G-class SUVs."

"It's a fantastic car," she said. "Are you looking to trade in that Audi?"

"Oh, no. That one is mine. This is going to be a surprise for my wife."

"Oh, my goodness, Tim, what a lucky woman she is to have found you." I could practically see the wheels turning in her head. Kristy was a pretty lucky woman herself. She'd just hooked a live one.

"I have a G 550 right here on the floor, and it's fully loaded," she said, walking me toward it as she spoke.

I checked the VIN. Not on my list. I got behind the wheel and was listening to her extol the virtues of the state-of-the-art cockpit when Delaqua arrived. Redwood showed up a minute later, and each headed out to the vast parking lot of new and used cars, with a salesman in tow.

My target was the service area. Logic dictated it was the best place to secure the coke.

"I'm sold," I said to Kristy in the middle of her sales pitch. "My wife, Deirdre, is going to love this car."

"I can't wait to meet her."

"It's a surprise, so you won't get to see her till her first service appointment. Speaking of which, can I take a look at the setup back there?"

"Absolutely," she said, leading me to the promised land.

It was late, and most of the cars that would have arrived in the early morning rush were done and gone. I counted the service bays. Twelve. Three of them had cars on the lift that were probably going to spend the night. Only one still had a mechanic working on it.

And yet, there were eight other men in the area: one sweeping the floor, another cleaning tools, two more sitting at desks—every one of them trying their damnedest to look like they had something to do.

"As you can see, it's a state-of-the-art service center," Kristy said, using her go-to superlative for automotive excellence.

I tuned her out and let my eyes drift over to the cluster of five SUVs parked against the far wall. The eight men who were just hanging about were also looking in that direction, then shifting their gaze back to me.

"That blue one over there," I said, interrupting Kristy's spiel. "I think Deirdre would love the color. Do you mind if I get a closer look?"

"That one is already sold, but I can have her in one just like it in a couple of days," she said, steering me toward the sequestered vehicles.

Like sheepdogs protecting their flock from wolves, the eight men went on high alert. One of the two behind the desk got to his feet, and the sweeper began pushing his broom in my direction.

I ignored them, kept chatting with Kristy, and stopped at the car long enough to admire the gleaming blue finish. Then I glanced at the windshield and checked the VIN.

Jackpot. It was a match. And I was willing to bet that the other four members of the quintet were the Mercedes mules we'd been looking for.

"Perfect color," I said. "Let's do it."

She ushered me back to her desk and started the paperwork. I didn't blink at the price, but when she took me through the options, I held up a hand. "I had no idea I had so many choices. Wheels, upholstery, entertainment package—wow. Do you have something I could take with me so I can make an intelligent decision tonight over a glass of wine?"

"Absolutely," she said, handing me several brochures. "If you don't mind me asking, what's the gift occasion for your wife?"

"Deirdre is turning the big four-oh in two weeks. She's dreading it."

"Well, Tim, I can promise you she'll forget all about it when she sees this car sitting in her driveway."

I stood up. "Thanks," I said. "You've made my job a lot easier. I'll be back in the morning."

It was true. She had made my job a hell of a lot easier. I just didn't tell her that by "morning," I meant the middle of the night. And I wouldn't be coming back alone.

CHAPTER 59

ONCE AGAIN TRACE BAKER HAD DELIVERED. He had recruited twelve more combat-ready NYPD veterans—nine men and three women—and by seven p.m., we were all gathered around the conference table.

"First, thank you for coming," I said. "I've worked with you and trust you all. But this is going to be different. Look around. Except for one other man who will join us during the operation, this is the team. There's no backup, no support group. This won't be police work as you know it. This, as they say in the CIA, is Secret Squirrel shit. We will be risking our lives, breaking the law, going to prison if we get caught, and getting zero credit if we succeed."

"No problem, Danny." It was Brandon Mattingly. "As long as we can still get drunk together when it's over, we're in."

Laughs and head nods all around.

"Trace briefed you all on the big picture," I said. "Now I'm going to take you through a well-thought-out, finely tuned tactical plan, which I carefully crafted in the ninety minutes since we located the cocaine."

I threw a satellite photo of Shelter Rock Motors up on the big screen. "Here's the target," I said. "The showroom faces the main drag. The service department is in the rear, butting up against the ass end of a lumberyard, which will be our entry point."

I brought up a labeled schematic of the dealership. "There's only one vehicular entrance to the service area from the outside—an oversize accordion garage door," I said, highlighting it with my laser pointer. "A few feet away, there's an employee entrance door."

I moved the laser dot to the far wall of the service area, where I had added five colored squares. "Five factory-fresh Mercedes G-class cars, each holding two hundred kilos of coke. I was only able to confirm the VIN on the blue one, but the whole lot of them were so heavily guarded that we have to assume all five are dirty. We'll confirm the other four upon entry."

I slid the bright-red dot back to the employee entrance door. "This is where we get in. We're going to blow it open and immediately deploy flash-bangs. But first we need a distraction. Bob will take us through that."

Bob Beatty, another decorated marine, had spent most of his twenty-plus years in NYPD working auto crime. We could bring him a piece of a grille recovered at the scene of a hit-and-run, and just by eyeballing it he could give us the make, model, and year of the car we should be looking for. I had asked Trace to get me the best car guy in the business. Bob was that guy.

"There are three hundred twenty-seven vehicles in the parking lot and twelve in the showroom," he said. "This afternoon, using pinhole cameras, Chris Redwood and Frank Delaqua filmed the VINs on all of them. We already had the VINs on the five target cars. With that data, I was able to create virtual key fobs. I can now sit at my console and lock or unlock doors, start the engines, and set off the alarms of any piece of rolling stock on the lot. There's your distraction."

More head nods. I'd meant what I said. This was beyond anything they ever experienced with NYPD.

I stood up. "When I was there this afternoon, I saw eight hired guns in the service area," I said. "There will probably be more patrolling outside. I'm hoping that when fifty car alarms go off, at least half the guards will head for the chaos. That's when we blow the door, throw the flashbangs, and eliminate any resistance."

I threw a final slide on the wall—the five colored boxes, each one representing a car. Below each car were the names of two team members.

"Here are your assignments," I said. "Ten of us will be in the target vehicles. Five drivers, five shotguns. Yannick and Musto will be driving the transports that bring us there and get us home. Wiley and Ballard will be with Beatty in the electronics van."

I knew that seeing and hearing their names would add another dimension to the mission. We were a team, but now every individual's role was defined. I paused to let it sink in.

"Once the door blows and the enemy is neutralized, go to your assigned vehicle, confirm the VIN, and get in the car. Bob will have already opened the locks and started the engines. Chris and I will be in the lead car. I'll be behind the wheel, and he'll open the garage door. It's not very sophisticated. Green button, red button. Any questions?"

Karlina Padilla raised a hand. "Danny, methanol is volatile and flammable. Let's say we hit a pothole on the way to the disposal site. What are the odds of it lighting up?"

"Great question," I said. "This is where I am totally relying on the genius of Joaquín Alboroto. This shit has bounced along a couple of hundred miles of mountain roads in Mexico, been driven over speed bumps rolling onto the cargo ship, and been banged around at sea for the better part of a week. If he got it this far, I think we can drive it another eleven miles, potholes or no potholes."

Three hands shot up.

"Eleven miles?" It was Dennis Collins. "No matter which direction we go in, we'll still be in a pretty densely populated part of Nassau County. Are we burning it in somebody's backyard?"

"No." I told them the rest of the plan.

Silence followed by a few murmured "holy shits."

And then my fellow marine Chris Redwood pumped his fist in the air and let out a thunderous "Oorah!"

CHAPTER 60

I CAN'T BEGIN TO COUNT THE NUMBER of missions I've been on in over a quarter century as a member of the United States Marines and the New York City Police Department. But this one was unlike any that had gone before it.

I was a guardian without license. I had power without jurisdiction. Justification without authority. Some might say I was just another vigilante, as criminal as any of the lawbreakers I'd brought to justice, as misguided as any of the religious fanatics whose quests I had cut short.

And yet, as I sat there with five of my comrades in the Ford Transit cargo van, I knew in my heart that whether the world saw me as good or evil, this was the most important mission in my lifetime of public service.

We arrived at the lumberyard at 0130 hours. A bolt cutter was all it took to get through the front gate, and we pulled our trio of vans behind the warehouse.

Wearing goggles that transformed the moonless night into green-tinted day, ten of us, in black tactical vests and helmets, silently made our way to the chain-link fence that connected the property to the parking lot at the rear of Shelter Rock Motors.

Dennis Collins expertly cut through it and peeled back a section that would allow us to get in and out fast. As soon as he stepped away, I signaled Beatty in the electronics van.

Within seconds, the night resounded with the clamor of car alarms coming from every vehicle parked in front of the building. The racket served two purposes. First, it drew four of the guards to come running through the showroom door. It also muffled the sound of four gunshots as Redwood and Mattingly, our two best shooters, took out the million-candlepower floodlights that had lit up the entire front end of the complex.

Staying in a tight formation, our entry team double-timed across the rear parking lot and lined up alongside the service employees' entrance door. Ryan, a twenty-five-year veteran of the NYPD Bomb Squad, rigged it with just enough explosive-packed det cord to blow the door without taking down the entire wall.

At least four guards were still inside the service area. I signaled Beatty a second time, and with a few keystrokes, all twelve cars on the showroom floor suddenly sprang to life.

The men who remained in the service area would either respond to the chorus of roaring engines or not. Either way, they'd be distracted. Ryan triggered the fuse, and the metal door flew off its hinges, launched across the room, and ripped through the roof of some hapless customer's top-of-the-line S-class sedan.

Before the guards had time to react, we lobbed three percussion grenades into the room. We were wearing earplugs. They weren't. The sound would totally disorient them and, if we were lucky, blow out a few of their eardrums. But they wouldn't be deaf for long. We raced in, and before they could get off a single shot, we surgically eliminated every guard who had stayed behind to safeguard the drugs.

I signaled Beatty to start the five SUVs we came for.

"Danny!" It was Redwood, his voice filled with an ominous urgency. I turned, and he didn't have to say another word. The guards had been one step ahead of us. Sometime after I left the dealership that afternoon, they had brought in a fifty-ton wrecker capable of lifting a city bus and parked it broadside across our exit door. There was no way we could move it.

"Plan Bravo!" I yelled. "Plan Bravo!"

By now our four drivers were already in their assigned cars, which meant they had checked and confirmed the VINs. We were now in control of the drugs. But we were trapped inside the building.

The only way out was through the showroom. There were two problems. First, we'd be running into a barrage of bullets from the guards who had run in that direction when we set off the alarms. And second, the doors from the showroom to the street were designed for people, not three tons of metal, glass, and volatile cocaine.

I knew that the cars on the showroom floor had all entered the building from the rear and had been carefully driven through an interior set of electronic pocket doors that separated sales from service. I ran toward them, reached for the control panel, and punched the green button.

Nothing.

I hit the button again.

And then a joyful electronic *thunk.* As the doors began to part, I could see the flashing lights and smell the exhaust of all the vehicles Beatty had started. And I could hear the sound of automatic weapons as the rest of Alboroto's crew came racing toward us.

I ran for the blue Mercedes and got behind the wheel. Redwood was already in the passenger seat, his window down, firing into the darkness.

If I had to guess, I would say that on a normal day the speed limit on the polished marble floor at Shelter Rock Motors was about three miles an hour. This was not a normal day. I gunned it and immediately clipped the rear end of a silver-gray GLC coupe. It was too dark to see where it wound up, but I could hear the loud crunch of metal on metal as it careened into yet another German-engineered masterpiece.

Redwood, an action junkie to the core, was in his element, yelling, "Go, go, go, go, go!"

I veered to the left, barreled through a block of sales cubicles, and had executed a perfect turn around the marble reception desk when a bullet tore through our front windshield.

"You okay?" I yelled.

"Never better," Redwood said as he leaned out of his window and strafed the forty-foot-wide sheet of glass that separated us from the outside world. Thick shards came cascading down on our hood and roof as the window opened up and became our doorway to freedom.

I plowed through the opening, the other four cars right behind me, the open road in front, and a hail of bullets coming at us from all angles.

I ripped through a manicured patch of grass doing fifty, hopped the curb, and as my wheels slammed down onto Shelter Rock Road, Redwood let out another whoop. "This fucking thing is a beast!"

I dropped to the speed limit to give the rest of the team time to catch up. One, two, three sets of headlights fell into place behind me. I slowed to a crawl and keyed my radio. "Team Leader to Team Five, what's your status?"

No answer.

"Does anyone have an eye on Five?" I said.

Collins, in Car Four, responded. "We were already on the street, and I could see some of Alboroto's men making their way to a car. Team Five stopped to take them out. Permission to double back and assist."

Before I could answer, Delaqua's voice cut in. "Thanks, but no assistance necessary. Team Five needed a little extra time to neutralize the rest of our welcoming committee."

"Outstanding, Team Five," I said. "What's your location?"

"We're about six blocks behind you, Team Leader," Delaqua said. "And there's nobody behind us." He paused. "At least, not yet."

Not yet. He was right. We'd made it this far, but we weren't out of the woods. Alboroto would have had his watchdogs calling in a status report every thirty minutes. As soon as they failed to check in, he'd scramble another team and hunt us down.

And it wouldn't take them long. Knowing Alboroto, he would have planted multiple tracking devices in each of the cars, including in the one place we couldn't disarm it: the compartment under our floor plates.

The best we could do was outrun him and destroy the drugs before his next assault. Easier said than done. If I were still a cop, I could call on a unit of hazmat specialists who would meticulously remove every granule of coke, load it into an EPA-approved hazardous-waste transport vehicle, and escort it to a safe facility where it could be stored, tested, held as evidence for trial, and eventually incinerated. The entire process could take years.

But I wasn't a cop. I had hours, not years. And I couldn't think of a single place where I could burn this poison without contaminating the air for miles around.

Fire was out of the question. That left only one other option. Water. Specifically, the bottom of the Atlantic Ocean.

CHAPTER 61

ANDERS THORDSEN SPENT HIS ENTIRE CAREER as a cop patrolling the 150 miles of New York City's waterways. When he pulled the pin after thirty-five years with the NYPD Harbor Unit, the department gave him a memorable sendoff: helicopters, bagpipes, and, of course, fireboats shooting arcs of water in the air.

His farewell speech was short and memorable. He thanked a lot of people, and then he closed with this: "And for those of you who have been asking me what I'm going to do next, here's my answer. Tomorrow I'm buying a ferry."

I never dreamed we'd be working together again. Earlier that night, I had called him and told him what I needed.

"I'm in," he said.

"We're going to run into some really bad dudes who are going to try to stop us," I said.

He laughed. "I'm armed."

"And we have absolutely no jurisdiction. What I'm asking you to do is totally against the law."

"Sorry, Danny," he said. "But dropping five cars and a ton of cocaine into the deepest part of the ocean sounds like God's work to me."

His boat, *Forever Blue*, was perfect for the job. Anders wasn't interested in ferrying fun-lovers to Nantucket, Martha's Vineyard, or Fire Island. He was much happier moving excavators, concrete mixer trucks, and other construction vehicles from the mainland to the islands and back.

"Best place to rendezvous is Garvies Point Road in Glen Cove," he said. "There's a boat launch adjacent to Mercadante Beach. At that hour of the night, the whole area will be deserted, but I'll wait offshore just to be safe. You call me when you're fifteen minutes out. I'll pull up onto the beach, drop my ramp, and you can drive right on. With five cars, we can be underway in less than a minute."

"Where can we get rid of them?" I asked.

"I'd like to take the whole lot to the Marianas Trench, which is seven miles straight down," he said. "But it would take us about a month to get there."

"What's our second choice?"

"There's a spot out past Montauk. It's only a hundred and fifty feet deep, but it's an old unexploded-ordnance field, so once we scuttle the cocaine, nobody's going to try to recover it. By the time it hits bottom, the pressure of the water should burst the packaging, and the coke will slowly leech over time."

"So it'll kill some fish," I said.

"I doubt it," Anders said. "It's been a government-sanctioned hazardous-waste disposal location for more than forty years, so fish and smart people don't go near it."

"How long will it take us to get to the drop point?" I asked.

"If we can get underway by oh-two-hundred, we can be there by sunrise."

That was the plan. And our caravan of bullet-riddled Mercedes SUVs arrived at Garvies Point and rolled onto the *Forever Blue* by 0153. We were seven minutes ahead of schedule.

"The less weight the boat is carrying, the faster we can get where we're going," Anders reminded me when we were laying out the tactics. "I can offload a nine-thousand-pound forklift and another fifteen hundred pounds of nonessential equipment. You can help if you cut back on crew."

He was right. I decided that five of us—Redwood, Delaqua,

Mattingly, Padilla, and I—could handle whatever Alboroto threw at us. Yannick would take one of the cargo vans and pick us up in Montauk when the mission was completed. Everyone else would return to base.

As soon as we were underway, we covered the five SUVs with tarps, opened our vests, and helped ourselves to the food and drinks Anders had brought.

Redwood, Padilla, and Mattingly ate first. Delaqua and I stood on the deck and kept watch.

"Thanks, Frank," I said.

Delaqua looked at me. "For what?"

"You bought us some time. If you hadn't gone back and taken out the rest of those guards, Alboroto would have been on us that much sooner."

"Hey, I couldn't walk away with two of them still standing," he said. "You know how I hate loose ends."

"Well, it still took balls. Well done," I said, and patted him on the back.

He doubled over and dropped to his knees.

"Frank!" I said.

He looked up at me and smiled through the pain. "Sorry, boss."

I looked at my hand. It was covered with blood. I grabbed my knife and sliced open his shirtsleeve, knowing what I would find even before I shined a light on it. The round had entered his left shoulder from the rear, but there was no exit wound. The bullet was still inside him, continuing to do more damage long after it had stopped.

"You should be in a fucking hospital," I said.

"No," he said. "I'm exactly where I'm supposed to be, Danny. I started this war with Alboroto. I have the death and destruction of so many lives on my conscience. I'm not quitting until I make this right."

I wanted to scream at him. I wanted to throttle his arrogant, self-centered ass for compromising the operation and for putting his need for redemption above our mission.

But I couldn't. Or at least, I didn't. The best I could do was live with his stupid mistake and pray to God that it wouldn't get us all killed.

CHAPTER 62

KARLINA PADILLA AND I CLEANED AND DRESSED Delaqua's wound. We both had enough medical training to know that what we'd done was rudimentary—a battlefield Band-Aid.

Delaqua was upbeat through it all. He assured us repeatedly that if the bullets started flying, he'd have our six, and waxed poetic that dumping a hundred million dollars' worth of Alboroto's blow into the briny deep would be the culmination of his career in law enforcement.

"Do you think the lead poisoning has gone to his brain already?" Padilla asked when we were alone, "Or are all FBI agents delusional douchebags?"

I smiled. "Dealer's choice," I said.

"I can kick myself," she said.

"For what?"

"My partner got shot, Danny. How did I miss it?"

"You didn't miss it," I said. "He covered it up. Now, stop thinking about it and get your head in the game."

She nodded and looked up at the stars. "There's a lot of sky up there, Danny," she said. She lowered her head and scanned the horizon. "And a lot of sea. And here we are, sitting ducks. Do we have a plan?"

"Yeah, but it's not original. I borrowed it from Sun Tzu. 'Let your plans be dark and impenetrable as night, and when you move, fall like a thunderbolt.'"

"Translation, please."

"They're not going to drop a bomb and sink us. Their orders will be to board us, kill us, and retrieve the cars," I said. "Our plan is simple: when they get here, fight like hell."

"One question," she said. "If the cars are all they're after, why don't we just roll them down the ramp right here? There's plenty of water."

"And there are plenty of people traveling this waterway night and day. We don't know the toxic effects of these drugs. Dropping them right here might be the equivalent of leaving them in a hole under Times Square. Anders came up with an area east of Montauk that's already a designated hazardous-waste zone. That's the target."

"Pretty narrow target," she said.

"We're not looking for a bull's-eye. It's about sixteen square miles, so we've got some wiggle room."

Nobody slept. Even in the middle of the night, the Long Island Sound is well trafficked—pleasure craft, barges, and, of course, fishing boats, both private and commercial. We each took our assigned positions and checked and crosschecked every vessel that entered our field of vision.

We were passing the Montauk lighthouse into open sea when Mattingly called out, "Large fishing vessel at ten o'clock."

I trained my binoculars on the boat. It was a late-model trawler, casting a wide wake as it cut through the waves at high speed.

Anders was in the wheelhouse. I yelled up from the deck. "She's coming pretty fast, isn't she?"

"And straight at us," he said. "I'm changing course."

We made a hard turn to port. The trawler turned toward us.

I had no doubt. This was it.

"Positions!" I ordered.

The team regrouped against the gunwale on the port side while I climbed up to the wheelhouse and locked a hundred-round belt into my M60E6 machine gun. "On my go," I yelled.

The trawler bore down on us, emerging as a shadow against the dark sky, lights off, engines roaring and coughing up billows of thick black diesel smoke. I thought of what Padilla had said earlier. "Sitting ducks" was an understatement. All that was missing was the theme music from *Jaws*.

We waited.

The trawler was still outside our effective kill zone when I heard a loud boom and the distinctive whistle of a .50-caliber bullet as it traveled through the air. It was followed by the scream of metal against metal as it ripped through the rear end of the ferry. The round had struck nearly thirty feet from where any of the team was positioned. I had no idea what he had been aiming at, but I knew one thing for sure: Alboroto didn't hire snipers who missed.

I looked up at Anders. He knew exactly where the bullet had hit. "He took out the motor for the stern ramp. We won't be able to—"

Another bullet hissed by. This one shredded the motor at the front end of the ferry.

"He knows what he's doing, Danny. He just took out the other one. We can't offload these cars unless we can drop one of those ramps."

"Is there a manual override?" I asked.

"Yes, you can crank it by hand, but you'll be totally exposed."

"How far are we from the drop zone?"

"At this rate, twenty minutes," Anders said. "I can give her more throttle and get us there in fifteen, but this old bucket will seize up if I push her too hot and too long. And if that happens, we're fucked."

"Do your best!" I yelled at him. "We'll buy you as much time as we can."

The engine strained, and the lumbering craft lunged forward.

I zeroed my scope on the trawler: 1,300 yards out . . . 1,250 . . . 1,200 . . . "Light 'em up!" I barked, and in Sun Tzu's words, the five of us finally unleashed the thunderbolt.

CHAPTER 63

THE NEXT FIFTEEN MINUTES were the longest fifteen minutes of my life. I'd been in my share of firefights, but I had always felt I would walk away and live to fight another day. Not this one. For the first time in my career, I had the sobering thought that our journey had escalated into a suicide mission.

I had never been prouder to lead people into battle. With tracers lighting up the last gasps of darkness, and bullets buzzing past their heads, my team of four bravely stood their ground while our virtuoso sea captain jockeyed his graceless craft through the water.

We were the Baltic Avenue Group, funded by four billionaires and able to tap into law enforcement resources around the world. The day before, I was on a $36 million submarine capable of accessing the Department of Defense's global armament network. Now my resources had dwindled down to five ex-cops on a twenty-year-old ferry that was bought with a dream and one man's retirement savings.

Alboroto's men outnumbered us, outgunned us, and pretty soon would outrun us and kill us. But I'd made a decision. If Anders Thordsen could get us to the drop zone, our last act would be to somehow, some way, take those five cars down to the ocean floor with us.

Early morning light was just breaking over the horizon when

Anders pushed a button on his console, and the *Forever Blue* belched three loud horn blasts that cut through the incessant sound of gunfire.

We had arrived.

I parkoured from the wheelhouse to the roof of a Mercedes, to the deck below and rolled to the gunwale.

"As soon as Anders turns the boat, I need you guys to cover me with as much suppressive fire as you can," I said. "Once he's positioned the rear ramp between me and the bullets, I'm going to lower the forward ramp by hand."

I signaled, Anders spun the wheel, and hundreds of spent shell casings rolled across the deck as the ferry leaned into a hard right turn. She had almost righted herself when Delaqua yelled, "I got this!" then jumped in front of me and squirreled his way toward the manual override.

I didn't have time to vent the anger that exploded inside my head. I turned and joined Redwood, Maddingly, and Padilla as they sprayed the trawler with automatic fire.

Delaqua dived to the floor and squeezed behind an iron column that supported a six-foot-wide stretch of roof built to protect the crew from the elements. He found the oversized handle that would allow him to lower the ramp by hand, inserted it into the mechanism, and started cranking.

"He's wounded," Redwood said. "He's not going to be able to get it down on his own."

"Stay where you are!" I yelled. "Your job is here."

The ramp had been stuck at an eighty-degree angle, its highest position, and Frank, grunting like a powerlifter, began to lower it. With our boat pitching, it would be difficult for Alboroto's men to tell that the giant steel plate was inching its way down, but as it cleared sixty degrees, they realized what was happening. They fired another .50-caliber, this time at Frank. It took a chunk out of the iron column, but he was wedged so deeply into his nook, and the trawler was rocking so unpredictably on the swells, that he would be hard to pick off.

The shooting stopped, and without warning, the enemy backed off. I looked up at Anders, still safe in the wheelhouse that we had outfitted with ballistic shields before the onslaught.

"The only way they can keep us from outmaneuvering them is to stop us," he yelled. "They're getting ready to drag the net. If it snags our engine, it'll foul the prop and then we're dead in the water."

The ramp was now at a forty-five-degree angle, but Frank, who was bleeding through his bandages, was depleted. He stopped and wiped the bloody gashes where the flying shrapnel had chopped up his face.

The trawler found a spot fifty yards ahead of us, lined up perpendicular to the *Forever Blue*, and then, plowing ahead, dragged its net straight across our path. I braced myself for the sickening sound of our engine as it caught up in the net, choked, sputtered, and died.

But all I heard was Anders letting out a victory whoop in his native Swedish. We had cleared the net.

This time.

I looked over at Delaqua, both hands back on the crank, slowly making headway with whatever strength he had left in his arms.

Somehow, he managed to lower the ramp to thirty degrees as the trawler made a second pass across our bow.

They failed again, but this time Anders wasn't cheering.

"They went too fast the first time," he called out. "The pilot adjusted his speed on the second pass, and he missed us by a few feet. If we can't get that ramp down this time around, we'll be caught up in that net like a school of bluefish."

"It's not budging," Frank called back. "It's jammed."

We were out of range as the trawler swung around to try again. I raced across the deck and put all my body weight against the crank. With a violent crack, it gave way, and I lurched forward. But the ramp didn't move. The only thing I had managed to do was snap the crank.

I looked up at Frank Delaqua, blood dripping from his hands, his face, and the open wound on his shoulder. His eyes were fixed on the trawler as it came about for one more run. And then he looked at me.

"Best damn job I ever had," he said. "Thanks, Danny."

He sprinted toward the cluster of pockmarked Mercedeses and yelled up at Anders. "Hold your course! When they cross your bow, don't turn away."

He climbed into the blue car at the front of the pack, and it roared to life. At first, I thought it was an ingenious plan—hit the ramp just hard enough to knock it off its hinges, jam the brakes, and then try to push the cars into the water before we were boarded.

I waited for him to move, but he held fast, eyes riveted on the trawler. And then it dawned on me. The same sharpshooter I had watched put a perfect shot group in the target at a hundred yards that first morning in Matamoras, Pennsylvania, was lining up his next shot. But this time the target was moving. And this time he wasn't firing bullets. He was launching a guided missile.

He timed it perfectly. Seconds before the trawler crossed our path, Delaqua revved the engine, dropped the legendary high-performance car into low gear, and gunned it. The smell of burnt rubber filled my nostrils as he catapulted across a short runway of about thirty feet. His front tires caught the incline, and the Mercedes lofted into the air as its rear end ripped the giant metal ramp clean off the boat and into the water.

I will forever hold that single image in my visual memory bank. Like a modern-day Evel Knievel, Frank Delaqua, sitting behind the wheel of the battle-scarred Mercedes, was airborne, sailing over twenty feet of blue water, backlit by the blinding rays of a red, orange, and gold morning sun.

And then it was over. The Mercedes came down hard on the trawler's wheelhouse. Every piece of electronic equipment on the bridge erupted in a supernova of sparks, igniting the fuel that surged from the ruptured gas tank.

The trawler was instantly engulfed in flames, and within seconds they found their way to the methanol-infused cocaine. A hundred-foot fireball shot straight up into the air, and we hit the deck as debris flew in every direction.

I could hear the grinding of gears as Anders threw his engine into full reverse, managing to avoid colliding with the trawler, which had listed to its port side and was taking on water fast.

There were no survivors.

Anders killed the engine, and in the eerie morning stillness, Redwood, Mattingly, Padilla, and I silently pushed the four remaining cars over the side, to rot forever in their watery hell.

CHAPTER 64

NOBODY KNEW. Not the ineffectual pompous-ass mayor. Not the bumbling, self-righteous police commissioner. And certainly not the unsuspecting public.

The evidence was buried at sea. The chaos at the car dealership would be swiftly and expertly covered up by the cartel. The heroism of Francis Michael Delaqua would go unrecognized, but Kaori made sure it did not go unrewarded.

A certificate commemorating his sacrifice in the line of duty was hand-delivered to his only surviving relative, a brother in Hawaii. And on behalf of a grateful nation, a sizable, but untraceable, sum of money went along with it. That was the hallmark of the Baltic Avenue Group: awesome power tempered with deep compassion, wrapped in absolute secrecy.

One day after the greatest drug bust in the history of mankind, the Russians reopened the supply chain. Fresh product from Colombia returned to the streets, the clubs, and the usual haunts of cocaine-addicted New Yorkers. Blow had returned, and once again all was right in the city that never sleeps.

Cloaked in anonymity, a handful of ex-cops had broken every law in the book and saved the lives of so many. But there was no celebration.

We had lost one of our own. And I had failed my family. Deirdre's sister Kirsten was still behind bars awaiting trial.

I commiserated with Redwood over a beer.

"It's a county jail," he said. "How hard can it be to break her out?"

For the first time in more than twenty-four hours, I laughed. "Thanks, 007," I said. "I needed that."

"You need a lot more than that, bro," he said. "You've got to stop torturing yourself."

"What is that supposed to mean?"

"Hey, just because I'm young and incredibly good looking doesn't mean I'm stupid. We had Jason Harding. How we got him was illegal as fuck, but given enough time, we could have talked him into meeting with the DA, copping to Phil's murder, and spilling everything he had on Alboroto in exchange for a reduced sentence."

"We didn't exactly have the luxury of time," I said.

"I know. But you're still blaming yourself for turning Harding over to Malenkov instead of the DA. You're thinking you gave up Kirsten's shot at freedom to make a deal with the devil. You're forgetting that the devil told us how to find el Portugués, and we wound up keeping a couple of hundred thousand Seeing Eye dogs from getting work in New York City."

"The most frustrating part of this whole fiasco is that Kirsten is in jail for a murder she didn't commit," I said. "And I have the killer on video admitting he did it, but I can't take it to the DA without getting thrown in jail myself."

"I remember that from law school," Redwood said. "The justice system tends to frown on confessions when the confessor is kidnapped, drugged, and tied to a chair. Look, Danny, you made the right decision. And I will bet you a truckload of Bitcoins that if you tell Kirsten what went down, she'll agree in a heartbeat."

She did. Of course she did.

"Deirdre would have made the same call," she said. "So would my dad."

"Maybe, but I'm the one who did," I said, "and I'm sorry."

"Don't be," she said, her smile warm and consoling.

We were sitting in a visitation booth, a thick piece of Plexiglas between us, phones pressed to our ears. She'd lost weight, but she hadn't lost hope.

"Look, I don't know when I'll get to see my kids. I don't know when I'll get back to my life. But I do know this. I didn't kill my husband. And now that you've told me who did it and that there might be a video of it somewhere, I have faith in you. You'll find it."

"I won't stop looking until I do," I said.

But my team had already searched every inch of Harding's apartment, his office, and his car. Marina had tapped into his computer, accessed his cloud storage, and combed through every file on his phone. So far, we'd found nothing.

And we were fast running out of places to look.

CHAPTER 65

THE DINNER HONORING LUCIANA AND SEBASTIÁN ALBOROTO was by invitation only.

Of course, those who had received the card announcing the event knew that it was hardly an invitation. It was a summons, a command performance, and not to attend would be to insult a man for whom disrespect was punishable by death.

And so they came, the lofty and the lowly; the politicians, the judges, and the police; the field workers, the packers, and the enforcers—more than three hundred loyalists, the lifeblood of Joaquín Alboroto's empire.

As instructed, no one wore black. This was not a wake, not a memorial. It was an evening for Joaquín Alboroto to celebrate the lives of his wife and son with food, drink, music, and a stunning announcement.

It was all a ruse.

Alboroto was still reeling from the economic disaster that had rocked his business. The attack on Central Park cost tens of millions. Another hundred million was now resting at the bottom of the Atlantic Ocean. And it had cost him hundreds of millions more to convince his distributors to stop selling drugs.

His resources were depleted. It would take months to get his production back up to speed. The sharks already smelled blood in the water, and the Colombians, Peruvians, and Bolivians were circling, trying to fill the gaping void in the market before he could recover.

Tonight, he would send them all a message: *I am as rich and powerful as ever.* The party would be lavish. And at the end of the evening, he would announce his plans to build a glorious art museum for Luciana, and a state-of-the-art sports stadium to honor Sebastián.

He would project spectacular architectural drawings onto the giant screen at the front of the room. And finally, he would reveal the budget for both structures: five hundred million dollars. It was money he didn't have, but his enemies didn't know that, and this show of strength would make them think long and hard before they tried to upset the balance of power.

In time, he would cripple them all. He would also track down and kill the mercenaries who destroyed his cocaine. He knew that they were only hirelings, soldiers of fortune. The real enemy was those who had funded their operation. He would find them as well and turn their final days on earth into an eternity of pain.

But tonight, there would be no thoughts of revenge. Tonight, Alboroto mingled among his guests as they wined and dined in the grand ballroom of la Casa de la Fortuna.

A hundred years earlier, the building had been the headquarters of the largest bank in Mexico. That heritage had been carefully preserved when it was transformed into a banquet hall, and the space was still dominated by towering stone columns, stained-glass windows, hand-carved paneled walls, and flickering copper gas lamps.

At ten p.m., as his guests sipped Gran Patrón Platinum and puffed on Cohiba Robustos, Alboroto walked to the front of the room, to cheers and thunderous applause.

The room was filled to capacity. No one would even dare go to the bathroom while *el Jefe* spoke. All activity in the kitchen stopped, and the entire staff filed into the dining room and stood in silence. All except one busboy, who slipped out a back door and sent a single-word text.

Ahora. Now.

Inside the vast ballroom, Alboroto addressed the crowd. He spoke without notes, the tribute to his wife and son pouring from his heart. Less than three minutes into the homage, the first salvo came hurtling through the windows.

Grenades.

Most people are familiar with the fragmentation grenades used by the military—the kind that explode when detonated, sending steel shrapnel flying in every direction. These were incendiary grenades—fire starters packed with magnesium, napalm, and phosphorous.

They landed on tables, on the carpeting, and, one of them, on the lap of a bank president, each igniting to a white-hot two thousand degrees, cremating whatever it touched and sending a shower of fire into the crowd.

Alboroto watched as a few brave souls tried to beat out the flames with tablecloths, jackets, or whatever else they could grab. He knew that their efforts would do nothing but add fuel to the blaze. He turned his eyes to the front of the room. Men in dinner jackets and women in embroidered gowns clawed at the exits, unable to get out.

He waited for the doors to fly open and his security team to burst in.

Nothing.

Which meant they were dead.

His mind raced. There must be a way out. There was always a way out.

And then the miracle happened. A geyser of water cascaded down from the ceiling.

He looked up. The sprinkler system. Old, but still functional. *Agua fria* pelted his face. Mouth wide open, he could taste the rust as the life-saving water that had been sitting in those pipes for years hit his tongue.

He would survive. He would live to fight another fight. *Next time,* he thought, *I will not underestimate my enem . . .*

The ancient pipes sputtered and began coughing up air instead of water. Once, twice, three times, until finally, they rattled and belched, releasing another torrent of liquid.

But this was not water. It was gasoline. The walls erupted as the high-octane fuel hit the gas lamps.

Joaquín Alboroto was a fighter, but he was also a realist. This time, there was no escape. The smoke was so thick that he could barely see the destruction around him. But he could feel the intense heat, hear the screams, smell the burning flesh.

In his final moments, all he wanted was to know who had done this to him. There were the enemies he had made over the past fifty years. There were the allies who were ready to turn on him because he had upset the delicate ecosystem of the drug culture. There was even the possibility that some of his own men, who appeared to be loyal, might have—

With a loud *whoosh*, his gasoline-drenched suit ignited, and like thousands of his victims before him, el Carnicero, one of the most feared men on the planet, died screaming in pain.

Outside the building, a camera crew filmed the blaze. Their credentials stated that they were local press, but the footage would never be seen on Mexican TV. It was being transmitted to a private server in Brighton Beach, New York, where it was being screened by Fyodor Malenkov, who was still grieving over the death of his brother Oleg.

"I've seen enough," Malenkov said in his native Russian to one of his lieutenants. "Turn it off. I've got a business to run."

CHAPTER 66

I CAN'T REMEMBER ANYONE EVER CALLING ME in the middle of the night with good news. But there's a first time for everything.

The sound of Metallica blasting from my work phone jolted me awake. I squinted at the caller ID. Sergeant Inés Bolano calling from Mexico.

"Inés," I said, my voice fuzzy, my body still clinging to the last vestiges of sleep.

"Danny, I'm sorry to call so late," she said.

"S'okay. Wassup?" I slurred.

"Joaquín Alboroto is dead."

"When? How? Who?" I sat up and threw my feet over the side of the bed. I was wide-awake.

"A few hours ago. He was hosting a big party. Whoever did it locked the doors, firebombed the building, and when the sprinklers went on, there was gasoline in the pipeline. The fire is still raging. No survivors. Hundreds dead. From what we know, everyone from his organization was there. Not just the workers, but every judge, every cop, every politician he had in his pocket. It's over, Danny." She paused. "The Alboroto cartel is wiped out." Another pause. "Forever."

"Do you know who did it?"

"Not yet, but check your Twitter feed. Everybody has a theory: a rival cartel, the CIA, the Federales. And you'll love this: some people are saying your mayor and Police Commissioner Ennis organized the whole thing. Hashtag NYC Payback."

"Hashtag Never Happen," I said. "Those two guys couldn't piss downhill if they were standing on a ladder. If they tried to organize a firebombing, Alboroto would still be alive, and they would both be burnt to a crisp."

I could hear a chorus of laughter behind her.

"Sounds like I've got an audience," I said. "Who's there?"

"Vadillo, Ordóñez—all the usual suspects."

"Hey, guys. I don't care what the internet thinks. My best guess is, the Russians did it."

"Do you have an address for them?" Inés asked.

"They're in Brooklyn, but it's a little bit out of your jurisdiction."

"Oh, we don't want to arrest them," she said. "We just wanted to send them a couple of cases of tequila."

More laughter. Me included.

"Guys, I can't begin to tell you how great this news is," I said. "Thank you all for your help and your cooperation. If there's anything I can ever do for you in return, let me know."

We said our goodbyes, and I hung up wishing I had been able to share my good news with them, but I couldn't. Only the handful of us involved in the operation knew about it, and that's as far as it would ever go.

I looked at the clock on my night table. 3:13 a.m. The world as I knew it had just become a safer place. I never had any doubt that Alboroto had plans to come back to New York again and again and again. He would continue to murder innocent people, and I would feel the burden of their deaths weighing heavily on me because I had failed to stop him.

But now he was dead, his entire organization wiped out. "Forever," I said out loud, trying to capture the same somber joy that was in Inés's voice when she said it.

I closed my eyes and took several deep breaths. I could practically feel the weight being lifted off my chest.

Now I could devote all my energy to figuring out how to get Kirsten out of jail. But first, I needed that energy restored. I needed time off. I needed to get away from everything and everybody—everybody except Marina.

I looked at the clock again: 3:14. I called her.

She picked up on the first ring. "Danny, are you okay?" she said.

"Better than okay. Alboroto is dead."

I repeated the story Inés had told me practically verbatim. When I was finished, she asked the obvious. "Now what?"

"Get out of town and recharge my battery."

"Good idea. Where are you going?"

"Depends. First I'm hoping to hook up with a traveling companion."

"Hell, you're a good-looking guy," she said, her voice getting playful. "I'm sure you'll find someone. I'll bet Kirsten's lawyer would jump at the chance."

"Cut the shit, Marina. I hate to play the sympathy card, but I'm kind of a tortured soul here. I know what I did, and I know why I did it. And now that I have time to think about it, I keep asking myself, did I do the right thing? I was hoping to spend some quality time talking it through with one of the few people on the planet that I can talk to."

"You realize that going away together is outside our arrangement," she said.

"So that's a no?"

"I'm not finished," she said. "Damn right I know what you've been through. I got a little taste of it myself. I wasn't out there dodging bullets, but I borrowed a couple of billion dollars' worth of US military technology to disable that cargo ship. I tried not to leave any breadcrumbs, and I pray to God that nobody is smart enough to catch it, because if they do, I'll be spending the rest of my life in a federal prison for espionage, treason, piracy on the high seas, and whatever else the government decides to throw at me."

"This is starting to sound like a yes."

"Yes, it's a yes. Did you notice I wasn't asleep when you called? I was lying here awake because my dead mother came to me in a dream and she kept asking me if I was a good girl or a bad girl, and I didn't know the answer."

"Then let's go someplace together," I said. "I'll give you a chance to be both."

CHAPTER 67

"MEET ME IN CHARLESTON, SOUTH CAROLINA," Marina said.

"What's there?" I said.

"An airport. Everything else is a surprise." She hung up.

I booked a ten o'clock flight out of JFK, threw some things in a bag, and managed to grab another three hours' sleep.

By the time I landed, Marina was waiting for me in the terminal with a smile on her face that lit up my world.

She threw her arms around me and kissed me. It caught me by surprise. It was our first public display of affection, and she had initiated it. Nobody seemed to care. Of course, we did catch a few judgmental stares, but I guess that's to be expected when a Black woman kisses a white man in the middle of a busy airport in the Deep South.

"We're going to Kiawah Island," Marina informed me as she merged our car onto the interstate.

"Never heard of it," I said.

"It's a private community with very few people, beautiful beaches, spectacular sunsets—"

"Stop," I said. "You had me at 'very few people.'"

Less than an hour later, we checked into a grand seaside mansion called the Sanctuary.

It was aptly named. The Sanctuary was an escape from the rest of the world, and for the next five days, we lazed on the beach, got pampered at the spa, ate breakfast on the terrace of our oceanfront suite, drank wine as we watched the sun magically disappear into the Atlantic, and for the first time in our relationship, we made love knowing that we wouldn't have to go our separate ways in the morning.

And, of course, we talked. But for the sake of sanity, we decided to limit our soul-searching to a single two-mile walk on the beach every day. A typical session went something like this.

ME: On the plus side, we saved the city of New York from an attack that would have destroyed the lives of millions and had a devastating psychological, emotional, and economic effect on millions more.

MARINA: Yay, us.

ME: But we had no legal right to do any of that.

MARINA: The law is riddled with gray areas, Danny.

ME: I turned a dirty cop over to the Russians, knowing that he'd be put to death. Is that gray?

MARINA: Probably not. Bad Danny.

ME: One of Alboroto's men told Delaqua to go fuck his mother, so Frank responded by blasting a giant hole in the man's chest. Is that gray?

MARINA: In Mexico? I'm thinking yes, but I'll let you win that one. Bad Frank.

ME: And you—

MARINA: I know what I did. But in my defense, we were serving up some hard justice. Move on, Counselor.

ME: This whole good guy, bad guy shit is up for grabs. Was Robin Hood a bad guy?

MARINA: The sheriff of Nottingham thought so. The townspeople, not so much. Can I ask you a question?

ME: Go for it.

MARINA: Knowing what you know, and knowing that you couldn't do it any differently, would you do the same thing all over again?

ME: In a fucking heartbeat.

And so it went. For two miles a day. And then we would drop it for another twenty-four hours.

On the fifth day, we arrived at a verdict. We had broken the laws of God and man. But there wasn't a man on earth qualified to judge us, so in the end, we decided to turn it over to God. Each in our own way.

Marina was deeply rooted in her faith. I, on the other hand, am not religious, but I pray. Sometimes to an unknown ethereal quantity in the sky, and sometimes to my dead wife.

I had faith that the answer would come. We both did. But neither of us was in a hurry for it to be revealed. We were too busy living in the moment, enjoying the best vacation of our lives.

CHAPTER 68

I don't know if it was a sign from God, but on the final evening of our stay at the Sanctuary, one of my prayers was answered decisively.

Kevin Cavanaugh called.

I didn't tell him I was with Marina, but I knew it was business, so I put him on speaker.

"Danny, I'm back in Mexico shooting a piece on this firebombing. You wouldn't believe the carnage. The death toll is up to two eighty-nine, with at least another thirty still missing. The good news is that every one of them was either working for or in bed with the cartel. The rival gangs are circling like vultures hoping to take over Alboroto's distribution channels, and if we're lucky a lot of them will get killed off in the turf war until one of them eventually comes out on top."

"I wish I were down there with you," I said. "I'll bet the locals are dancing in the streets."

"It's like the night we found out Osama bin Laden was dead, only with mariachi music," he said. "And the Federales—they're reveling in it. They're like pigs wallowing in shit, and the farmer just told them that a dozen more truckloads of manure are on the way."

There was a laugh in the background. A female laugh. Marina and I both heard it. She gave me a knowing smile.

"I'll bet the Federales are happy," I said. "They can go to work every day with a lot more confidence that they're going to come home to their families that night."

"Oh, yeah, but it's a lot more than that," Cavanaugh said. "What's the best asset seizure you ever had?"

I thought for a few seconds. "It was a drug bust in the Bronx. Dominicans. Between cash and other property, I think the department netted out a little over three hundred grand."

"Peanuts," he said with a laugh. "Our friends down here took over Alboroto's compound the day after the fire, and they're still tallying it up. So far they've seized cars, trucks, boats, two helicopters, a 737, artwork, jewelry—they figure they can get fifteen million or more at auction, and they haven't even begun to count the cash. They're going to use it all to fund the war on drugs."

Marina raised her hand, and we gave each other a silent high five.

"That's incredible, Kevin," I said. "Thanks for calling."

"Wait, I'm saving the best for last," he said. "A lot of the Federales told me they have relatives in America, so of course I interviewed a bunch of them for the piece. I told them, when the show airs in the States, I'm going to make them look like Super Bowl champions. They were so grateful, they gave me a gift."

"What did you get?"

"They found Alboroto's personal laptop. They went through it, and there was a folder in there marked 'Nueva York.' They copied it onto a flash drive and delivered it to my hotel room. It's in my computer now, Danny. Videos labeled Central Park, Brooklyn, and—hang onto your hat, kiddo—there's one marked 'Bedford Hills'—and it's time-stamped the night your brother-in-law was murdered."

"And?" I said. "What's in it?"

"I don't know. It's password protected. I was going to call Marina to help me open it, but I wanted to call you first."

"I'm right here, Kevin," Marina said.

He exploded with laughter. "Wow," he said. "You realize you just outed yourself to an internationally known crime reporter with a television audience of millions."

"And you realize I can push a button and send a BGM-109 Tomahawk missile straight up your Irish ass."

More laughter, followed by a familiar voice.

"*Hola, Danny. Hola, Marina.*" It was Inés Bolano. "Don't worry. Kevin is not going to tell anybody. You keep our secret; we'll keep yours."

"I think we've come to a mutual understanding," Cavanaugh said. "Now, how long will it take you to hop on my computer and open this file?"

It took less than three minutes. It took another fifty-seven minutes to watch the GoPro footage Jason Harding had streamed to Alboroto.

It was all there: Harding breaking into the house, surprising Phil, Kirsten coming home, walking into the living room, and then just as she saw her husband sitting in silent terror on the sofa, a hand came from behind her and covered her face with a large red bandanna.

"No wonder she tested positive for heroin," I said as I watched her drop to the floor. "That thing must have been laced with it."

We watched as Harding put the gun in Kirsten's limp hand, fired at Phil three times, lowered her to the floor, left the house, and walked to his car. Then, with the video still running, he called 911 and made the Good Samaritan call that would send the cops to the scene before Kirsten regained consciousness.

It was soul crushing to watch. But it was also exhilarating. We had evidence. Solid, irrefutable evidence.

"Kevin," I said when it was over, "you just saved Kirsten's life. Thank you."

"*De nada, ese,*" he said.

"Do me a favor," I said. "Can you send a copy of the video to Kirsten's lawyer, Marjorie Becker, and another to the district attorney? I'll text you their contact information."

"I can do the lawyer immediately," he said. "But let's hold off on the DA for another twenty-four hours. This footage is going to air tomorrow night, and I want my viewers to see it before some overzealous prosecutor tries to stop me from showing it because it's undeniable proof that the cops and the DA's office did a piss-poor job."

"You're a total cynic," I said.

"All reporters are cynics," he said. "I'm just better at it than the rest of them."

I thanked him again, said goodbye, and turned to Marina. "Let's not check out of this paradise tomorrow," I said.

"Okay," she said.

"Let's not check out ever."

"Oh, you're Mr. Big Talker right now," she said, "but as soon as that work phone goes off, you'll be three feet in the air before Kaori even has a chance to say 'Jump!'"

"Maybe," I said.

"There are no maybes about it, Captain Corcoran. You may be conflicted, but you love this work. You're not giving it up. You *can't* give it up."

She knew me well. Sometimes I felt that she knew me better than I know myself. "You're right," I said. "I can't give it up. I believe in Trace Baker, and I believe in the mission."

"It's more than that, Danny. You don't just believe in the mission. You're willing to lay your life on the line to make it succeed. Like every cop and every soldier who ever went to war, you may question some of the choices you made on the battlefield, but don't ever question your moral compass. Don't ever apologize for your commitment to defending the lives and freedoms of others."

Her words took my breath away. I took her in my arms and whispered a soft thank-you.

"Just one more thing," she said. "Promise me that next time you put yourself in harm's way, you'll take me with you."

"Hell no," I said, stepping back a little and giving her my best marine drill sergeant glower. "I've seen your file, Whitney. You are not exactly combat ready."

"Don't pull that crap. You know what I mean. I'm not asking to go into the trenches, but whatever you do next, you're going to need cybersecurity."

"I know. Trace will find somebody else. I can't keep asking you to break the law."

"And I can't sleep nights knowing that someone who is not as good as I am is sitting behind the console, doing their best to keep you alive. If you're in the game, so am I," she said. "It's not an ask, Danny. It's a deal breaker."

"Wow," I said. "That sounds like emotional blackmail."

"Please, don't resort to denigrating my negotiating prowess. Just man up. Are we or are we not in this together?"

"Yes, ma'am. It appears to me that we definitely are."

"You promise?"

"I swear on a stack of Mercedes G-class SUVs."

"Good," she said with the same triumphant little tell that lights up her eyes every time she gets what she wants.

"You realize, of course, that my . . ." I pretended to grope for the right word. "My *commitment* . . . yes, my commitment to this partnership signifies a dramatic change in what we've been loosely calling our *arrangement.*"

She smiled, and those enchanting brown eyes locked on mine. "Some things will change," she said.

And then, ever so slowly, she started unbuttoning my shirt. "But some things are perfect just the way they are."

ACKNOWLEDGMENTS

Tom Clancy famously said, "The difference between fiction and reality? Fiction has to make sense."

So if the story of a Mexican drug lord going to war with the city of New York made sense to you, it's because I had a lot of help from a real NYPD detective, whose name also happens to be Danny Corcoran. Thank you, Danny, for helping me give this unbelievable fictional concept the ring of truth, and thank you, Angela, Samantha, Nina, and Ryan for sharing him with me.

Thank you also to my friend and ophthalmologist Dr. Diane Kraus for making sure I got the details of Joaquín Alboroto's evil plot medically accurate, and to my pilot buddy Dan Fennessy, who helps me fly right every time I write about aircraft.

Thank you to Bob Beatty, Bill Harrison, my daughter Sarah Charles, and my agent Mel Berger, who are always there when I reach out for their wisdom.

To Josh Stanton and Josie Woodbridge at Blackstone Publishing, thank you for welcoming me into your stellar group of authors and for supporting me with an exceptional team who guided *Snowstorm in August* from manuscript to finished publication.

Major bro hugs and fist bumps to Michael Carr, a world-class editor whose innate sense of story, character, and dialogue made this a better book and me a better writer.

As always, I am grateful to the booksellers, librarians, fan magazines, bloggers, and readers who continue to support my life of crime.

And finally, thank you to my wife, Emily, who understands that the term "neurotic writer" is redundant, and that the faraway look in my eyes at the dinner table almost always means that I have someone to kill, a body to bury, or a weapon to hide.

ABOUT THE AUTHOR

MARSHALL KARP is an international #1 bestselling author, TV and screen-writer, and playwright. He wrote the critically acclaimed Lomax and Biggs novels, featuring LAPD detectives Mike Lomax and Terry Biggs. Then, with James Patterson, he cocreated and cowrote the NYPD Red series, featuring Detectives Zach Jordan and Kylie MacDonald, who are part of an elite squad sworn to "protect and serve New York's rich and famous." After six bestsellers, Marshall will carry the series forward on his own with *NYPD Red 7*. For over twenty years Marshall has worked closely with the international charity Vitamin Angels, providing tens of millions of mothers and children around the globe with lifesaving vitamins and nutrients. More at www.KarpKills.com.

THE #1 BESTSELLING NYPD RED SERIES IS BACK!

PREVIEW

MARSHALL KARP

AVAILABLE NOVEMBER 2022

CHAPTER 1

My phone chirped, and I looked down at the gray text bubble on my screen. It was from Selma Kaplan at the District Attorney's Office. The message was one I had seen or heard hundreds of times over the course of my career as a cop. Six words that I knew had the power to change people's lives. What I didn't know—what I could not even have possibly imagined—is that this time those words would change my life. Forever.

THE JURY HAS REACHED A VERDICT.

I looked up at my partner, Detective Kylie MacDonald, who had gotten the same text. "It's about goddamn time," she said. "How long have they been sequestered? A week? A month? A year?"

"Four and a half days," I said.

"It doesn't matter, Zach," she said. "You know how it goes. The longer the jury deliberates, the worse it is for our side. Convictions come fast. Acquittals take forever."

"Four and a half days isn't forever."

"It is this time. Our testimony was airtight. Selma's closing was brilliant. The case was a slam dunk. If they were going to find him guilty, they could have done it in four and a half hours."

"Ye of little faith," I said, grabbing a radio. "Let's go. Judge Hollander isn't going to wait for us."

"Twenty bucks says Hellman walks," Kylie said.

"You're betting *against* us?"

"I'm betting with my head, Zach, not my heart," she said as we headed down the stairs. "Warren Hellman is filthy rich and has the power to turn ordinary mortals into superstars. There were five women on the jury, and he was eyeball-fucking every one of them. Juror number seven barely looked at me when I testified. She just gawked at him. She probably went home every night, flipped on the TV, and masturbated to his reruns. If anybody turned the jury, it was her."

A minute later we were speeding toward the Manhattan Criminal Courthouse at 100 Centre Street. Normally we're too busy to drive downtown and sit through the proceedings just to hear the verdict read. We wait for a call from the DA's office, and win or lose, we move on without missing a beat.

But this was different. This time it was personal, and we both wanted to be there when Warren Hellman went down. He'd killed a cop.

The first time I met Jonas Belmont, I was working in the Three-Two up in Harlem. I was a rookie, and he was a legend—a detective first grade with more Medals of Honor than anyone in the history of the department.

That night, I brought a homeless guy into the station. The desk sergeant got one whiff of the man and asked me what the charges were.

"He was jaywalking, sir."

The sergeant exploded. "Are you fucking serious, Jordan? Give that bag of shit a summons and get him the hell out of here."

"I will, sir," I said, "but if I could just talk to a detective for two minutes."

"Get him out of here," the sergeant repeated. "Now."

I started to leave when a voice boomed out. "Hold it right there, Officer."

I turned around. A hulk of a man was walking toward me. Six six, ginger hair, muscled chest straining against his suit jacket, and steel-blue eyes that were lasered in on me and my homeless persona non grata.

"Detective Jonas Belmont," he said.

I knew who he was. Everybody knew who he was. "Jordan, sir. Zach Jordan."

"How much time do you have on the job, kid?" he said.

"Two years next month, sir."

"And how many foul-smelling, raggedy-ass jaywalkers have you arrested?"

"This is my first, sir."

"And I'm betting you're smart enough to know he doesn't have the means to pay for a summons even if you slapped him with one."

I felt a smile coming on, but I held it back. Belmont was on my wavelength. He knew what I was up to, and he was ready to inform the sergeant that he was about to join the party.

"You're going to have to hold your nose a little while longer, Hank," Belmont said. "This astute young officer and I are going to take this egregious jaywalker upstairs for questioning."

The sergeant gave him a sour stare. "You working traffic violations now, Detective Belmont?"

Jonas pointed at the derelict's feet. "The shoes, Sergeant. The shoes."

The man, a human dumpster from his head to his ankles, was wearing a brand-new pair of rich brown Ferragamo alligator leather oxfords. As soon as I saw him shuffling across Broadway against the red light, I figured they had to cost a thousand bucks. I was wrong. They were twelve thousand, and two days earlier they had been inside a suitcase that disappeared from a taxi rank outside the Pierre Hotel.

Belmont took it from there, and I watched in awe from the other side of the two-way mirror as he sweet-talked a confession out of the man and got him to give up the name of the pawnshop that was dealing in stolen luggage.

When he was done, he gave me his card. "Good job, kid. Keep in touch."

Did I ever, hanging around the squad room like a fanboy. Even after he retired, we stayed friends, and every couple of months I'd meet him for dinner and listen to him tell war stories and, of course, brag about his kids.

Evan, who had always wanted to be a cop like his dad, was now a detective working out of the Tenth Precinct in Manhattan. Vivian, who'd had the acting bug ever since she was a kid, had followed her dream to the High School of Performing Arts, then NYU, and was now out there occasionally landing a small part and waiting tables at a restaurant near Lincoln Center, hoping for her first big break.

And that's where she met Warren Hellman. It started with a simple "Here's my card. Call my office." Then came the audition. She was perfect to star in his upcoming series. But of course, other young women were also perfect. The way Hellman spun it, beauty and talent were just the cost of entry. If he was going to work with an actress week in, week out, for the next five years, he had to make sure they had chemistry.

Vivian knew what that meant. Fuck the producer; become a star. The classic show business quid pro quo. She didn't hesitate.

It was heady at first. Restaurants, clubs, paparazzi, a key to his suite at the Sherry-Netherland. She knew there was a price to pay. Sex with a man who repulsed her in every way. But she could do it. She was an actress, and his bedroom was just another stage. The alcohol and the cocaine helped.

The heroin came later. One night she was soaking in the tub, a glass of champagne at her side. The bathroom door opened. "I'm Jeff," the man said. "Warren had to go to London. He sent me."

"For what?"

"To keep you company till he gets back," he said, peeling off his clothes.

"Jeff, please . . . I think . . ."

"No," he said. "You don't think. Warren doesn't want you to think. That's not part of the deal."

He stood there naked except for the gold wedding band around his pudgy ring finger. "I'm an executive producer on the new show. The networks love the premise, love you, but they're screaming for script changes before they sign off. Fucking networks, right?"

He produced a glassine envelope and tapped some powder onto the edge of the tub. "Help yourself."

She put her finger to one nostril and snorted the white line with the other. Nothing. He licked his lips, waiting. It was like nothing she'd ever felt before. Her body slipped back into the tub as the first wave of heroin bliss enveloped her. She felt his hand between her legs.

"Beats the piss out of cocaine, doesn't it, sugar?" he said, sliding into the tub with her.

She couldn't stop him. She didn't want to stop him. She never felt so good in her life.

Three months later, hooked on heroin, forcibly removed from the hotel suite, unable to face her friends and family, Vivian Jean Belmont went down into the Columbus Circle subway station and threw herself in front of a moving train. The last dozen calls on her cell phone were all to Hellman. He never picked up. He was three thousand miles away in Hollywood, no doubt exploiting the dreams of other young beautiful women.

A month later Kylie and I were called to a town house on East 71st Street. An intruder had broken in, and the homeowner had shot him in self-defense. The shooter was Warren Hellman.

My knees buckled when I saw the body. The man sprawled on the rug with a bullet through his head was my friend, my mentor, my hero: Jonas Belmont.

CHAPTER 2

There are three classes of people in New York City: the haves, the have-nots, and the most rarefied of them all, the have-lots. They are the superrich, the overprivileged few, the 1 percent of the 1 percent. Of course, there's a downside to having all that money. A lot of people want to get their hands on it.

One of those people was Stanley Spellman, our former mayor. Stanley came up with an ingenious plan for winning the love and financial support of his richest and most powerful constituents. He ordered the police commissioner to create a special squad dedicated to solving crimes committed against them.

And so NYPD Red was born. Mayor Spellman lost his bid for reelection, but by then the Red team had made its mark, and the new mayor wasn't about to deprive the city's movers and shakers of their elite task force.

On the night that he shot and killed Detective Jonas Belmont, Warren Hellman made two calls. One was to 911. The system identified Mr. Hellman as one of New York's platinum frequent flyers, and his case was routed to NYPD Red. When Kylie and I arrived at the house, Sonia Blakely, Hellman's lawyer, met us at the front door. She was the first call he had made, and phone records would verify that there was a ninety-two-minute gap between the time he called her and the time he reported the crime. A solid hour and a half for the two of them to concoct a believable story.

She led us to Hellman's office, where Chuck Dryden and his crime scene investigators were already at work. Kylie pulled Chuck aside while I knelt beside Jonas, whose ginger hair was now caked with dark-red blood, his blue eyes fixed in a death stare.

"His name is Jonas Belmont," I said to Blakely. "He was a police officer."

"I know who he is, Detective, and don't try to hide that man behind a badge," she said. "He's a deranged psychopath."

I knew her reputation. I'd seen her in court. She's a barracuda who attacks perfectly reliable witnesses, chews them up, and decimates their testimony. Her favorite defense tactic is to vilify the victim, and she wasted no time in creating the myth that my dead friend was a monster.

I stood up. "Counselor," I said, my jaw clenched, "Jonas Belmont was a decorated cop."

"Of course he was. That's the culture at NYPD. Kill someone, get a medal. So why stop just because he retired? Your *hero cop* came here to murder my client."

She was baiting me to do or say something I'd regret, and I might have if Kylie hadn't stepped in.

"Is your client okay?" she asked. "Does he need medical attention?"

Kylie almost never plays the good cop. It doesn't matter who she's up against. She doesn't kiss ass; she butts heads.

"We can have an officer drive him to a hospital," she said, gilding the lily.

"That won't be necessary," Blakely said. "He's in the living room trying to regain his composure."

"I'm sure he's in shock, and the last thing he wants to do is rehash what happened," Kylie said. "But as you know, the best time to talk to him is now while the details are still fresh in his mind."

"Right," Blakely said, leading the way. "But make it brief."

Warren Hellman was sitting in a wing chair, regaining his composure with the aid of a bottle of Johnnie Walker Blue.

"It was self-defense," he said as soon as we entered the room. "He came at me with a gun. He was going to kill me."

"Calm down, Warren," Blakely said. "Let the detectives ask the questions, and then you answer them to the best of your ability."

"Oh, yeah, right," he said, which I took to mean he'd already forgotten the ground rules she laid out for him earlier.

"Let's start with how you discovered the man was in your house," Kylie said.

Hellman gave her a vacant look. "I didn't discover him. He rang the doorbell, said he was a cop and he wanted to talk to me, so I let him in."

"Oh, I was confused," Kylie said, "because you told the 911 operator that he was an intruder. Now you're saying you invited him in."

"Stop right there, Detective," Blakely said. "The man rang the bell, flashed a badge, and my client did what any law-abiding citizen would do. He *granted* him entry. But he was a total stranger, not an invited guest. He used his police credentials the same way a burglar would use a crowbar. He *was* an intruder."

"I understand," Kylie said. "Did he say what he wanted?"

"Yes. He was here to serve me papers. He was suing me for the wrongful death of his daughter. I . . . I was dumbfounded. I said that's impossible. Who is your daughter? He told me her name—Vivian Belmont."

"Did you recognize the name?"

"I did. She was a wannabe actress. Not very good at all, but I didn't want to tell him that, so I said I never heard of her. That was my mistake. He went berserk and started screaming, 'You killed my daughter, and now you're going to deny even knowing her?' He pulled a gun from his waistband. He was standing between me and the door. I had nowhere to run. I was in fear for my life, but I knew I had a gun in my desk drawer."

"It's perfectly legal," Blakely said. "I can get you the permit."

Kylie ignored her. "Go on, Mr. Hellman."

"I backed away and sat down in my desk chair, sobbing, begging for my life. I said, 'You're a police officer. How can you do this?' He said, 'The best thing about being a cop is getting away with murder,' and he began to move toward me. I reached into the drawer, pulled out my gun, and I shot him."

"Which drawer was your gun in?" Kylie asked.

"Bottom right drawer of my desk."

"And you keep it loaded?"

"Yes."

"Thank God for that," Blakely said.

"So you backed away from the assailant, sat down in your chair, pleaded with the man not to shoot you, but he kept advancing toward you, so you opened that bottom right drawer, pulled out the gun, and shot him," Kylie said. "Is that basically it?"

"Yes," Hellman said. "That's exactly it."

"Detective, I think you got what you came for," Blakely said. "My client has cardiac issues. He's been through enough stress for one night."

"Absolutely," Kylie said. "Your client's well-being is our primary concern. If you give me your card, someone from the District Attorney's Office will want to speak to you tomorrow. I think it best if Mr. Hellman finds another place to spend the night. Our crime scene people will be here for several hours. Thank you so much for your help."

Blakely handed over a business card, and Kylie and I returned to Hellman's office.

"*Your client's well-being is our primary concern? Thank you so much for your help?*" I said. "What happened to the nasty-ass cop I used to work with?"

"Have no fear," Kylie said. "She's back, and she's going to nail that dirtbag's balls to the wall." She bared her teeth. "One at a time."

She wiggled a finger at Chuck Dryden, who has a not-so-secret crush on my blond, green-eyed partner, and he came right over, thrilled to be the man she wanted, even if it was strictly professional.

"Chuck, tell Zach what you told me," she said.

"Well, this is strictly preliminary. Nothing official," he said, giving his standard disclaimer. "The weapon that killed Detective Belmont is a

Glock 9mm Model 43. The bullet penetrated his head, just above the left eyebrow at about a forty-five-degree downward angle. The autopsy will give us the exact trajectory."

"Which means that Hellman, who is at least eight inches shorter than Jonas, could not have been sitting in his chair pointing the gun up at him," Kylie said. "He was standing up, aiming down. My best guess is, Hellman pulled the gun, and Jonas bent down to retrieve his from his ankle holster."

"He never got to it," Dryden said. "Detective Belmont's weapon, a Smith & Wesson .38 special, is still in the holster."

"But Hellman said that Jonas pulled a gun from his waistband and came at him with it," I said.

"That would be the Taurus .357 Magnum Model 65 that was found next to the body. It hadn't been fired," Dryden said, "and I would be surprised if Detective Belmont had it in his waistband. It's a heavy gun, and he wasn't wearing a belt that would secure it."

The story that Warren Hellman and his attorney had slapped together was full of holes, and three days later the DA's Office decided they had a strong case against him, and he was charged with murder two.

He spent one night in jail and the next ten months confined to his home, an electronic monitor strapped to his ankle. The trial took three weeks, and the jury was out for almost another five days.

Nearly a year had passed since the deaths of Vivian and Jonas Belmont, and as Kylie pulled the car into an illegal space two blocks from the courthouse, I was more than ready for the verdict.

What I wasn't ready for was the shitstorm that would follow it.

CHAPTER 3

The trial had blossomed into a media circus. The private tragedy that had befallen the Belmont family had turned into a public spectacle. Centre Street was lined with satellite trucks, and Collect Pond Park, the tranquil urban green space that sits directly opposite the courthouse, had given up its serenity for as many as fifty camera crews, all jostling for position to get the best shot of the key players as they entered the building for their day of reckoning.

The first row of the gallery on the prosecutor's side was reserved for family and friends, and Kylie and I sat down next to Jonas's son and daughter-in-law, Evan and Trish. Next to them were five cops, all retired—Jonas's crew from back in the day.

Normally, fewer than half a dozen court officers are on hand. Today, I counted twenty-eight lining the walls, and there was another contingent in the hallway outside.

Every seat was filled. Noticeably absent was Warren Hellman's brother Curtis. Three years ago, Curtis was also responsible for the death of a young actress. According to TMZ, he picked up the woman at a party in LA and invited her to drive with him to his house near Joshua Tree National Park.

Starstruck and high on coke, she said yes. Two hours later, Curtis pulled over onto the side of a dark desert highway, yanked her out of the car, and sped off. Her body was found the next morning. Cause of death: snakebite.

The rest of the details were sketchy because he paid her family three million dollars for their silence, but the smart money says that he wanted sex, she said no, so he dumped her on the side of the road because nobody says no to the king.

It was Sonia Blakely's decision to keep Curtis out of the spotlight. During the trial, she had painted a grim picture of Jonas. He was a failed father whose daughter grew up to be a hopeless junkie—a gun-happy cop who would rather settle a dispute with a bullet than with a law book. The last thing Sonia needed in the courtroom was for Curtis to show up and remind the jury of the evil that coursed through the Hellman family bloodlines.

Instead, she made sure that the gallery was peppered with Hollywood's biggest and brightest. The entourage changed daily, and it had to have an effect on the jury. If these superstars support Warren Hellman, how bad can he be?

The bailiff announced, "All rise," and the assemblage stood as Judge Mark Hollander entered the room.

I liked Hollander. He was fair, impartial, and less of a hard-ass than most. He took the bench. "Please remember that this is a courtroom," he said. "I respect that emotions are high but I will tolerate no outbursts from the gallery."

It was a standard speech at the close of any case as charged as this one. The crowd was divided. No matter what the outcome, a lot of people were going to be unhappy. Outbursts were inevitable, and I suspected Hollander would bang his gavel, but he would let the crowd have their moment.

The jury filed in, and finally, the moment of truth had arrived. "Will the forewoman please read the verdict?" Hollander said.

The woman, a fifty-year-old professor at Baruch College, stood up. "In the case of the People of the State of New York versus Warren Hellman," she said, her voice shaky, her pitch high, "we the jury find the defendant not guilty."

Bedlam. The zero-tolerance speech forgotten. The rapping of the judge's gavel echoed through the chamber.

Selma Kaplan, the prosecutor, who had done an outstanding job, buried her face in one hand and shook her head. I closed my eyes and felt that gut punch of emotions cops go through when they know the charge was good, but a person of wealth and power has beaten the system.

But Evan Belmont couldn't keep his outrage to himself. He jumped to his feet, waving his fist at the jury. "How could you!" he screamed. "My father dedicated thirty-five years to protecting this city. And this is the payback he gets?"

Hollander had had enough. "Officers," he yelled above the din, "remove Detective Belmont from my courtroom!"

Two officers approached. Evan held his arms up in surrender, turned, took his wife's hand, and walked down the aisle and out of the room. Kylie and I, along with the five retired cops, joined him in solidarity.

We followed him out of the courthouse into the bright summer sunshine. A podium and a phalanx of microphones had been set up, and a swarm of reporters who now knew the verdict began yelling questions, none of which were worth responding to.

Evan stepped up to the podium, and the noise died down.

"My father always left this courthouse knowing he did the best he could for the victims he was representing. But today that didn't happen for him," he said. "My father did not go to Warren Hellman's house that night to kill him. He went there to expose him, to tell him that my sister Vivian's tragic death was on his hands and that he would dedicate his life to finding every woman whose lives Hellman destroyed, and bankrupt him in civil court. Hellman's response was to shoot my father in cold blood."

"Why do you think the jury found him not guilty?" a reporter yelled out.

"Hellman is a Hollywood showman," Evan said. "He lied, and despite the prosecution's brilliant job of refuting those lies, the jury bought it. My family and I are heartbroken, and I'm sure that many

New Yorkers who knew and respected the legend of Detective Jonas Belmont are equally devastated."

A barrage of questions, but Evan waved them off. He'd said his piece. Just as he finished, there was another roar from the crowd.

Warren Hellman and Sonia Blakely, flanked by a cadre of Hollywood royalty, exited the courthouse and walked toward the media frenzy.

Hellman, smiling, ebullient, took center stage. Two fingers of each hand were raised high in a V, and he stood there beaming, obnoxiously victorious, without a trace of humility or concern for the lives he had crushed.

"He got away with murder and he's proud of it," Kylie said to me.

He stepped up to the microphones. "This has been quite an ordeal for my family and me," he said. "But justice has prevailed. I'd like to thank my attorney, Sonia Blakely, and her outstanding team, and I'd especially like to express my gratitude to the twelve men and women—a jury of my peers—who believed in my innocence. Thank you for giving me my life back."

Bullets can travel faster than the speed of sound, so I saw the geyser of blood erupt from his neck a split second before I heard the gunshot.

Kylie and I instinctively hit the ground, drawing our pistols, scanning the surroundings for the shooter, and scrambling for cover before the next bullet ripped through the air. But there was no second shot.

"Thank you for giving me my life back" would be Warren Hellman's last words. His life was over even before his body crumpled to the ground. And while we didn't know it at the time, the assassin, wherever he was hiding, was already breaking down his weapon and following through with his exit strategy.

The crowd, conditioned by mass shootings over the years, ran for their lives. People in the courthouse evacuated out the back. Judges were secured in windowless offices. Within ten minutes, NYPD had locked everything down, and the area was secured.

There were no eyewitnesses who could help us pinpoint where the bullet came from, but half a dozen earwitnesses all agreed that it came from somewhere north of the courthouse.

A team of cops fanned out to canvass the area. Kylie and I zeroed in on the nine-story office complex on Centre Street between White and Walker. At least two dozen people were standing outside.

As soon as they saw the shields on our lapels, several of them pointed at the roof.

"The gunshot came from up there," one man said.

"What did you see?" I asked.

"Nothing. But I heard it loud and clear. I was in the waiting room at the dentist's office on the ninth floor. It definitely came from the roof."

"Did you go up there?"

"Hell, no. I raced down nine flights of stairs. I'm an accountant. Going up there is your job, man."

I nodded. I was going up there. But I sure as hell wasn't going alone.

CHAPTER 4

There were at least a hundred cops on the street. Kylie saw the one she was looking for. "Captain!" she yelled.

He turned and glowered at her. This man was not used to being barked at.

"Sir," she said, "Detectives MacDonald and Jordan from Red."

Red was the magic word. He walked toward us, the scowl fading rapidly.

"Sir, we believe the shot came from the roof of this building. Can we get some backup?"

"What do you need, Detective?"

"A team to cover the lobby. Nobody comes in. Anybody wants to leave, they get searched. A floor-by-floor canvass and another team to accompany us up to the roof."

Within seconds, dozens of uniformed police poured into the building. Six got in the elevator with us. We drew our guns, got off on the eighth floor, and took the stairs to the roof.

Kylie and I weren't wearing vests, so two of the uniforms took the lead.

The rooftop door was open. "The screamer's been disabled," one of the cops said, pointing at the wires dangling from the alarm.

Whoever killed Warren Hellman had silenced the security system, found his position on the roof, and taken the shot from here. Odds were, he didn't stick around for the cops to show up, but we weren't taking any chances.

My adrenaline kicked up a notch. I split the eight of us into four teams and hand-signaled the game plan to breach the roof. On my go, we charged through the door and fanned out in our assigned directions. The shooter was gone.

"Okay, guys, let's shut it down and wait for Crime Scene to get here," I said. I radioed Central to let them know that the roof was clear.

One by one, the cops went back into the building.

"Zach," Kylie called out. She was standing on the east side of the roof, looking out at the courthouse.

"What have you got?" I said.

"Look at this," she said. "There's a clean line of sight from this spot to the podium where Hellman was standing. Dryden can verify it with a laser, but the evidence is starting to mount up. There's no security, the building is easy to get in and out of, the rooftop alarm was cut, and the guy in the dentist's office one floor below heard the shot loud and clear. This has to be it. And our shooter was a pro—a long-distance sniper who was smart enough to take the shot, disassemble the weapon, and leave without a trace."

"Yo! Dee-tee. Dee-tee."

Hearing the street slang for "detective," we both looked around.

"Yo! Dee-tee. Up here. The Tombs."

Directly across the street from where we were standing was the Manhattan Detention Complex, better known as "the Tombs" because the original structure built in the nineteenth century was inspired by a picture of an Egyptian tomb.

Today it has been replaced by two towers that house close to a thousand male inmates, most of them awaiting trial at the courthouse. One of those men was desperately trying to get our attention. He was on the top floor of the jail, three barred windows in from the corner of White Street.

"I saw him take the shot," he hollered.

Kylie pointed to a spot on the parapet.

"No. Not there. Over more."

She started to her right.

"No. The other way."

She walked along the rooftop wall.

"Keep going."

She took a few more steps.

"Right there! You got it. Right there."

She bent down and studied the limestone slab on top of the parapet. "Looks like traces of gunpowder stippling," she said. She took a deep breath. "I can smell the burnt powder."

She stood up.

"I told you! I told you!" the man yelled triumphantly. "I saw him. Come over here and get me out. Tell the CO you want to talk to Elroy."

"Looks like we've got a witness," I said.

"But altruism doesn't permeate the halls of the Tombs," Kylie said. "Elroy is going to be angling for a get-out-of-jail-free card in return for his generous cooperation."

"If he gives us the guy who just put a bullet through Warren Hellman's neck," I said, "I'm pretty sure Selma Kaplan will escort him out the front door herself."

My phone rang. It was our boss, Captain Cates. I put her on speaker.

"Jordan," she said, "where are you and MacDonald right now?"

"We're on a roof two blocks from the courthouse. It's where the shot came from," I said. "Crime Scene is on the way, but we're running over to the Tombs to talk to one of the inmates who witnessed the shooting."

"No, you're not," she said. "I'll send another team down there. I need the two of you uptown forthwith."

"Captain," I said, "this has been our case since the day Warren Hellman killed Jonas Belmont. We have an eyewitness to the shooting. What's going on uptown that's more important than this?"

"A runner was stabbed to death on the West Side Highway jogging path," she said.

"And you can't lay that off on someone else?" I said.

"No, I can't," Cates said. "And even if I could, you wouldn't want me to. Your newest victim is your current victim's brother—Curtis Hellman."